ISBN 978-0-9973240-2-0

Tsuga's Legacy Publishing Company
PO Box 488
Cuero, TX 77954

I0739456

Dedicated to Travis. Thank you for always believing in me.

Tau

Volume Two of
The Loss of Magic

Pangaea
Unknown Lands
Maelven Isles
Teeth of the Wyrm
Zardri
Devali
Gilead
Dulai

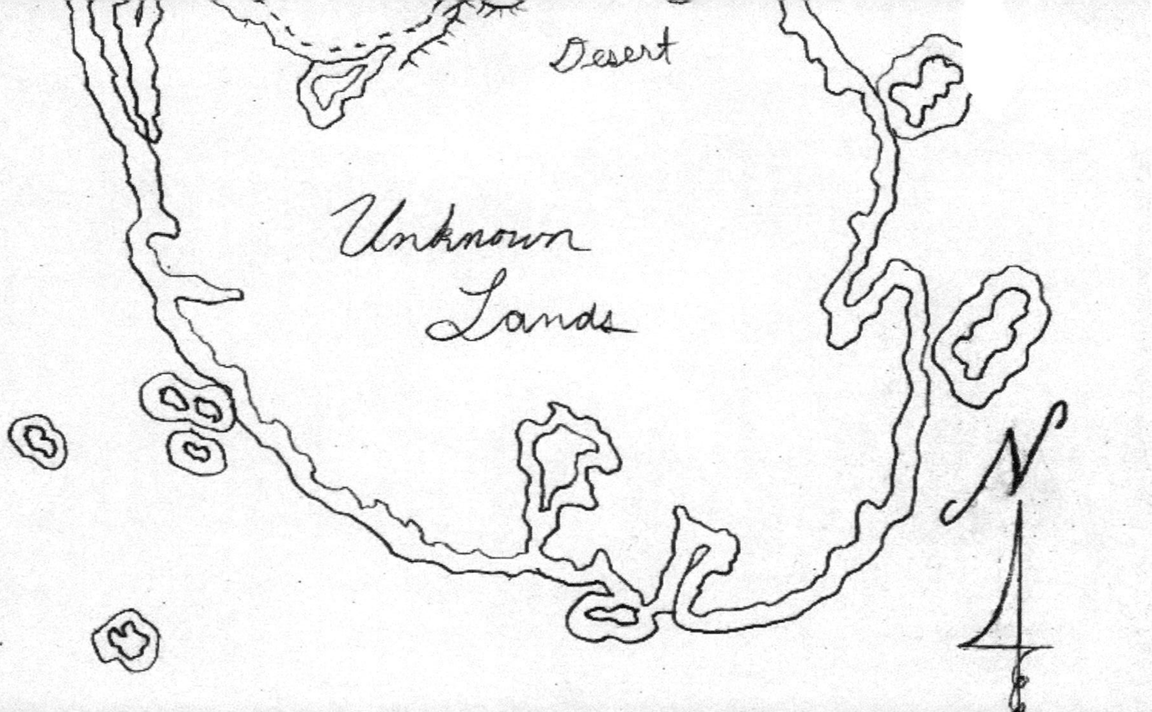

Desert
Unknown Lands
N

Chapter 1

"We are *not* binding her power!"

The sound of her mother's raised voice was nothing new. Neither was the surge of emotion Tau could sense from the tall, thin woman. What *was* new was this other feeling in her head, this sense of something coming. Her father gestured to her from across the room, and though she couldn't feel his emotions as plainly as she could her mother's through his empathic shields the anger was plain in his green eyes.

"She is four years old. Four! Already she's mindspeaking and sensing our emotions. She's a danger, not just to those around her, but to herself."

Tau was used to this argument; they'd rehashed it a dozen times or more. She knew her mother would win, as she always did. What drew her attention now was the powerful urge to go outside. She *needed* to be out there, even if she didn't know why.

"Wasn't it you who told me a mage who ignores her abilities is a danger? If you're so concerned, Ramiq, then here's a thought: teach her! Show her how to control her magic so that she *doesn't* hurt anyone."

The child was no longer listening. Her small, olive-toned brow was wrinkled in concentration, her green eyes – a match for her father's – closed, and hair the same shade of brown as Tsuga's fell forward to cover her face. She could picture the courtyard of the Mage's Complex where they lived with perfect clarity, almost as if she were there. She *should* be there, in the shade cast by the giant fountain. She didn't know why, but she felt the need like a physical pull.

The world turned over, shifted, and then spit her back out. She landed hard, and the impact jarred her so much that tears sprang to her eyes. She shook her head and sniffed loudly, but a quick look around startled her out of her tears.

How'd I get out here...?

The grass was soft under her hands, and when she pushed herself to her feet she realized that she stood in the shadow of the towering, mystically-shaped fountain. Her robes, a miniature green and gold imitation of those her father wore, stirred slightly in a light breeze.

As she turned a slow circle to take in her surroundings, Tau became once again aware of the sense of growing excitement stirring her insides. The mages and students who passed smiled and waved at her, and many also called a hello. The daughter of the Queen's Mage was well known in the Mage's Complex. She wasn't looking at them, though; indeed, she scarcely even registered their presence. Rather, she stood staring intently to the north. Whatever was coming seemed to be approaching from that direction. She could only see a small section of blue sky between the roofs of the surrounding buildings, but still she strained to look into the distance.

When the breeze stirred again, she thought she heard screaming. The sound distracted her for a moment – but only a moment, because before she could think to wonder what was wrong her attention was grabbed by what she saw flying over the roof of the servants' quarters.

The creature was roughly the size of a large horse, with a wingspan more than three times the height of her Daddy, who was the tallest man she'd ever seen. Its long, graceful neck bent as the animal turned its triangular head to scan the ground. Tau laughed aloud and clapped her hands as the creature cried out before spiraling down to settle just a few lengths away.

Now that it had landed Tau was able to make out more detail – once the dust stirred up from the process had cleared, at least. She – for Tau felt it had to be a female – was a brilliant copper, the same bright color as the wire caging that wrapped her mother's mage stone. The color darkened slightly to a more burnished shade on her extremities and around her eyes and joints, while her belly, like the underside of her wings, was the color of coals glowing in the hearth. She was, to say the least, beautiful. Her eyes – her bottomless, green-gold eyes – met and held Tau's gaze, and in that moment the world turned over. Again.

She was still shaking with reaction when the change in air pressure that marked a teleporter's arrival popped in her ears. Moments later she was snatched up in her father's strong arms and turned away from the creature, her Daddy's back between them. She squirmed until she could see over his shoulder.

"A dragon! Imagine! Tau, how did you get out here? What were you thinking?! You could have been hurt!"

"Lilae wouldn't hurt me. She couldn't."

Her mother moved up to pull her gently from her daddy's arms.

"Lilae? Is that her name?"

Tau nodded eagerly, only now able to tear her gaze away from the beautiful dragon.

"Yeah."

It came out as two syllables, more of a "yea-yuh," and Tsuga smiled as she set Tau upon her hip.

"How do you know her name?"

Tau looked at her mother in surprise. She hadn't thought to wonder *how* she knew. She simply knew it, like she knew to take in a breath and let it out.

"I just do. She's in my head. And in here, too." She thumped her chest. Her mother and father exchanged a look over her head, and then her father moved around so she could see him, too.

"Tau, are you saying she's your guardian?"

She turned to look at the dragon again and felt her face split in a wide grin. Her guardian. A dragon! She laughed aloud in delight.

"Yeah!"

Chapter 2

"They're not even supposed to *fly* this far south! Everyone knows dragons prefer mountain ranges, volcanoes, coastline cliffs. As far away from civilization as they can get!"

"Well, obviously this one is different. If she's Tau's guardian she has no choice but to live where Tau does. What concerns *me* is feeding her. Do you have any idea what dragons eat? Or how much?"

Tau, who had been staring out the window at Lilae, turned to answer her Ma's question. Leave it to Tsuga to be the one to voice the pragmatic questions, while Ramiq still struggled with accepting the unexpected turn of events.

"She can feed herself. 'Sides, she says she only needs to eat once every week or two. Maybe more when she hits a growth spurt." She grinned at that. "Like me!"

"Fantastic!" Her father, dramatic as always, threw up his hands and strode across the room to take up his daughter's vacated place at the window.

"She only has to eat every two weeks! We live in a *city*. Where is she going to hunt? Everything around here is domestic!"

"What's do-me-stic?" Tau pronounced the unfamiliar word carefully.

Ramiq turned to look down at her; she could see his expression soften when he met her earnest gaze.

"It means they belong to someone. They're pets, or else they're the way someone makes his living and keeps his family fed."

"Oh." Tau frowned. "She wouldn't eat someone's pet."

"But how will she be able to tell the difference?"

Tau frowned in puzzlement and paused to consider this problematic question.

I will ask them.

When Tau relayed this answer – still delighted at hearing her dragon's speech in her own head, just like when she mindspoke a person – Ramiq's frown deepened.

"What?"

Tau shrugged. This all seemed very obvious to her. She couldn't see why her daddy didn't understand; as a mage, this innate magical stuff should be easier for him to accept.

"She can ask them, sorta. See their thoughts and stuff, and know if they're safe to eat."

Tau heard the sound of a chair scraping back, and then her mother's footsteps. Tsuga stopped in front of her daughter and crouched down until she was on eye level with the young girl.

"Tau, does Lilae have animal mindspeech?" Tau nodded excitedly.

"Yeah!"

"What else can she do?" This question came from Ramiq, who had turned to face his little family, his back to the window. Tau giggled and pointed behind him.

"Why don't you ask her?"

Lilae, curiosity piqued by Tau's relaying of this conversation, had abandoned her comfortable place

in the sun and come up to peer in at this little tableau through the window. Ramiq turned to look where Tau pointed, and the girl had to stifle a giggle when he yelped and stepped back from the vertically slitted, gold-flecked green eye – nearly as big around as his fist – that peered in at him through the glass.

Tau walked over to pat her father's arm comfortingly and drew him back to the window.

"She won't hurt you, Daddy. Why don't you say hello?"

She could hear him swallow, obviously still uncomfortable facing the unblinking stare of an actual dragon.

"Hel-" his voice caught, and he had to clear his throat before he could manage a full "Hello."

Hello, Adept.

Ramiq tensed, and Tau could feel the emotions that boiled just beneath the surface; in physical contact with him like this, his shielding was far less effective against her strong empathic ability. In fact, she realized, she could feel *everyone's* emotions. Not just her daddy's and her mother's, but *everyone's*. She could pick out more than a dozen different sets of emotions just in the few surrounding rooms. How peculiar.

You can speak into my mind.

Tau's eyes widened when her father's voice sounded in her head. She was used to hearing mindvoices by now; she had heard them since before she could talk. But her father's thoughts had always been well shielded before; she only heard him when he spoke directly to her. Maybe it was because he spoke to her guardian?

Or maybe it's because she's so close to us both?

Dragons were inherently magical creatures, or so she gathered from Lilae's memories. The great green eye still peered at them through the window.

Of course I can.

What else can you do?

The dragon's pupil dilated, the previously thin line of black widening until her green iris shrank to half its previous size.

I am a dragon, mage. You use magic. I *am* magic. I can do all things. More than you can imagine.

Why are you here?

Because of Tau.

Tau? Why?

She is the other half of my soul.

But why her? Why my daughter?

That remains to be seen, mage. Such knowledge of the future is veiled, even to me. I know only that Auriga wills it so.

Ramiq nodded dazedly, and though he seemed outwardly calmer than he had all day, Tau could sense the many emotions that warred within him.

What now?

Now, mage, life moves forward.

Chapter 3

"Tau, sweetheart, I know you've been surrounded by magic your whole life. It was a part of you even before you were born. You've seen both your mother and me perform magic, and have even used it yourself. But do you really understand what it is?"

Tau sat on her daddy's lap and looked up into his eyes, the same color as her own, though the shape was slightly different. Today she wore a miniature version of mage robes in various shades of pink and purple.

"Course I do. Magic is life."

Ramiq blinked, looking surprised by this intuitive answer.

"Well, yes, that's true. Magic is what powers life and allows the world to exist. But that's not all. Magic is a tool, Tau. Like an axe, or a hammer, or a sewing needle."

Tau giggled at the image this called up as she swung her feet in glee.

"Magic is a sewing needle?" She giggled again, but her father shook his head, expression serious.

"In a way, it's like one. If you use it correctly and with patience and skill, you can make something beautiful. But imagine trying to write with one, or using one as a sword. It's not the right tool. At best, it would be useless, and at worst, could get you seriously hurt or even killed."

Tau had started to laugh again at the images this analogy called up, but at the last word, she sobered quickly.

"Do you see what I mean, Tau?"

"Not really."

"You have a very strong talent for magic, Tau. One day you'll be like me: a Queen's Mage, one of the most powerful people in the world. And with a dragon at your side, you'll be even more so. But only if you train and practice really hard."

"That doesn't sound like much fun."

Ramiq laughed at her face and tapped her lightly on the nose – prominent and angular, just like her mother's.

"It's not always going to be fun, you're right. But parts of it will be. At any rate, it's time for us to get started. And the first thing you will learn is how to see magic."

"But Daddy, I see magic all the time! The lights on the ceiling, when you or Mama start a fire or light a candle. And I watch the trainees practice all the time!"

Ramiq shook his head with a little smile.

"You see the results of magic all the time, Tau, but not the magic itself. Think of it like … hearing thunder without seeing the lightning that caused it."

Her brow wrinkled in thought and she stuck out her lower lip as she contemplated this new idea.

"Then how do I see the lightning?"

His smile broadened, and he reached out to place two fingers over her eyelids.

"First, close your eyes. Just relax. Feel the world around you: the heat from the fire, the draft around the windows and the door. Listen to the sounds of life: the birdcalls, the people talking and laughing. What else do you notice?"

"I can feel Lilae, and how good the sun feels on her back. And I can hear everybody going about their day and how Cook is mad at the serving girl for doing something she shouldn't have with one of the students, and … and I can feel you. And that surprises you. Why, Daddy?"

Ramiq cleared his throat and she could feel him shake his head as though to clear it, even with her eyes closed.

"Never mind that. You're doing well. Now, open your eyes slowly, and keep that awareness. What do you see?"

She did as instructed, and when her eyes focused again she gasped in delight.

"Oh," she breathed. "Daddy, you're so pretty!"

She felt his surprise, but it lasted only a moment before fading to amusement.

"What do you see, sweetling?"

"You're like a rainbow! All glowy and shiny! And you have all these different layers to you, and each one is a little different color, but they're all *you.*"

Ramiq made an odd sound that she didn't recognize, but he smiled at her.

"The 'rainbow' is the color of my magic. As another Queen's Mage, yours will look similar. All the layers are my shields, which protect me from attack, but also protect everyone else from harm I might otherwise cause them by accident. This is very good, Tau; you're doing splendidly!"

Tau flushed with delight at his praise and clapped her hands

"What's next, Daddy? I want to keep going!"

She could sense his hesitation, so in the way she'd somehow always known to do she smiled up at him and *leaned* with her mind to push him the way she wanted him to go. His eyes narrowed, and she felt him, for the first time, resist. She could see his shields shimmer oddly as he strengthened them and, seeing how he pulled and then directed and shaped the power around him, she tried emulating him.

Abruptly, she was the only person in her head; she could no longer sense her father, even though she still sat on his knee. She couldn't hear the thoughts of the passers-by, and the little knot of "everybody else" that always resided in the back of her mind was suddenly gone. She blinked in surprise, but her father's jaw had dropped open in shock.

"Tau, sweetling, what did you just do?"

She shrugged, still trying to figure out why her sense of the rest of the people had suddenly disappeared.

"Nothing bad, Daddy. I just did what you did."

"But … you shielded. Without being trained. Without having any idea what you were doing. And it – it's perfect."

She felt a pressure that she'd never felt before, and in response did as she'd seen him do when she had tried to influence him. The pressure left, and Ramiq shook his head in awe.

"And strong. That's … that's enough of a lesson for today. Bring your awareness back down to just the normal level and your vision will return to normal. You can leave the shield for now; in fact, it's probably a good idea. Can you still feel your guardian?"

She did as he bade her and let her senses drop back into the normal range. She didn't even hesitate at his question; the dragon was right there in her mind, just like she was supposed to be.

"Course."

"Good. Then run along. I've got classes to tend to."

She reached up to throw her arms about his neck and gave him a quick kiss before sliding down from his lap and heading outside to play.

Chapter 4

Ramiq sighed and hung his head as he allowed Tsuga to knead the knots of tension out of his shoulders.

"How did the lesson go?"

The Queen's Mage frowned to himself. Tsuga had fought him on the subject of Tau's magic every step of the way. She was so afraid that her daughter would share her early fear and distrust of magic that she had insisted Ramiq begin the child's training as soon as possible. She refused to listen to his logical arguments in favor of caution and allow Tau some years to mature before thrusting her into mage lessons. He had relented to her wishes, and after the way things had gone today, he was glad he had.

"She has a natural affinity I've never seen before. She learned mage sight like she'd been using it all her life, and ... Tsu, she shielded."

"Well, that's wonderful! Now that you've taught her to shield, we won't have to –"

Ramiq reached up to place his hands atop hers, and she broke off mid-sentence.

"I didn't teach her. She saw me reinforce my own shielding – once, and at normal speed – and produced a perfect mental shield without even *trying.*"

Her hands lifted from his shoulders and he heard her steps as she walked around his chair. He opened his eyes to see her crouched before him, her face only inches from his as she met his gaze.

"You can't really be all that surprised. Ramiq, she's been surrounded by magic since the night she was conceived. It only makes sense that it should come so easily to her."

Ramiq sighed and scrubbed his face with his hands.

"I know. I expected it to come easily to her, but not *that* easily. I mean, Auriga's tits, she saw it *once*. And did it without even being told how. That shouldn't be possible!"

"I seem to recall another young mage who did things that shouldn't have been possible. What did you call that thing you tried against me? A sun snake, or something?"

Ramiq grinned ruefully.

"A finger of the sun. I stand corrected."

Tsuga chuckled and stood to walk around him and resume the massage.

"So, what now?"

"Now her training starts in earnest. Immediately."

Chapter 5

*T*au sat next to Lilae in the shadow the dragon cast in the courtyard, basking in the radiant heat she produced. In the past year, while Tau had thrown herself into her magic lessons with the kind of enthusiasm only a child could muster, Lilae had become somewhat of a favorite pet among the other residents of the castle.

A dragon was a rare enough sight under any circumstances, but a clever, beautiful young dragon who enjoyed the company and attention of the people who doted on her was simply unheard of. Dragons were supposed to breathe fire and steal away young girls in the night, not lounge on the paving stones and converse with young trainees. Consequently, her tough hide – rather similar to a lizard's skin with its fine scales – shone with the oils her friends rubbed into it.

She had nearly doubled in size since the day of her arrival, so that her head alone was roughly the size of a hand cart. Her body had taken on a firm musculature, her build filling out until her feline conformation spoke of the power needed to thrust her massive bulk into the air.

In that same time Tau had grown as well, though at what seemed a more normal rate. Her skill in magic had grown, too – by leaps and bounds.

What did you learn today?

Tau looked up at her guardian's mindvoice and smiled.

"We started targeted thought-sensing and distance mindspeaking."

Oh? And how does that work?

Everyone knew dragons were innately magical creatures. Even Tau knew that, at five years old (though to be fair, Tau knew more than most about dragons, having one for a guardian as she did). What few people ever seemed to realize, though, was that dragons were not merely made of and steeped in magical energies; they also used and manipulated them, largely by instinct.

As a practically immortal species, dragons gained knowledge, power, and control as they aged. Fire was the first thing most young dragons learned, which was why it was the thing most associated with them, at least in the stories told to scare little children into good behavior. They were largely solitary creatures, and the young, consequently, were left to learn their skills and abilities through trial and error.

Lilae, the first dragon in living memory to be soul joined to a human as her guardian, had the good fortune to have bonded to a child who stood to be one of the most powerful mages alive. And so as Tau progressed in her lessons she shared the knowledge and skills she gained with the dragon, and the two worked over any problematic techniques together until they had them right. At the rate they were currently progressing, they would both reach – or surpass – the level of Journeyman before Tau turned ten.

Already it was obvious that Tau's strengths were the healing and mind-magics. Physical power manifestations were more challenging for her, so her skill in them grew more slowly – slowly by her standards, though still faster than many pupils, as her father was wont to point out when she grew frustrated over a lack of mastery.

The techniques she'd learned today put her near Journeyman level for telepathy, but in order to reach full Journeyman status as a Queen's Mage-in-training Tau would have to achieve the same level of proficiency and status for each ability she possessed, until which time she would still be considered an Apprentice.

"Well, distance mindspeaking is pretty easy, but you have to know the person. You need to have seen them, know how their mind feels, that kind of thing. Then, you just kinda picture them and think *at* them, just like normal mindspeech. Only, it takes more effort the further away they are."

So it is only an extension of the skill we have already learned. Simple enough. Now, what about this targeted thought-sensing?

"Oh! Now *that* is interesting. When not shielded, a thought-sense is overwhelmed with the thoughts of everyone within range. For someone like me, that's a lot of people over a pretty big distance. But sometimes, it's useful to be able to listen in on someone's thoughts. So, to do that without dropping your shields completely, you have to change them some, like this."

The technical vocabulary associated with magic rolled off of her tongue after a year of intense study, making her sound far less like a typical five-year-old and more like one of her teachers. Her father did not teach her everything, as some of his skills were too weak to be of much use in instruction; the other Masters and Adepts took care of those skills with which he was least comfortable.

Despite her new-won knowledge of the words necessary to communicate about magic, she still found it easier to simply demonstrate. The trick to this technique was to adjust her mental shields and make them more porous, so that she could let in what she chose to, while still keeping out everything else. It had taken her a few tries to get the knack of it – and even longer to learn how to listen in without being detected – but she had it down now; her father had made certain of that before he dismissed her for the day.

For the purposes of this demonstration, Tau focused her attention on a person, rather than a group, room, or train of thought (a skill that, until demonstrated, she had not known existed; it allowed the mage to scan for something like "kill," as her father described, and was useful for a Queen's Mage who was expected to act as magical bodyguard to the queen whenever in her presence).

She knew her mother would be riding back from the council meeting – as Weaponsmistress, Tsuga was among the queen's advisors, and so was a key part of the country's decision-making process. Her thoughts should be agitated and powerful this time of day, and therefore easy to read. Sure enough, Tau had only to open her awareness for her mother's thoughts to bloom in her own mind.

She's completely irrational where Devali is concerned. There was a pause before the next

thought, as though she listened to only half of a conversation.

Well of course, but she is the queen; she cannot afford the luxury of personal grudges. Not when they run counter to her people's best interests!

Tau realized that her mother must be speaking with her guardian. Curiosity piqued, the young mage expanded her awareness to catch the horse's thoughts as well.

It is seldom an easy thing to reconcile one's duty with one's emotions. She has every right to hate Devali.

She has every responsibility to seek peace for her people! One bad apple does not mean the entire tree is rotten! Why can't she see that?

Her family was killed when she was scarcely more than a child. Assassinated. That kind of thing leaves emotional scars that may never heal. As you well know, Tsu.

Yes, of course. But I don't have to like it. And I have a responsibility to my trainees as well as to my friends in the field – in both countries – to try to find a way to spare their lives.

You can't go against the queen; she may never be persuaded, and in this she is likely to declare you a traitor first, and ask questions of our corpses.

I know. I must find a way to work within the laws and with her blessing to achieve the end she cannot yet reconcile with her conscience. This will require a great deal of thought and careful maneuvering.

Tau carefully brought her awareness back to herself and restored her shields to their normal, impenetrable state. She shook her head, unable to

make much sense of what she had overheard. Lilae's careful shifting next to her brought her attention back to the task at hand, and she turned to smile up into the enormous green eyes.

"So, you see the trick. Think you can do it?"

A mischievous spark ignited in the vertically-slitted draconic eyes, and Lilae rumbled her confidence.

Of course. It is only a matter of finesse. I shall practice this one until it comes as naturally to me as speaking to you.

Tau laughed and obligingly reached up to scratch the soft patch of skin under her guardian's jaw bone when the dragon lowered her head and looked at her imploringly.

Tau's stomach chose that moment to loudly announce its emptiness, and a quick glance at the sun's position in the sky confirmed that it was in fact time for dinner.

Go.

Dragons could not manage human expression, but Lilae's mindvoice held the warmth of a fond smile.

Eat. I will practice.

Tau threw her arms around the great neck of her dragon – they didn't reach much more than half way around; the beast's neck was as big around as a grown man – and Lilae reached down to nudge her gently before the girl released her hold and turned to run inside.

Chapter 6

$\mathcal{T}$au sat outside the tent and watched the hustle and bustle of construction crews as they clamored over the scaffolding and set stones in place. This far north in Sennor, autumn meant a decided nip in the air and a frigidity to the frequent rains. She may even get to see her first snowfall this winter.

Today had dawned clear, though the temperature meant she was bundled up in a warm cloak, and the workers were taking full advantage of the fair weather. Personally, Tau would have preferred to use magic to warm herself to the bulky woolen clothes she now wore – it was a simple manipulation of fire energies – but her mother was of the opinion that such a squandering of power was frivolous. Her father, who held no such qualms about the ready expenditure of power in favor of human comforts, was so paranoid about their use of magic drawing attack here on the border that he had stood firm with his wife on this point. Even her magic lessons were now conducted inside such shields that not even a whisper of power escaped to be detected.

Late spring had seen their departure from the capitol, and a few weeks' travel had brought them to this place. When Tau had asked why they were leaving, Ramiq had told her that he was starting a new mage school on the Devalian border, and Tsuga had added that the students would be trained in physical weaponry as well. As she would be. And, true to her word, her mother had begun instructing Tau in the use of light weaponry suitable to her size and strength as they traveled. Now her mornings were spent learning these mundane skills, while her lessons in magic came in the evenings, when it was too dark for the construction work to continue safely without the use of mage lights.

At the moment, Tau enjoyed a rare chance to simply be outside without having to worry about lessons of any sort. It seemed her reprieve was destined to be short-lived, however, for already she sensed her mother's approach.

Tsuga came to stand beside her, and Tau peered up at the tall woman with a feeling of resignation. She did not particularly enjoy her weapons' lessons, but she knew they were necessary – or at least, that her mother thought they were.

"Are you ready?"

Tau stifled a sigh.

"Yes'm." When she turned to walk towards the cleared patch of ground Tsuga used as her interim training arena, a hand closed on Tau's shoulder and stopped her.

"Not that way. We're going to do something special today."

Tau looked up at her curiously, but followed her mother through the maze of tents and half-erected structures until they were well clear of the camp. It didn't take her long to realize that they were headed in the direction of Lilae's favorite spot – a clearing where the sun warmed her hide and the music of a small stream burbling over the rocks at its bottom lulled her into a peaceful state of mind.

When the dragon came into sight Tau broke free of her mother's gentle hold and ran forward to hug her guardian's large snout and breathe her in.

Lilae had a smell unlike anything else Tau had ever encountered. It was a little like the sharp, musty scent of a snake, but with the tangy under-currents of ash and the sense of energy that hung in the air just before a powerful storm. It was comforting and invigorating all at once, and Tau's blood quickened in response to the hum of immense power that surrounded the dragon.

Tsuga stood back and watched this greeting for a moment before she cleared her throat. Tau reluctantly pulled her attention away from her guardian and turned to face her mother.

"Are you ready for your next lesson?"

Tau nodded, resigned to some unknown – but surely unpleasant – task. Tsuga smiled and moved forward to place a hand on Lilae's large foreclaw.

"Good. Then get on."

Tau blinked in surprise.

"Get on?"

"Yes. Get on your guardian."

"But –"

"What? Didn't it ever occur to you that you could *ride* her? After all, Bane is my guardian; I ride her."

"Well, yes, but Lilae's a *dragon!*"

"All the more reason. She can fly. And she's a living, breathing source of magical energy – incredibly useful to you as a mage. Once you two can work together physically as well as you do magically, you will be an incredible pair."

Her voice trailed off slightly as she continued, almost as though she spoke to herself.

"Of course, we'll have to work up some sort of saddle or harness to help hold you in place before you can try any serious flying...."

"Flying?"

Tsuga broke off and smiled at the interruption and the obvious excitement in her daughter's expression.

"Yes, dear. Bane is a horse, but Lilae *is* a dragon. Play to your strengths, as I always say. Now come on; up you go!"

Tau looked from her mother to her dragon with a growing sense of excitement.

"But how?"

Lilae craned her head around to look at the small girl with one warm green-gold eye.

I will help you.

As she spoke the dragon offered her forearm, and Tau stepped onto it and giggled with delight as the creature lifted her up so that the child could climb atop the dragon's neck where it met her torso. She settled herself in the comfortable spot she found there, somewhat surprised to find a rope looped around Lilae's neck.

After a moment of consideration, she realized her mother must have put it there for her to hold on to. This suspicion was confirmed when Tsuga came forward and showed her how to hook her feet into the loops that had been tied in the rope and where to grip it with her hands to hold on. Once Tau was secure, Tsuga patted her leg and stepped back.

"Now, she's not a horse; you'll have to get used to how she moves and learn to move with her. But luckily, you also won't have to worry about steering or controlling her, since you can speak mind-to-mind. Now, I want you two to stay fairly low, since this is your first time together. Just circle the camp a few times."

She paused to frown at Lilae.

"Don't let her fall."

Of course not, Weaponsmistress. She is part of me. She shall be as safe on my back as she would be asleep in your arms.

Once Tsuga had moved far enough away, Lilae spread her wings and rose to a crouch, head raised as she tested the winds for a favorable current. When the dragon's muscles bunched Tau held her breath, only to have it forced from her by the power of Lilae's leap upward.

The first downstroke of the expansive wings created a rough hop-like motion that made Tau's stomach churn, but after a second and third wingbeat the dragon found a warm updraft that smoothed the movement out and lifted them quickly into the air.

Tau had half expected to feel some alarm at being so far from the ground, the but the only thing she felt now as she looked down on the receding form of her mother was a sense of elation.

As Tsuga had warned, Lilae's movements were vastly different form the horses she was used to riding. She found, however, that adjusting to the oddly rolling gait – much like a leaf must feel on the surface of a puddle when carried forward on a ripple – was so natural it seemed almost as though she were born to it.

How are you doing?

Oh Lilae, this is wonderful! Everything is so pretty from up here! I feel so free!

A laugh escaped from her when the dragon dipped one wing and executed a lazy turn. As they circled

back to where her mother watched from below, Tau found the courage to release her hold on the rope long enough to wave. Lilae's rumble of laughter vibrated the great beast's throat beneath her.

Your mother says to tell you to keep your hands on the ropes and your mind on what you're doing.

Tau giggled at her mother's overprotective warning, but did as she was told. Tsuga did not have any mindspeech of her own, but Lilae could hear anyone's thoughts she chose to, without being bombarded by them constantly. Her shielding, like so much else, was purely instinctive, and when a thought was directed to her, she could hear it easily even if she was shielded.

I know you won't let me fall, but she's my mother. She worries, even when she knows I should be safe.

That is what mothers do.

This time when they turned, it seemed almost as though Lilae pivoted in place; Tau was thrown to one side and forced to find her balance again once she had righted herself.

Are you alright?

Fine. Just caught me by surprise.

Here, let's try something. Do you trust me?

Perhaps this was a moot question a few hundred feet in the air, but she answered nonetheless.

Of course.

Open your mind to me.

Tau did, loosening her shields in the way she had learned so that the separation between girl and guardian blurred until she could no longer distinguish where she ended and Lilae began.

It was an odd sensation to be able to feel the dragon's muscles bunch between her legs at the same time she felt the power in Lilae's wings as though they were her own. The changes in the air currents that told her where the thermals were; he knew each wingbeat instinctively before it happened, could sense how to lean into each turn before it came. She learned what each movement meant, the intricate workings of the dragon's body that made flight possible, and was shown how to work with her guardian so that she did not interfere with the miracle that was a dragon's flight.

Gradually Tau realized she was aware of herself again. Once her shields had been restored, she had to give herself a little shake to bring her mind back to its own thoughts before she could concentrate enough to speak.

That ... was incredible.

When we fly together in battle, it will be something like that. Working as one, and yet with the abilities and knowledge of both. Not quite so complete a meld, but ... similar.

Oh.

Tau hadn't given much thought to *why* they were beginning this training together. The thought of riding into battle sobered her a great deal. Lilae seemed to sense the change in her mood.

Are you ready to go down?

Tau fought back a sigh of regret and nodded with no little reluctance – not that Lilae could see the gesture, but she knew the dragon could feel her assent through their bond.

I guess so.

The landing was a little rough, but after having meshed so completely with her guardian Tau was able to adjust her seat and keep from being flopped around too gracelessly. By the time the dust raised from Lilae's wingbeats had settled, her mother was there at her side and had begun to untie the knots that secured her.

"Well? What did you think?"

Tau could feel the grin splitting her face as she slid down into Tsuga's arms.

"That was the best lesson ever! Can we do that every day? Did you see how high we were? Flying is such an amazing feeling! You've got to try it!"

Tsuga laughed and gave her a tight hug before letting her go.

"I did see. The two of you looked very at home up there."

"It felt … right." Tau's brow furrowed as she searched for the words to convey her meaning. "Like it's where I've always been meant to be."

Tsuga smiled in answer and nodded as she turned to smile at her own guardian where the horse waited to one side of the clearing.

"It's a good feeling, isn't it?"

Tau looked over her shoulder at the large dragon and smiled wider.

"It really is."

Chapter 7

$\mathcal{T}$au furrowed her brow in concentration as she watched her teacher. In the school they had established here on the border shortly after construction of the fortified castle, mages and warriors trained together, worked together, and lived together.

That was, ostensibly, the primary purpose of the compound her parents had built almost three years ago. In truth, though, a great deal more went on here than anyone back in the capitol suspected. Her parents worked together with the select few friends who had entered into this undertaking with them to harbor friendlier relations between Sennor and Devali.

What amazed Tau most was not that such a big secret had been carried out for fully three years now; it was that her parents' efforts were working. Here, at least, Sennorrans had begun to view their neighbors as humans rather than monsters. There were even a few – a very few – people from Devali itself who had taken up residence in what was, on paper at least, the newest of Sennor's border fortifications.

Now her older brother Trag – a native-born Devalian with Sennoran parents – sat at the table across from her and demonstrated how he was able to manipulate metal into various states, shapes, and consistencies. She did not bother to ask how any such feats were accomplished, for she could see the ebb and flow of magical energies as easily as she could see the table between them. She brushed a strand of unruly hair back from her brow and bit her lower lip in thought as something occurred to her.

"Is there a way to set something you've made permanently to its shape so that another mage can't manipulate it? Shielding is obvious, the way the lights here are shielded against natural fluctuations in magic so they are steady and do not go out, but any shield can be broken or bypassed. Is there another way?"

Trag smiled at her question – their mother's smile – and leaned back slightly in his chair.

"The fact that you thought to ask such a question shows that you are thinking ahead. So far no one has found a permanent solution, but I have been experimenting. The best I have managed is a self-perpetuating shield tied to the object."

Tau frowned and considered the little silver figurine on the table between them.

"What about a spell?"

Trag shook his head.

"Spells are unpredictable at best. We still don't fully understand how they work. They tie into the old magic somehow. But they don't always work, and when they do, the degree of success is varied."

Tau considered his words a moment, then reached out to grasp the finger-length dragon she had made. The proportions were off – the wings too small to support the body in flight – and she began manipulating it to correct the error.

"There must be something we're missing."

"We?"

Tau nodded and changed the position of the dragon's head so that it leveled its unblinking stare at her brother.

"Daddy has been after me to choose a Journeyman project. He says I am almost ready to be tested, and that I will need a focus for my studies. And nothing else interests me quite the way spells do."

Satisfied with her creation at last, she looked up to see Trag considering her with an odd expression.

"What?"

He shook his head.

"Nothing. Just imagining the reactions of the old fuddy-duddies when you figure out what has taken them decades to gain so much as an inkling of."

Tau beamed, and she saw his eyes light up as he grinned in answer.

"You really think I'll be able to?"

"Well, little sister, if anyone can it will be you."

Why would you want to write a spell for teleportation? You're a Queen's Mage trainee. You can teleport without a spell.

Yes, but spells take less energy from the mage. All they require is a little jolt to get them started, and the rest comes from the old magic in the world around the mage. And if I can get this right, the mage won't have to be a teleporter. It opens the ability up to anyone with magical talent.

Concern was plain in Lilae's mindvoice when she responded.

That could be dangerous. Armies could be moved in the blink of an eye.

Tau shook her head.

The spell I'm working on is only meant for one. To add anyone else to it would require a change in wording, ritual, timing….

But it would be possible.

Tau sighed and set the graphite stylus she was using aside and rubbed her forehead with her palms, leaving a gray smudge behind.

Yes, Lilae, it would be. But it could also mean getting help to those who need it. If healers could teleport to the wounded…. The good that can be done far outweighs the possible ill. I need your support in this, Lilae.

You have it, of course. I know your intentions are good, Tau. It's everyone else's that concern me.

I know. But it is no different than a sword, or than any other magic. In the wrong hands, it becomes a tool of destruction. But in the right hands —

—It is a tool for great good.

Exactly.

I know. Just … be careful.

I will. Now, if I could just get this wording right….

Read it again.

Tau did so, reading aloud in the hopes that hearing the words might help her think of the right phrasing.

"Speed my travel, here to there. Move my body through the air. Take me to the place I seek, that I may spare my aching feet."

Hmm. The rumble of the dragon's exhalation reached her as though Lilae were in the room next to her, rather than curled atop the roof baking in the sun.

That may fling you through the air, or remove your feet, or bespell you to run the whole way.

Good point. So how do I avoid anything like that?

The phrasing has to be just right. What about 'My mind holds the place I seek. Take my body where my mind leads. Speed me safely here to there. Transport me now, take me there?'

I could see a problem there, too. What if it separates my body from my mind? Or leaves out anything I carry – like clothes? Or ... here, how about this? 'My mind holds the place I seek. This destination I must reach. Transport me there instantly, along with all I have with me.'

That ... may work. Interesting tactic, adding that last part. But again, that is too easy to manipulate into something that will put too much power in the wrong hands. Maybe 'along with all that I carry?'

I like that! She wrote it down quickly, before she could forget the wording, and then set the stick down again to look at the page in satisfaction.

When will you try it?

Why not now?

Now?! Is that wise?

It's mid-morning. If this works the way I hope, I'll be back in a matter of minutes. And if it doesn't, you will be able to find me and fly me back after you let my parents know what happened.

But Tau, I–

I won't go far. I know just the place. We flew over it a few days ago. It's only a couple of miles from here – far enough to really test it, but not so far that I'll be in any real danger if anything happens.

Before Lilae could protest again, Tau pushed back from the desk and reached through the mage stone she wore about her neck into the magic around her and seized the power. She centered and grounded herself with the ease of long practice – a necessary precaution to keep the power from fighting her overmuch – and began to chant the spell. As she finished, she gave a slight twist to the power she held.

The world dipped, shrank, and then abruptly expanded. Her ears popped and her head spun slightly, so that she had to blink her vision clear. As she did, she became aware of the sound of running water, distant shouts, and the unmistakable clink of armor. Before her she saw the small stream she had pictured as her destination.

It worked!

Filled with elation, she turned to take in her surroundings – and the world dropped out from under her again.

"Seize her!"

The words scarcely registered; she flung raw magical power against the shields that had been thrown up around her. Or tried to. She felt panic rise in her throat when she realized the shields had cut her off from her magic. Only now did she register the armed men around her. A few advanced towards her, but her attention snapped to the man in the robes. He was the one who had shielded her.

"That won't be necessary. She is shielded. And a child."

The mage approached her, and when he was about an arm's length away he crouched down to look her in the eye.

"You are a powerful mage, child. What is your name?"

As though his words had been a release, Tau felt her mind begin to work again. She forced herself to relax as her parents' training took over.

"Molly." *If you are ever kidnapped, lie about your name. If they don't know who you are, it could very well save your life.*

The man arched an eyebrow.

"That's a lie. But that's alright. You're going to come with me. There is someone I have no doubt will be interested to meet you."

Chapter 8

"What do you mean, 'gone?'"

Lilae shifted uncomfortably and dropped her head to the ground so that she was closer to eye-level with the human.

I can't hear her. I know she's alive, but she's blocked from me.

"Well, where is she?"

The dragon moaned, a sound deep in her throat that hurt the ears and made Ramiq and Tsuga – the last to have spoken – wince.

I'm not sure. We were working on a spell – that's what she's chosen for her Journeyman's study – and I tried to stop her, but she wouldn't listen, and –

"What kind of spell?"

Ramiq's voice was low, and the unspoken worry there made the guardian whine again.

A teleportation spell.

"A what?" Lilae flinched. "Do you have any idea how dangerous that is?! What could have happened?"

"Ramiq." Tsuga reached out and grasped her husband's arm, and the mage stopped mid-tirade. She shifted her attention to the dragon again.

"Lilae, do you know where she went?"

Yes. She held the image in her mind as she said the spell. And the last thing I heard from her was that it worked.

"Can you show us?"

Lilae considered a moment, and then settled her wings as she assented and sent the image Tau had used into their minds.

"Good. Let's go." Ramiq gathered his robes about himself even as he gathered his magic closer, but once again his wife's hand on his arm gave him pause.

"Wait. I recognize that place. It's just a few miles away, on the Devalian side of the border. It's also where our scouts report an encampment of Devalian soldiers."

"What are you saying?" Ramiq's voice was tense, and Tsuga swallowed a lump in her own throat before she could answer.

"I'm saying the Devalians have our little girl. And if we teleport into the middle of them and burn them all in a fiery rage, it will undo everything we've worked for."

Ramiq visibly drooped, and Tsuga released him as his hand dropped from his mage stone.

"So what do we do?"

"We plan. We have to think through the best way to handle this."

"And what happens to Tau while we think?"

"She is eight years old, Ramiq. They won't hurt her."

"How can you be sure?"

"I have to be."

"Who are you?"

The older woman had a vaguely familiar look to her, but Tau couldn't quite place where she might have encountered her before. She could, however, see that she was a mage – and a very powerful one, at that.

She's a Queen's Mage, she realized as she looked more closely at the aura surrounding the stranger. *Maybe that's why she seems so familiar…. Aren't we related to the one in Devali somehow?*

The mage brushed a lock of brown hair – it was just starting to go to silver, with a light peppering here and there – aside and looked at her out of eyes that reminded Tau of her father.

"I suspect you know the answer to that, child. I can see your mother in you. And my cousin, as well. Their blood has marked you, in more ways than one. What I want to know is how you teleported into the middle of my camp without being magically detected? If Jason had not been right on top of you, he wouldn't even have known another mage appeared out of nowhere."

Tau did her best to keep her expression neutral, but her voice dripped with scorn when she answered.

"Your battle-tested mage cannot detect the magical workings of an eight-year-old child?"

The stranger had a great deal more experience schooling her reactions than Tau did, and so her expression did not change. Her tone was even when she responded.

"You are strong, child, and talented. But your skill is not yet so great as all that. So how did you do it?"

"Odds are you will be in enemy territory one day; possibly even captured. When that happens, you

must try to remain strong. Stay calm, and try to avoid giving any useful information away."

Her mother and father had drilled her on such eventualities her entire life. Her mother had preached caution; her father had taught her deceit and diplomacy. Tau drew herself up to full height and lifted her chin, jaw set in an unconscious echo of her mother's defiant mannerisms.

"If your magical abilities are so greatly lacking that you are unable to figure it out for yourself, that is your problem, not mine."

Tau had thought herself prepared for any reaction; had, until the older woman laughed aloud in response.

"You certainly do have your mother's fire, don't you? No matter; you can stay until you change your mind. Take her to my tent. Keep an eye on her, and keep her tightly shielded. She is a valuable hostage; we can't have her slip through our fingers."

The last was addressed to the mage who stepped forward at her words, and Tau felt him draw on his power, then cried out in surprise as her arms were seized from behind by invisible hands and bound there.

"Easy. Don't hurt her." The pressure lessened by a few degrees, and Tau eased the muscles in her shoulders. Before she could say anything else her guard turned her around and gave her a shove towards the tent flap.

Chapter 9

"What do you mean you're going to fly over?"

Just that. I know where she went. They can't have taken her far. I'm going to fly over and see if I can sense her.

Ramiq frowned and shook his head.

"It's too dangerous. All it would take is one well-aimed shot, and you'd both be dead."

The dragon's tail lashed in annoyance as she lowered her head to meet Ramiq's gaze.

I am a dragon, mage. I can hide myself when I wish. The only one who will know I am there will be Tau.

"That encampment is going to be crawling with mages. How are you going to manage that?"

Like this.

Ramiq blinked, and then blinked again, suddenly confused. Where a moment before there had been a dragon the size of a small house, there was now … nothing. Not only did he not see anything, but he didn't *sense* anything either.

Just to be sure he called upon his mage sight, but still everything seemed perfectly normal. There was absolutely nothing strange about the magical currents around him; they all looked as natural as ever. He couldn't even hear the dragon breathe, a sound like a bellows that he had grown accustomed to over the last four years.

"How are you doing that?"

Just as quickly as she had vanished Lilae reappeared, causing Ramiq to take a startled step backwards.

I told you. I am a dragon. I am an expression of nature's magic; made from the elements, by the elements, and for them. They protect me. Hide me, when I need it.

"That's incredible."

I am going to find her, Adept.

"I know you will. But I am her father. It is my job to protect her. And I don't know how."

His voice broke on the last, and Lilae touched her snout to his chest and breathed out softly in sympathy.

I know. I feel the same. We will figure it out.

Ramiq sighed and pinched the bridge of his nose between his thumb and fingers in an effort to alleviate his growing headache.

"I have to get back to my students."

Of course.

"Just … stay safe, okay? And bring our daughter home to us."

I will.

Tau sat on the short stool she had been provided and watched the morning bustle of the Devalians' camp. It wasn't all that different from what she was used to, really. The smells of wood smoke, horse, and unwashed bodies were all familiar to her, though the last was hardly pleasant.

She shot a glare at her guard. They had changed who watched her at some point in the night, for now instead of the young man who had captured her yesterday a middle-aged woman stood quietly off to one side. Almost absently, Tau probed at the shields that held her apart from her magic, the way she would worry at loose tooth with her tongue. She sighed as she completed the examination. There was still no change; she could find no weaknesses, no faults for her to exploit. The woman shifted her cool regard to Tau when the girl sighed, but didn't say anything. In fact, she hadn't spoken once today.

Tau could feel the magic around her, could even see it still when she used her mage sight. But the shield prevented her from touching so much as the slightest trickle of power. It was infuriating. She shifted her weight and frowned at the scene before her irritably.

A pressure was building within her. At first she dismissed it as frustration, but as it continued to grow, realization dawned.

It's Lilae. She's close. She must be scouting to make sure I'm alright!

Tau had to fight back the urge to look up and confirm her suspicion. If Lilae was up there, she didn't want to draw any attention to her guardian, lest she unwittingly put the dragon in danger.

Dragons are made of magic. And she's my guardian. That bond is deeper than anything else. They can shield me from mindspeaking her, but they can't shield us from each other completely – not without killing us. Which means....

Tau glanced around her to be sure everyone else continued to go about their own business, and then acted quickly, saying a quick mental prayer of thanks to her mother for drilling her so extensively. She hooked one foot around the leg of the stool on which she sat and shifted her weight onto the other so she could grip the seat with one hand. She stood, turned, and threw in one fluid motion and sent the stool flying at the mage's head.

"Hey!"

So she can *speak.*

Tau didn't stay long enough to see the results of her attack, but instead turned and fled. She had to do this quickly. As she ran she puffed out the words to her spell, picturing clearly the roof where Lilae best liked to sun herself. She could hear the mage raising the alarm somewhere behind her, but she could not spare a moment's thought for what it might mean. She reached out for that soul-deep bond, seized it, pulled on the inherent power it carried, and *twisted.*

Chapter 10

*H*er momentum threw her off balance, and it was all she could do to keep from falling on her face. Her arms windmilled wildly, but at last she regained her equilibrium and was able to gasp in a breath as she looked around.

Home.

A light breeze stirred the white-and-silver banners of Sennor displayed atop the gray stone wall, and from the practice yard she smelled the sulfur that bespoke a battle mage at practice. She reached out with her magical senses, eager to feel the power again at her fingertips.

Instead of the familiar rush of energy she expected, though, she met the same resistance she had when shielded in the Devalian camp. The shields she was used to broke when no longer in proximity to the mage who set them. Obviously, Devalian shields did not.

She groaned in frustration and turned as the wind changed direction, then moved off to the side of the rooftop and shielded her eyes against the dust of Lilae's landing. When she heard the dragon settle herself, she opened her eyes and turned to meet the bright green-gold stare with a worried frown.

"We have a problem."

"Well, the shields should be simple enough to break from the outside. That's not a problem. You're sure you're alright? They didn't hurt you?"

"No, Daddy, I'm fine. They only shielded me." She paused a moment, and then wheezed out, "Daddy? I can't breathe."

"Oh! Sorry."

She gasped in a relieved breath as he released his grip on her and she was able to pull her face back from where it had been buried in his voluminous robes.

"It's alright."

A moment passed, and then she felt the shields collapse like a dam suddenly giving way before the floodwaters. Magic flowed into her eagerly when she reached for it, but after years of practice she was able to brace against the torrent with little effort. She centered and grounded in the space of a moment and erected her own shields – ones that bent to *her* will, not anyone else's – to effectively soothe the raw exposure to every thought and emotion of every non-shielded person, guardian, and animal near the fortress. That brief moment of cacophony was enough to ensure that she reinforced and checked the protections a second time before she allowed herself a sigh of relief and smiled in satisfaction.

Lilae?

Glad to have you back again.

Not as glad as I am to be back.

She turned her smile to Ramiq, who still watched her worriedly.

"I promise, I'm alright. Where is Ma?"

Ramiq sighed and shook his head. Upon realizing that the Devalian shields had held through her teleportation – and *how* had they done *that?* – she had immediately sought his help. She had not even paused long enough to let anyone else know of her safe return.

"She is with her trainees. We both agreed to try to keep things running normally for as long as possible. Why don't you go let her know you've made it home? I'm sure she will want to see you."

Tau nodded and gave her father another hug before she turned and ran out of the room, already reaching out with her thoughts to pinpoint exactly where Tsuga was. She ran all the way, remembering a time a few years ago when she would have simply teleported herself the short distance.

"Tau, look at me."

Tau raised a tear-stained face at this command from her mother and choked back a sob as best she could manage.

"Oh, darling. I'm not angry with you. Come here."

Tsuga pulled her into a tight embrace, and Tau allowed herself to take comfort from her mother's arms.

"But you must understand that you cannot use magic for every little thing. Not only because it may exhaust you, but because it can be dangerous to rely on it. What would happen if you were lost and alone somewhere, shielded or so drained you could not use your magic? How would you start a fire to stay warm and cook your food?"

Tsuga relaxed her grip and sat back on her heels to brush Tau's tears away and smile.

"Your own feet will do you just as well as your power to teleport – sometimes better. You may need

to keep your magic a secret one day; you need to know how to do without it."

"But why would I want to keep it a secret? Magic is a gift to be proud of. Daddy said so!"

"And your father is absolutely right. But what of all the people who don't have such a gift? You are a powerful empath, Tau; you should be able to understand the pain jealousy can cause. If you can avoid giving someone that kind of hurt, wouldn't you want to?"

Tau considered these words for a moment, and then nodded.

"Yes ma'am. Of course."

"Good girl. Now, why don't you go and find your father? I'm sure he has a fun lesson planned for you today."

Tau slowed to a walk when her mother came into sight, and at last drew to a stop at the edge of the training yard, where she folded her hands before her and did her best to wait patiently without shifting her weight restlessly or fidgeting unnecessarily.

Tsuga was in the middle of drilling some of the students on form. She walked among ten or so young men and women as she barked out commands. A couple of the trainees shone with the light of mage energy to her other senses, and these were the ones who seemed to be having the most trouble. Tau watched with a critical eye as the pupils danced through the various forms her mother named. At eight years old, Tau had already been training with various light-weight weapons for three years.

This was a beginner-level class in swordsmanship. While Tau had not yet been taught to handle a full-size sword herself, she had often watched her mother conduct classes like this one. Many of the forms were similar to those she had learned for her small belt knives, though with some noticeable differences.

When Tsuga came around behind one of the students and turned to demonstrate a proper stance Tau caught her gaze and raised a hand in greeting. Her usually-composed mother let out a wordless exclamation and ran across the distance between them. Tau allowed herself to be scooped up into a too-tight embrace, and managed not to squirm too much as Tsuga squeezed her even tighter for a moment before loosening her grip.

"You're home! What happened? Are you alright? Did they try to hurt you? Does your father know you're here?"

Tau laughed and wrapped her arms around her mother's neck for another quick squeeze before she answered.

"I didn't check where I was going before I teleported, and there was a Devalian camp. They shielded me. But I'm fine. Daddy has already seen me. He had to break my shields; I couldn't." That failure still irked.

Tsuga kissed the top of her head in an annoying matronly fashion, but a moment later the Weaponsmistress rocked back on her heels and tilted her head to the side with a frown.

"If you weren't able to break the shields yourself, how did you escape?"

Tau smiled and glanced over her shoulder. She couldn't see Lilae where she sunned herself on the rooftop from here, but she knew the great copper beast was there.

"Lilae."

Tsuga's brow furrowed in confusion, and she, too, looked over Tau's shoulder as though she could see what Tau could not.

"But how –"

"We are the same." Tau shrugged. "They could shield me from my magic, and even from talking to her. But our bond was too deep to be shielded against."

Tsuga shook her head in wonderment. She looked as though she were about to say something more, but one of her trainees cleared his throat at that moment, and she recalled the presence of her class.

"Go get something to eat, Tau, and some rest. And no more teleporting, at least for now. I will be up to check on you as soon as I'm done here."

After one more rib-crushing embrace Tsuga stood and returned to the task at hand, leaving the young girl to her own devises. Tau couldn't help but feel somewhat slighted by this quick dismissal, but a light touch to her mother's surface thoughts – one of those morally gray practices of magic that her father encouraged while her mother cautioned against – revealed the Weaponsmistress to, in fact, be obsessively worrying over her daughter's well-being. It was only a strong sense of duty and common sense which held her from coddling her daughter and dropping everything else to see to her.

Tau sighed and turned towards the mess hall.

Maybe food isn't such a bad idea....

Chapter 11

"Now explain to me again just how it is you were able to use magic while shielded."

Tau heaved a long-suffering sigh and shook her head. She had been over this so many times she was beginning to think she could recite the answers by rote. Her father had asked the same question a dozen different ways, as though by phrasing it differently he might get a different answer or glean some additional information.

"Lilae and I are the same. Two halves of a whole."

"Yes, yes, two sides of the same coin. The same is true of any person and his guardian."

"Yes, to an extent. But Lilae is a dragon. She doesn't just use magic like we do; she *is* magic. Magic is woven into her bone and muscle – everything about her. And because of our bond, it is a part of me as well. They were able to shield me against using magic in the traditional sense, and against sending any messages out, but short of death there is no way to sever a bond with a guardian. You taught me that. So when she flew close enough, I was able to use her inherent magic as a source of power to start my spell and get me home."

Ramiq shook his head and Tau flinched away from the look he gave her. Where she had hoped to find her father's respect and pride in his daughter's accomplishments, she instead found herself looking into green eyes filled with bewilderment and no little fear. She sighed and allowed her head to slump forward; she lacked the will to hold it up.

"May I go now?"

When he didn't answer, Tau mustered the strength to look at him again. His expression had softened, and where moments before there had sat a Queen's Mage bent on understanding an unprecedented magical phenomenon, she now saw her daddy, the man who picked her up when she fell and held her when she cried over a broken toy.

"This has been harder on you than you've been trying to let on, hasn't it?"

She started to reassure him, but the words stuck in her throat. She didn't even realize she had started to cry until she saw the stain of her tears where they fell on her sleeves. She reached to dry her eyes with the cuff, but before she could finish the gesture Ramiq had come around the table and scooped her into his arms.

Caught in his warm embrace, she lost the last shreds of her restraint and turned into his shoulder, where she sobbed brokenly, shoulders shaking with the vehemence of her emotions.

At length, she was able to get herself under control again and pull away to dry her eyes and blow her nose on the handkerchief Ramiq offered her.

"Well, there will be plenty of time to figure this out. Right now, how about we go and get your mother and have dinner?"

Tau managed a weak smile, though she felt her eyes tearing again as she did so.

"That sounds nice."

Ramiq smiled and held out his arm to her as he stood.

"Good. Come on; let's go."

Tau dabbed her eyes again, then wadded the kerchief up in one hand and allowed herself to be drawn to his side. She was unable to stifle a sigh of relief at the feeling of safety and stability that washed over her in his embrace.

Tau lay awake in her bed and watched the play of colored lights she had enchanted into its canopy. Her father had first done this for her as an infant, as a safer alternative to a candle burning on the nightstand with three powerful fire mages in residence. Now that she was older, Tau still found comfort in the swirl of color.

She had put this magic in place herself, but tonight the slow shifting and changing only served to stir her to further restlessness. Eventually she gave up grasping for sleep and threw back the thin blanket she used in the warmer months and slipped her feet into the light slippers she wore for traipsing around the building at night – usually down to the kitchens for a snack, or to use the necessary. She seldom had nightmares anymore; there wasn't much for her to be afraid of, here in the fortress. There was no place safer for her, certainly.

It was not until she stood on the roof, her filmy pink night dress blowing in the warm breeze, that she realized she had begun walking. Lilae lifted her head to greet her, the rich, green-gold eyes glowing in the darkness as she watched the little girl cross the roof. It was a testament to the strength of their bond that Lilae did not ask any questions or comment on Tau's presence at this time of night.

The dragon lifted her wing and invited the child closer. Tau did not hesitate, but moved to the guardian's side and nestled down against the soft, leathery hide. Lilae folded her wing over the girl in the protective way a mother guarding her nestlings might. Tau closed her eyes and let the warmth radiated by the dragon's body wash over her and chase the tension and worry from her muscles and thoughts. It wasn't long before she was asleep.

"Well, she is definitely your daughter."

Tsuga couldn't hide a smile at those words. In so many ways, Tau took after her father – her aptitude for magic, her empathy for others, her joyful, exuberant personality – but, as he said, in this respect Tau was well and truly *her* child.

When Tau had not been at breakfast, neither of them had been overly surprised. But when Tsuga had gone to check on her and found the child's bed empty, a frantic search had been stopped before it had started, thanks to a quick check with Lilae. Bemused, both parents had made the trek up to the roof, where they found their little girl nestled safely in the embrace of her guardian.

"As though there were any doubt."

Tsuga smiled and moved to kneel beside the dragon where Tau slept nestled against her side. She held aside the great beast's wing with one hand and reached out with the other to touch the child's shoulder. Tau's eyes fluttered open, and Tsuga rocked back on her heels. *Her eyes are so like her father's.*

"Tau, sweetie, what are you doing here? Is everything alright? Your Daddy and I were worried about you."

Tau sat up reluctantly and rubbed her eyes as she stretched.

"Mmhmm, I'm fine. I couldn't sleep." She stifled a yawn and peeked out from behind the shelter of her guardian's wing to see Ramiq standing and watching their interaction. She waved at him.

"Sorry I worried you."

"We're just glad you're alright. Are you hungry? Let's get you some breakfast."

Once Tau had nodded her assent, Tsuga stood and extended a hand for the girl to take.

"You know, your daddy has never known what it's like to need to feel safe to sleep. I used to sneak out and share Bane's stall a lot before we married. If you'd like we can bring a bedroll up here, so that you'll be a little more comfortable."

"That would be nice. Thank you."

"Take as long as you need. Sometimes a girl just needs her guardian."

Tau giggled, and as Ramiq fell into step beside them Tsuga caught his eye.

Is that really the best idea?

Would you rather she feel like she needs to keep it a secret? I for one would rather our daughter feel loved and supported.

Fine; I trust you. But I still don't like it.

Where will she be safer than with her guardian? With us.

Ramiq. She's a dragon. *You may be the Queen's Mage, but Lilae is* magic. *She is the best possible protection for her. Tau* knows *that.*

I already said you're right.

Tsuga laughed and Tau looked up at her, squinting against the glare of the morning sun.

"Are you two talking about me?"

"No."

"Yes."

Tsuga and Ramiq exchanged a glance and tried again.

"Yes."

"No."

Tau giggled, and her parents shared a wry smile.

"You two are awful liars."

"We are, aren't we?"

Ramiq chuckled and ruffled Tau's hair as the three of them descended the staircase from the roof.

Chapter 12

*J*ust allow yourself to relax. Metal is hard and unyielding. It requires a soft touch. You can hammer away on it all day long and scarcely make a dent. Manipulation of the element requires a less direct approach, and no little finesse."

For once Tau was not dressed in one of her usual colorful costumes of layered mage's robes. Today she wore a plain cotton dress under the child-sized leather apron that had been designed to withstand the rigors of forge work. Her hair – long and straight, no matter how much she might wish it to curl – was pulled back in a tight braid, making the hawk-like nose and angular face she had inherited from her mother all the more prominent. She took a deep breath.

"A blacksmith can create beautiful, wonderful things out of all manner of metals and ores. But he does not accomplish this through brute strength. He makes use of a forge, water, an anvil and, yes, a hammer. All of these tools allow him to shape what he has into what he wants, first by heating – often even completely melting – the metal before cooling and shaping it. It is a process that takes time, effort, and care.

"A metal mage does not always *need* these physical tools – not if his gift is strong enough – but we often utilize them nonetheless. The physical steps help to ground and focus our thoughts, so that the end result is stronger and even more stable than it might be otherwise."

Just over a month had passed since her experience with the botched transportation spell – no, that wasn't quite right. The spell had worked perfectly; it had been its functionality that had landed her in hot water, after all.

The dust had settled fairly quickly, and her life had since returned to its routine of political and academic schooling, mage training, and tactical and weapons training. Her days were filled with these activities, and though exhaustion held her firmly by the end of each night, she still sought out the comfort of Lilae's warm body more often than not. Something about the proximity of her guardian helped to soothe her racing mind and lull her to sleep.

Today was her first lesson in metallurgy since the incident, and she was happy to learn that her teacher had not changed.

Trag Dafrin – Tsuga's oldest child, and Tau's only sibling (even if he was only a half-brother) – usually traveled with one lord's army or another. He worked as a blacksmith and made a living by crafting, repairing, and bespelling weapons and armor for the fighting men and women of both Sennor and Devali.

As a Devalian native who had received Auriga's blessing in the form of his canine guardian Temalon, his loyalties were understandably torn. Thus, he sold his services without discrimination to any who could afford them. It was the only way, he said, that he could keep his conscience clear and avoid giving what may become an unfair advantage to one side or the other.

"Therefore, today we will begin at the beginning." He smiled wryly at his own joke, and Tau giggled herself at the weak pun.

"Now, typically a traditional smith will have an apprentice – or several – who tends the fire to ensure that it burns hotly and cleanly. However, with your unique gifts, I want you to learn to control the fire and heat yourself. Today we will still use physical fuel and actual water to assist in the heating and cooling process, but eventually you will be able to heat, cool, and even shape the metal wholly with your magic, should you choose to do so. Like this."

Tau had only received one lesson from her brother before. Her parents often brought in other instructors or sent her to join a class with other pupils, but this was a unique experience. Trag was more than just another mage: he was the foremost metal Adept that anyone had ever seen. Tau was determined to learn absolutely everything he could possibly teach her.

She watched avidly as he lifted one of the iron ingots from the pile and held it out before her. It shifted and changed in his hand, until it formed a perfect miniature of the coyote that lolled in the cool shade under the bench outside the forge. The change was too fast for her to track all of it, but he smiled at her look of consternation.

"All in good time. Now, I stoked the fire just before you arrived, but as you can see with your mage sight – or even with your naked eye, which you will eventually learn to use and interpret as I can – it is producing a great deal of smoke and heating unevenly. Smoke will contaminate whatever you work on; once soot and ash gets into the metal, it causes flaws and impurities that can compromise the integrity. An experienced smith or a well-trained apprentice will maintain areas of varying temperatures in a forge – hot and cool spots, if you will. For example, a higher heat is needed to melt the ore than that which is needed to make it merely malleable.”

Tau nodded her acknowledgement as she slipped into her sight and examined his forge. To her enhanced vision the fire burned wildly, leaping and falling sporadically. Without any further prompting she reached out to it (fire had always been among her strongest elemental abilities, though she had nowhere near either of her parents’ strengths with the element) and soothed it. She had no other word for the process by which she quieted the fire’s angry roar and gave its heat purpose and direction.

As she did this the smoke changed from sickly black – the kind full of grease and soot – to a pale gray that was nearly undetectable in comparison. Trag made a sound – of surprise or approval, she wasn’t certain – and she shifted her attention back to him.

“Not bad. You maintained the hot and cool spots quite well. You may need to adjust the temperatures a bit as we go, but that should do nicely for a place to begin.”

Tau allowed herself a small smile at this praise and slowly withdrew her awareness from the flames, careful to ensure that her changes held stable as she did so.

“Now we can begin. This is copper ore.”

He held up a rock that shone slightly with a coppery hue, speckled here and there with a bright blue.

"Copper is a softer metal. Even when it is cool, pure copper can be shaped and molded fairly easily. For that reason, it is common practice for smiths to mix in other, harder metals to help the end result maintain its shape. However, as a metal mage, you can alter its properties slightly to achieve the same result without needing to create an alloy.

"There are times when this property is useful, though in most instances an alloy is more practical. Your first project, for example: a pot. Copper conducts a great deal of heat and spreads it evenly over its surface. It heats and cools much faster than, say, iron, which is more commonly used for cooking. However, the kind of pot we will start you on today is highly sought-after by alchemists and healers.

"Copper has several unique properties that makes it ideal for potion-brewing, not the least of which is that it is a magical barrier. You can imbue the contents of such a pot with a spell or other magicka without affecting the surroundings or container at all."

Tau frowned as something occurred to her.

"If magic can't pass through copper, why don't we make all of our armor and weapons out of it?"

"It would seem logical, wouldn't it?"

Tau nodded.

"But copper is soft – too soft to withstand the rigors of physical battle, or even routine wear. It would have to be an alloy, but once copper is combined with another metal, it loses its resistance to magic."

"What about just coating the armor with it?"

Trag smiled indulgently at her, but shook his head.

"Copper is very expensive – almost as much so as gold. Not even the queen can afford to coat her soldiers' armor that way."

"Oh," Tau breathed. It was too bad, in a way; magic-proof armor could shift the tide of the war drastically. Or, if it were made available to both sides, would even the playing field and all but eliminate a highly unpredictable factor.

"Now as you can see here, this is copper ore; it is as yet unrefined. Our first step will be to smelt, or purify it. We accomplish that through a process of careful, repeated heating, pouring, and cooling, through which all of the contaminants are filtered and removed. For non-mages, this process is lengthy and very tricky to master. It requires near-perfect conditions of heat and air, and uses charcoal to separate the pure metal, then limestone to filter out any remaining impurities. There are other, less effective methods, such as melting the ore and then cooling it in water with a specific concentration of salt, but today we will practice smelting."

So far the process sounded simple enough; control the heat and environment, pour off the good stuff, and do it again, until all that was left was a pure metal. But in practice, she knew, it would be extremely difficult.

"Smelting is by far the most common method of refinery, despite being one of the most difficult to master. It is also the method most closely resembling what we do with magic, so it will make that transition more natural for you when the time comes."

He carried the small chunk of ore to his work bench, where a small pot about the size of her head with walls thicker than three of her fingers side-by-side sat filled to within a couple of inches of the top with similar chunks of ore. He added the last to the top of the pile and handed her what looked like a long pair of blunt scissors with a sharp curve in the ends.

"When you get the hang of using your magic you won't have to rely on these any more, but for now, this is what you use to handle the smelting pot. Now, the tool is a little heavy, and the pot will be hard for you to lift by yourself until you get a little older, so for now I am going to help you to make sure it doesn't get dropped, okay?"

She nodded, and he moved to stand behind her and cup his hands – burnt brown from the fires of his forge and rough with the callouses of hard work – around hers so that he could adjust her grip on the handle and help her lift the pot. They turned together, and he helped her set the pot in the coals in the appropriate place.

"Now, we will have to let that melt for a while. Once the metal is liquefied it will bubble slightly as the impurities begin to separate. We will help the process by aerating it – we can do this magically, but regular smiths require much larger and more complex setups for this step. This is part of what allows me to travel so freely; what I need is comparatively little. You will, some day, be even more flexible; a mage who can also control fire, earth, and water could do this kind of thing entirely of her own power – or over a campfire by a stream, or any number of other such locations."

Tau nodded to show she was listening, but her gaze remained riveted on their small pot where it rested in the furnace. She had, out of curiosity, slipped back into mage sight, and the activity in the pot fascinated her. Not only could she see how the heat spread in the furnace and across the pot, she could watch how it affected the copper ore itself and make minute adjustments. She surmised Trag was watching with the sight as well by his next words.

"What did you do just there?"

Tau started guiltily. It was, after all, her first time to try anything like this. Perhaps it had been overly presumptuous of her to take it upon herself to make adjustments.

"The pot was spreading the heat unevenly, so I fixed it. Now everything will heat all over at the same speed and temperature."

She was not looking at her brother to see his eyebrows raise towards his hairline, but the lift in his voice bespoke his surprise clearly enough.

"That is an observation I would expect the third or fourth time an apprentice underwent this process. Not the first. What else do you notice?"

Tau furrowed her brow and took a step closer to the heat of the forge.

"At this rate, the fuel will need to be replenished in about ten minutes to maintain the current level of heat. The forge is fairly efficient in design – very little of the heat escapes through the smoke hole, and a good amount of air is taken in through the grates near the bottom. The majority of your loss is through the open front, and there's really no way to avoid that short of sealing it off somehow, and that would make it nearly impossible to work with. The copper heats faster than the impurities – it would be in a liquid state already, if it were pure."

She paused to take a breath, and Trag held up a hand to forestall her.

"Alright, alright. I forget you are the daughter of the Queen's Mage. I shouldn't be surprised at your magical aptitude, I suppose."

Tau tore her eyes away from the furnace long enough to flash him a wolfish grin.

"Momma says that underestimation will always be one of my biggest challenges."

Trag nodded.

"And she is absolutely right. In battle – whether the fight is physical, magical, political, or purely mental – a young girl, or when you age, a woman, will often be misjudged. Many perceive women to be weaker or of less intelligence."

He tapped his nose and winked at her with a conspiratorial smile.

"But anyone who has spent more than ten minutes with our esteemed mother knows how very wrong such an assumption can be."

Tau giggled. She could not imagine anyone ever mistaking her mother for weak or stupid.

Tsuga Dafrin was a name widely known and respected, and often times even feared, in both Sennor and Devali. Not many women could boast two years' travel and training in the male-centric Devalian military. In fact, to date her mother was the only one to hold such a claim, so far as Tau knew. She had held the position of Captain in the Sennorran army, and had run her own band of mercenaries for nearly a decade. She currently held the title of Weaponsmistress for the Sennorran military – one of many – and so far as anyone could tell, she was the foremost authority on just about any weapon there was. Tau knew first hand just how quick her mother's reflexes were, both on the field of battle and off it. She had a tactical eye most generals would kill for, and a mind many scholars envied. Or so it seemed to her daughter.

She returned her wandering thoughts to the task at hand and nearly shouted with excitement.

"It's melted!"

She could even see a few large, slow bubbles forming on the surface.

"So it is. Now, a metal mage could, at this point, simply pull all of the pure metal away from the contaminants and be done with it. However, that is not the purpose of today's lesson. Today is about learning technique and getting familiar with the element in the most basic and fundamental ways possible. You've had some training in air magic, correct?

Tau frowned.

"A little."

"You can move it, shape it, and confine it?"

"Yes, but I can't control the winds yet."

"You don't need to for this. Just concentrate on the copper. Create lots of little bubbles inside the metal, then let them go so they rise and pop. Not too vigorously, or we will have quite a mess. But if it's done too gently, we won't get the desired effect, either. It's going to take some finesse."

Tau nodded to show her understanding and shifted her full focus to the task at hand. Air was a fairly new element to her as well; she had only just begun to grasp it last week. It was tricky; she was used to the firm, direct approach she used when dealing with fire, or even earth. But air was different. She couldn't seize it or hold it in her hand. She couldn't even *see* it without her mage sight, only what it did when it moved the leaves of the trees or stirred the dust at her feet. It had taken her a long time to learn how to even begin to use and control the elusive element.

She took a deep breath and concentrated on the little pot where it sat in the fire. She pictured forming little balls of air – the size of a drop of ink – and pulling them downward into the pot. She let one go experimentally, breath held in anticipation. She watched as it rose slowly to the surface and created a little bubble of molten metal. She released her breath with a sigh – it had worked! – and when she did, the other two dozen or so bubbles rose all at once to the top of the pot, where they burst through together with a loud POP and a small but spectacular explosion of molten metal.

She took a step back in alarm, but stopped to stare when she realized the droplets had been halted midair before they made it more than a few inches from their container. She turned guiltily to meet Trag's gaze.

"You have the right idea, but you lost focus. For anyone but a metal mage, a loss of even this small amount of copper is a significant one."

As he finished speaking the droplets began to reverse their trajectory, and eventually the last of them dropped back beneath the liquid surface of the molten ore with a low plop.

"Settle your thoughts, and let's try it again."

Chapter 13

$\mathcal{M}$oments to herself were few and far between these days. If it hadn't been for the need to exercise Lilae and let the dragon hunt Tau might have never been granted so much as a minute to be free of the demands of her parents, instructors, or friends. Once in a while, a girl simply needed her solitude.

Tau currently lay on her back in tall grass warmed by a pale fall sun. She was dressed against the slight chill in the air in her typical layered robes. This particular set, a blend of coppers and golds, was sewn of heavier fabric than her breezy summer costumes. Over the sound of water running through the rocks in a shallow part of the stream by which she lay, Tau could hear Lilae crunching the bones of her kill – a couple of deer – and sucking out the flavorful marrow in the middle. The smell of roasted venison floated to her on the breeze, and Tau smiled to herself.

Most people believed dragons had the appetites of wolves, who ate their kills raw. Lilae had informed her with disdain the first time Tau had made such a comment that dragons were far more civilized. Only a dragon pushed beyond the limits of hunger to the verge of starvation – which most of the dragons who attacked towns or carried off domesticated livestock were – would ever stoop to such barbaric eating habits. Dragons preferred their meat cooked, and traditionally used the heat of their own magically-generated flaming breath to cook their meals.

Nonetheless, the sound of those massive teeth and powerful jaws cracking through bone made Tau shudder with a primal discomfiture.

As a cloud drifted along on a breeze that did nothing to stir the air on the earth below Tau squinted against the sudden light of the exposed sun. By its position in the sky she reckoned it to be just past midday. She would be obligated to return before long to the fort she called home, as she was due for a lesson in politics in about an hour. After that she had a magic lesson, and then her second round of weapons training before she took her evening meal.

They were only a short flight away from the fortified compound, but Lilae would want to allow her food to settle before exerting herself for the trip back. Tau rolled onto her side in the grass and drew the dagger she wore at her belt. Trag had given it to her for her ninth birthday last month, and she was still trying to grow accustomed to its weight on her hip. The well-oiled blade caught the sunlight as she tilted it to glimpse the ornate "T" inscribed on the metal beneath the hilt. This simple, unassuming blade had changed hands many times in its life. Her brother had told her a little of its story when he had given it to her.

Once her grandfather's, this dagger was made as a companion to the sword her mother still carried. The two weapons were all Tsuga had retained after her father's untimely death. When she had left her son behind in Devali she had left him this dagger as a link to his family; all that the thirteen-year-old rape

victim could give him as a legacy after running away from home in her shame.

Trag had eventually found her; the dagger had proven his identity to the woman who had employed magical means to forget the more unpleasant parts of her past despite the gaps in her memory, and the two were reunited in a rather dramatic public meeting. Now the weapon had been passed on to Tau.

"I don't need it anymore," he had told her. "I know who I am. But you, little sister, still have a lot of growing up to do. The world will try to change you, corrupt you, and wear you down. Let this be an anchor for you in the stormy seas ahead."

She frowned as she traced the line of the leather strap wrapping the hilt. When she shifted again the weight of her mage stone – a large, rounded diamond – pulled the copper chain around her neck to the side so that it dragged more heavily at her.

Tau sat up abruptly and pulled the chain over her head to hold the amulet in her hand as an idea occurred to her. It thrummed against her skin as though alive; its power was by now closely attuned to her through repeated use. Thoughtful, she turned it over, eyes tracing the delicate copper setting that held it in place. On an impulse she dropped the knife to her lap and unlatched the chain so that she could slide the stone free of it.

She took a moment to draw in a steadying breath, then picked up the weapon again, this time holding it so she looked directly down upon the unornamented pommel. It was, as she had thought, about the right size. With a little frown of concentration, she turned the pendant again and unwound the wire backing with a little help from her magic.

Once the stone was freed, she set it squarely atop the pommel and pressed it against the iron, softening the metal magically so that it embraced the gemstone. As she worked, she wove a spell into the metal of the weapon so that the use of her mage stone would strengthen the steel rather than melt it in the intense heat generated by raw magical energy.

When she was done she turned the knife so the stone caught the sun and splintered the light into a rainbow of colors. It almost seemed as though there was a glamour on the blade now; light rippled across it so that the metal seemed to all but glow with its new power.

And what was the purpose of that?

Tau jumped. She had practically forgotten Lilae watched her as she worked. She smiled sheepishly at her startled reaction and shrugged her shoulders.

"I don't know. It just felt right, somehow."

She gazed at the improved weapon a bit longer, admiring it absently, then shook herself and looked to the sky. A great deal more time had passed than she had realized while she had worked her magic. Her lesson should have already begun! She grimaced as she stood and sheathed the dagger.

"We're late! Are you ready to go?"

Ready when you are!

Tau stepped up onto Lilae's great copper forearm and braced herself with a hand against the dragon's neck as she was lifted into the air. When she was high enough, she reached out to grasp the leather straps of the saddle-like apparatus that helped her to keep her place astride the broad neck and swung

herself into the high-backed seat. Lilae waited barely long enough for Tau to get settled and slip her legs through the straps that offered her a way to brace and grip during aerobatic maneuvers before her legs gave a great thrust and she beat heavily with her wings to gain height.

Dragons were not built to launch easily from lowlands – they were large creatures, awkward on the ground, but the magic that thrummed in their bones allowed for the accomplishment of a great number of things that would be otherwise impossible. With little enough effort, Lilae found and caught an updraft that lifted them well into the air to begin the flight back home.

Chapter 14

$\mathcal{T}$au looked up from the book she was reading –
a copy of *The History of the World* that until now
had fully engrossed her with its details of the
establishment of Old Sennor back before civil war
had sundered the nation – with a start.

"What was that?!"

No one answered her, of course; there wasn't
anyone else in the room to hear the question she
voiced. The explosion had been more than merely
physical; her magical senses rang more loudly than
her ears in the aftermath of the concussive sound.

Lilae? Can you see anything?

Tau, stay inside.

That was her father's mindvoice, ringing in her
skull with clipped authority. Tau huffed out an
irritated breath and stood up from the desk where
she'd been reading under mage-light and crossed to
the window on the other side of the room so that she
could look out over the northern wall.

"Why can't I do anything exciting? I want to see!"

This view offered her no great insight, either; she
could see people scurrying to and fro, but spied no
reason for the chaos from the vantage point of her
bedchamber.

So it wasn't just a student.

Not that she would have been able to feel the
magical effects if it had been; students with the more

volatile magics were only allowed to practice under heavy shields, lest they inadvertently blow up half the castle.

We are under attack.

What?! But why? We are peaceful. We have made nothing but peaceful overtures! We even have a couple of Devalians here!

Perhaps that in itself is reason enough. There are those who do not wish to see cooperation between Sennor and Devali, let alone the kind of peace we have begun building here.

Another explosion shook the walls, and this time Tau smelled the distinct odor of sulfur that meant at least one of the protections had given way. A mage shield against physical assaults such as the one that would have been erected at the first hint of attack would block anything out, including smoke and scents carried on the wind after an explosion.

That's terrible! Will they break through?

We will see. They have only a handful of mages, but all quite powerful. They are ripping through our defenses as quickly as we can erect them.

We? But of course, Lilae *was* a dragon, and a powerful ally. Of course she would be doing her best to help the fort's defenders. And Tau was able to find reason to smile at last, albeit grimly. Finally, here was something she could do! And it wouldn't even require her to go against her Da's orders to stay put.

Tau reached a hand down to grasp the hilt of her dagger as a way to strengthen her physical link to the mage stone set in its pommel. Though she had moved beyond this need for contact in most cases, the gesture still gave her a sense of comfort and a feeling of being more grounded when she was off balance. As she did this, she mentally reached out to Lilae and delved into the pool of nearly-inexhaustible magical power. The dragon was like a deep lake, crystal clear and filled with the water of life.

It was, of course, possible to completely drain the dragon of power, but not without killing her – and by association herself. And it would take a great deal more than shielding to do it, especially with Tau contributing her own not insignificant powers to the cause.

With the dual buffers of Lilae and her mage stone, Tau could grasp the fiery rivers of wild magic without flinching away from their intensity and bend the power to her will. It took only a heartbeat or two – less time than a thought – for her to accomplish this so that she could turn her attention to the shields surrounding the fort.

Many mages and students already worked to repair the damages to the magical defenses, but they were faltering – both from fatigue and simple uneven numbers. There were relatively few air mages here (this would be the kind of shield erected to block missiles and physical attacks), and though the other mages all helped to shield against their individual abilities, none of them could shield the entire perimeter alone. There were gaping holes all along the line. She didn't need to see them; she could sense the disarray.

Tau could identify the magical signatures of each of the mages – there. That was Ramiq. Of course he would be spearheading the defenses; he was one of the most skilled and powerful mages alive, and had invented no few new techniques himself. But his talents would be better used elsewhere.

Da. She felt a small fraction of his attention shift to her.

Give the shields to me. I can do this as well as you. You need to be free to go where you must.

Tau had learned tactics and strategy from the time she'd been born. She could see the sense in better utilizing their assets in this defense, even at the tender age of ten. He knew her skill, her strength, but still she felt him hesitate. She was only a child; this was surely too much to ask of her. She reached out and placed her magical "hands" on the threads he knitted into shieldwork beside his and took hold without seizing control away from him.

I am not asking you to put me at risk. I can do this. Let me help where I can, so that you can go where you are needed.

He hesitated a moment more – she could still sense his reluctance – but he knew she was right, and in the end she felt him withdraw from the shields. Still, she was not alone. He had worked in concert with fully a dozen others, orchestrating them to work to patch holes in the existing shields or erect new ones as they were able. A blast hit the walls on the northeast side of the fort, and Tau shuddered as the impact ripped through her senses.

Jocelyn, Adam, Gabriel, reinforce the northern defenses. Miriam, Evelyn, Johan, the east. Charlotte, Michael, Byron, south. Antoine, Charles, Mitchell, west. I will act as center.

None of them hesitated. She had worked with all of these men and women, either under their instruction or side-by-side as a fellow pupil. They all

knew her and each had joined to her magically in the past. Familiar channels are easiest to follow. In mere moments she felt a dozen threads of magical consciousness extended to her. She grasped them and took them into herself.

Abruptly she saw through twelve new pairs of eyes – smoke and fire, blinding light – and smelled the blood, sulfur, and ash of battle. The screams of the wounded and the dying she did her best to ignore, though they made her want to weep for them and rush to their aid. She tasted her comrades' sweat as it streamed down their faces, felt fear, confusion, and fatigue straining a dozen sets of magical senses. All of this she registered in the space of a breath – taken in, let out – and absorbed it without allowing it to distract or overwhelm her.

With such a bond formed she suffered from their weaknesses, but she could also offset each of them in turn. Where courage flagged she sent waves of calm confidence to reassure them. When they tired she drew on the well of strength and power that filled as quickly as it drained from the dual sources of Lilae and the wild magic she held to bolster them.

She now grasped four strong but completely separate pieces of shielding. Each was – momentarily, at least – solid, but none touched on the other. With a wrench of will she melded the four together, blended the magic and shaped the pieces into one comprehensive whole. She tied this shield – a simple blocking shield to hold off the physical attacks, melded of all of their abilities and combined using her own unique skills as a future Queen's Mage – into the current of wild magic that would sustain it and carefully withdrew her hold on it until it required only a trickle of her own power to prevent its collapse. It shivered as it took up the new power source, then solidified and held firm.

Tau's lips pulled back in a grim smile. Though successful, this was only one shield of many they would have to build. Their faith in her resonated through the mage-bond; she showed them what needed to be done, and they set to without question. Shields of absorption, reflection, rebounding, and reinforcement were layered one atop the next. Barriers against physical weapons and magical assault both sprang up between the fort and their assailants. Each had a distinctive feel and flavor to it, like the wind when it blew from the stables, meadows, or kitchens.

She didn't know how long she worked. Gradually the impacts grew less frequent, the necessary repairs less extensive. At long last, the battle staggered to a halt and Tau was able to thank her fellows and withdraw her consciousness from the meld. She staggered a bit as she released her hold on the wild magic, and then narrowed her pull on Lilae's stores to a small trickle that would, hopefully, sustain her long enough to finish what must be done.

Her entire body ached as though she had fallen from a great height and hit the ground without slowing. Lilae's presence was somewhat diminished in her mind, but still strong.

Are you alright?

Yes. Tired. Hungry.

I will send someone from the kitchens with food.

Only if you call someone to tend you, too.

As Tau made it to her bed and sank down into the feathery softness, she realized just how much she

would need someone to see to her. She shook with hunger as much as fatigue.

I will.

She had never felt so famished in her life, but after she had made the arrangements – no one startled at receiving requests via mindspeech here, not anymore – she lay back and promptly fell into an exhausted sleep.

Chapter 15

$\mathcal{T}$au woke reluctantly. She was tired down to her very bones, and her tongue felt swollen to twice its normal size from thirst. Her stomach gnawed against her backbone, though, and the needs of her body – for she realized now that it was the need to pee that had ultimately roused her – dragged her all-unwillingly into wakefulness. After the first and most pressing of her needs had been addressed, she turned her attention to the small table set near her south-facing window.

I must have been asleep for a while.

Although there was still condensation on the pitcher of fruit juice, the ice in the bowl it rested in had long since melted into cool water. No steam rose from the flakey honey cakes on the plate, and the small fruit pie had cooled so much that she could pick it up and eat it from her hand as she used the other to pour herself a glass of the juice.

Also on the table was an assortment of nuts, sandwiches, fruits, and cheeses. She had no qualms about setting to; with so much of her life involving magic Tau was always hungry, though seldom so starved as she felt now. And since sugars and starches were necessary to restore the particular type of strength needed to manipulate magic, the child's typical diet was one that would ache the teeth of any person not so gifted.

She had finished the pie and two honey cakes when she heard a soft knock on her door. She reached to pick up a meat-laden sandwich as she stood and made a casual obeisance to her parents as they entered the room. Each moved according to his or her nature, and Tau smiled to herself as she took a bite, amused as always by the differences between them.

Every gesture Ramiq made was grand and flamboyant. He did not merely walk into the room; he swept in, his presence swelling to fill the space near to bursting. To her mage sight his aura crackled with strictly controlled and contained power.

Tsuga, meanwhile, made no motion without purpose; she was a finely honed tool. There was no waste of effort here. She did not exclaim or gesticulate as she took in her daughter's restoring color and the dark circles – like two massive bruises – under Tau's eyes.

"Good to see you up."

She didn't mince words, either.

"Yes ma'am."

"How are you feeling?"

It had taken her a while to reconcile the clipped words her mother often spoke with the turmoil of emotions always below the surface. Tau had been able to understand how people felt long before she had found the ability to grasp the why. Tsuga's question spoke not at all of the concern she had for her daughter's health – nor of the immense swelling of pride at her courage and endurance. Tau flushed, unsure how to respond to such glowing approval from both of her parents who, though always loving and supportive, were strict taskmasters and very hard to please.

"Like I've been dragged behind a galloping horse all day, and then thrown off a cliff. But I'll be fine. The food is already helping."

This last she said around a mouthful of the sandwich she still held – the meat was chicken, she decided, with a wonderfully spiced sauce – as her mother moved to sit on the edge of her bed.

"Your father told me what you did. That was very brave."

Tau shrugged, uncomfortable with such praise from her mother.

"I wasn't thinking about bravery. I just knew it needed to be done, and that I could do it."

She shot a sideways glance at her father, who was smiling to himself as he leafed through the book she'd left open on her desk what seemed like days ago.

"He wouldn't let me go out, even to see what was happening."

"And rightly so. Battle is a dangerous place. For everyone. It is no place for a child."

Tau started to retort – she was hardly a normal child, after all – but stopped herself by taking another bite. Honestly, she had no desire to see battle, as her mother had when *she* was in her teens. She had seen death, blood, and pain in the healers' hospital. She had no desire to inflict such hurts on another person. Not even one who was supposed to be her enemy.

Ramiq turned and crossed to her, and Tau wrapped her free arm around his waist as he pulled her against him for a hug.

"You are our little girl. Forgive us for wanting to shelter you from the horrors of the world where we can."

He released her, then rested a hand on her shoulder to hold her attention.

"Tau, you did well. Very well. No one but you could have taken over the center like that, let alone done it so effectively. Your shielding turned the tide of the battle. Do you know that? You saved lives today, Tau. I am *so* proud of you."

"We both are."

Tau flushed and found that she couldn't squeeze out so much as a word around the lump in her throat. Tsuga smiled and stood to cross to Ramiq and place a hand on his elbow.

"We will let you finish eating and get some rest. You've earned it. You did well, Tau. Be proud of yourself; we are."

Chapter 16

$\mathcal{A}$ handful of prisoners had been taken in the attack on the fort. Most of them were ordinary soldiers, a few were mercenaries, but there was one in particular that now held Ramiq's interest as he looked at their prizes. He had disabled her himself, and though she no longer fought against her magical or physical restraints, she still glared at him as though trying to kill him with a look.

"Take the prisoners to the cells."

As the more senior students and the handful of instructors – the closest thing to real soldiers the fort housed – prodded their captives to get them moving, Ramiq moved forward to stand in front of the mage, thus impeding her progress.

"Except for this one. She will be questioned now."

She spat in his face. He managed to keep a composed façade, though he wanted to retaliate – badly. When he was younger he might have indulged the urge, but now he only wiped his face clean with a sleeve and fixed her with a cool gaze.

"And what is your name?"

She glared at him, but didn't answer.

"I could take it from you, you know. It wouldn't even be difficult."

Her lip curled into a disdainful snarl.

"You would torture a woman?"

Her hair had a good deal more red in it than Tsuga's and was considerably darker, and this mage wore hers long and unbound. A few snarled wisps stuck to her face, curled from the moisture of her sweat. Her dress – for she apparently scorned the robes more commonly favored by mages in Sennor – was smudged with dirt and soot, as was her pale skin where it was visible above the low neckline. Startling green – or were they blue? – eyes sparkled with emotion as she glared at him. In another time she would have tempted him; she was intriguing with her striking looks, full figure, and fiery passions. But right now his thoughts were fixed on only one goal: gain information.

Students had died; so had their teachers. Many more were injured. The walls had taken damage. He wanted to know who was to blame, and why they had attacked.

"I wouldn't have to. I could take it from you. Pluck it right from your mind. I could read your entire life from your thoughts in the space of a breath."

A little white lie, but one she was unlikely to know enough to doubt.

"I could wipe your mind while leaving your body intact. I could make you flap and cluck like a chicken."

She had paled considerably as he spoke, swelling his aura and drawing himself up to his full height so that his presence loomed larger than life. Judging her sufficiently cowed, he pulled back a bit until he stood almost normally before her. She was trembling; he felt it as a change in the air more than he saw her hands shake.

"But," he continued in a softer tone, "I would rather I didn't have to. I would prefer that you tell me what I want to know. What is your name?"

She was stronger than he had given her credit for. She did not flinch away from him, nor even drop her gaze from his. But she did, at last, answer him.

"Pyrena."

Ramiq nodded curtly.

"Pyrena. You will not be going to the cells. I have a very special place for you."

One of the work rooms in the mage's tower would make a more appropriate prison for her, at any rate. Accustomed to holding a mage's shields while magic was being worked inside, such a chamber would make his job of holding her apart from her own powers easier. He gestured behind her to the tower with a mocking flourish.

"After you."

No doubt a few days of isolation, cut off from the magic that was a mage's life-blood, would encourage her to talk. He could be patient, when it benefitted him. And in this instance, it was likely best that he not simply strip the information from her. Such reckless use of magic could cause permanent damage, and she may yet serve a purpose for him. But only if she was left intact.

The mage spat again – at his feet, this time – but turned and walked stiffly in the direction he'd indicated.

Chapter 17

"Where is my husband?"

Over the past couple of weeks Tsuga had seen even less of Ramiq than their mutually full schedules usually allowed. He had been spending a great deal of time interrogating the prisoners captured in the attack on the fort, and as a result his presence stayed shielded from her much of the time.

"He is in the mage's tower, Weaponsmistress."

Tsuga frowned.

With her, *no doubt.*

The novice gulped and wrung his hands nervously, and Tsuga forced her expression to lighten. It wasn't his fault her husband was late to dinner, after all.

"Thank you."

The boy stumbled over a courteous response and hurried on his way, though Tsuga scarcely registered his words or his departure. Ramiq had always been a bit absent-minded, but the more significant events seldom escaped his notice. It was unlike him to be busy so late on a day like this. It was, after all, nearly midnight.

Surely he has not forgotten what tomorrow is.

They were soul bonded, after all. She *knew* he had been feeling her dread and confusion. She'd been growing increasingly more agitated over the past week, and her paranoia was running especially high tonight. A sense of impending doom shadowed her everywhere she went, and she couldn't seem to shake the feeling that something was horribly wrong.

He knows *how hard my birthday is for me. In thirteen years, he's never forgotten it. Something isn't right.*

With a start Tsuga realized she was standing alone in the shadowed corridor as though rooted in place, muttering darkly to herself. With an effort, she set out on the path to the tower that housed the mage trainees.

The night air was cool. The wind rose as she crossed the courtyard, and though she did not shiver from it, there was a definite edge to the breeze. It was not unusual for the weather to turn colder so near her birthday. In fact this year the warmth of late summer had held on longer than was typical. But now, as the wind gusted and picked up strength, Tsuga found herself thinking that their luck was about to run out. The scent of rain was heavy in the air, and indeed, as she reached the door to the tower, she heard thunder growl.

She tugged the door closed behind her – a struggle, with the wind fighting her every inch of the way – and set off down the corridor to the stairs that wound up the center of the tower. He would be three stories up, in the room he had converted into the mage's prison.

The hallway was dotted every few feet with shields – many of the novices (and a small few of the journeymen) tended to lose control of their abilities, especially in their sleep, and so their personal shields were always reinforced before sleeping and an additional shield placed on the rooms themselves while they slept as an added precaution.

Such a shield was erected around the room where the mage prisoner was held, as well, lest she manage to break through the shields held on her directly. This would, ordinarily, account for Ramiq's utter absence from Tsuga's mind over the past weeks. But even at times when she knew he was teaching a class and should have been able to feel his presence, hear the whisper of his thoughts at the edges of her consciousness and sense his state of mind without any actual effort, the corner of her mind he usually inhabited remained puzzlingly blank. It was time she found out why.

Tsuga had seen the mage on the day she had been captured, though not since. She had been pretty; a full figure, no sign of disease, with a presence that crackled like lightning and charged everyone around her. No doubt men found her fascinating. And unsurprisingly, Tsuga was jealous of the amount of time – however innocent she reassured herself it was – that Ramiq spent in her company. His weakness for the flesh (before he had committed to her, at least) was no secret, least of all from her. But in all the time they had been together, he had never strayed.

She had no real reason to suspect him of anything now. Only her own insecurity. Just this sense of doom glowering behind her and an unfounded jealousy.

Chapter 18

Autonomy was a difficult thing to maintain in a marriage, and the presence of a child – however much he adored her – made it even more elusive. For someone used to being one of the most powerful men in the world not only magically, but politically as well, it had been hard to adjust. Where before he had prized his position as Queen's Mage as what defined him, here in this backwater fort they had established on the border he was just another (incredibly powerful) mage. He was so far removed from the court politics that had for so long been his life-blood in the capitol city that he may as well have been dead.

He could have teleported to the castle, of course – the journey that had taken their caravan the better part of a year would have been no more than the passing of a few moments for him. He did precisely that when the queen needed him. But the expenditure of energy necessary to span such a distance was staggering, and except in the most dire of circumstances utterly unjustifiable.

The excitement around the attack and the capture of prisoners had been a welcome reprieve from the daily monotony of classes, negotiations, and quiet home life. But the initial buzz had faded quickly, and he found himself burdened once more by the mundane drudgery of overseeing repairs and preparations for the winter. The weather spells on the gardens and buildings – even the stables – had to be reinforced, the food stores tallied, the wool and linen meted out appropriately…all of the horribly boring things usually left to a steward, which in the absence of anyone else willing and able had fallen to himself and his wife.

In an effort to distance himself from reality – however briefly – he sought out the prisoners. Initially he had the legitimate excuse of seeking information, but of course the men in the dungeons knew little beyond the orders they were given. The mage, he suspected, knew a great deal more, but he could not at first bring himself to face her.

She was powerful, but it was not her magic he feared; he was still her better. But being around her charged him as nothing else did these days. Her personality crackled with an intensity like the one he had first fallen in love with in Tsuga. Her face was animated, her emotions explosive, and her passion intoxicating. After a few days he found himself drawn increasingly often to her room, to the point that he had to drag himself away to attend to his more mundane responsibilities.

He knew his attraction to her was dangerous – she wanted to destroy everything they worked for here, and possibly even kill him – but that knowledge only spurred him on. For the first time in years, he felt alive. He even found himself driven to distraction by the thought of her during the day – and, perhaps worse, at night.

She was everything Tsuga was not – at least, not to the degree she had been. Tsuga had restrained her passions out of necessity; a commander had to appear controlled and level-headed in any and all situations. She was no longer prone to lighting his clothes on fire or starting conflagrations that consumed entire buildings at the drop of a hat. The fire he had fallen in love with had cooled; it was no longer a raging inferno, but rather a tame beast, like a hearth fire kept carefully restrained. Still warm, still comforting, but confined.

Tsuga was gone much of the day, for like him she had students to oversee, administrative duties, and…well, whatever else kept her occupied. She was difficult to pin down; it was rare that they saw each other while the sun still burned above the horizon. They did make an effort to spend what time they could together; dinner was typically a meal the two shared alone in the quiet of their chamber. It was always late (Tsuga seldom made it back before more than an hour after dark, and Ramiq was occasionally kept busy by one thing or another until even later), but it gave them a chance to relax in each other's company.

He knew he should tell Tsuga how he had been feeling; she loved him as deeply as he loved her, and would do anything she could to help him out of his slump. But he was sure she would take his lack of enthusiasm too personally. He had no desire to hurt her, and he knew such a conversation would be painful beyond belief for both of them. Better to spare her that, if he could.

So he walled off a little corner of his mind – and his heart – so that she could not see into it. In this secret place he stowed all of his tortured thoughts, his twisted emotions, and even his lust for this captive mage – this woman – Pyrena.

There was only one problem with this. The more he hid from his wife, the more things he *needed* to hide. His guilt grew until he felt it might crush him. Rather than have such a strong emotion resonate along his bond to Tsuga, he walled it off. The more he retreated from her, the more he was drawn to Pyrena – and so he would retreat further to keep his shame hidden. Before long he was such a tangled snarl of anguish, guilt, and frustrated lust (he could not lie with his own wife for fear that their physical intimacy might lower the mental and emotional barriers he had built) that he was forced to hide himself completely from her awareness.

The loss of her presence almost broke him. He had grown so accustomed to his unconscious awareness of her that to suddenly *not* hear the active chatter of her busy mind, to not feel a surge of pain when she stubbed her toe or snap at an unsuspecting student when she involuntarily overwhelmed him with her own irritation left him feeling broken and empty. So he sought comfort where he always had: in the flesh.

The first time had surprised him. He must have been more transparent than he'd thought; Pyrena had approached him, then. It hadn't been a hard sell. He knew she had her own reasons – no doubt she thought to soften him, to gain his favor, or at the very least some information. He told himself that because he knew what she wanted, he was safe against it. And so he sought her out again.

He had avoided the tower for two days, not wanting to draw suspicion to his actions. He fully expected Tsuga to read the guilt of what he'd done in his face – as though "adulterer" had been branded across his forehead – but she must have been preoccupied with her own troubles, for she made no mention of anything out of the ordinary. Without the aid of their emotional bond he could not read below her smooth surface without prying into her privacy with a use of magic, so he let himself believe that all was as well as it could be. He should have known better.

Had he not closed himself off from her so completely, he would have had some warning. By sensing her approach, he might have had time to disentangle himself from Pyrena's embrace, straighten his clothes, and put on a convincing charade. But in the end it was his very desire to spare his wife pain that proved his undoing.

His guard was so far lowered, his mental and emotional state so chaotic, that he did not even hear the door open. He was pressed against the mage in a passionate embrace, one hand braced on the wall while the other sought under her skirts. There was no way for him to know how long Tsuga had stood there, nor how much she had seen.

A noise he could not identify – something between a choked-off sob and a grunt of pain – caught the edge of his awareness and caused him to look over his shoulder to seek its source. And time froze. His breath stopped; his heart ceased its beating in his chest. As though in a dream, where the blink of an eye may seem to take a day, he watched her heart break. She shook her head, unable to speak, and turned away from him with tears in her eyes to flee back the way she had come.

Chapter 19

I knew it. She hadn't wanted to believe it, of course, but deep down she had known something wasn't right.

Tsuga?

That was Devilsbane. No doubt her guardian was alarmed by the emotions churning within the Weaponsmistress, but Tsuga couldn't manage to respond to the concern in that mindvoice – especially not to offer anything like a reassurance.

I don't know why I'm surprised. Surprised that he waited so long, perhaps?

There he stood in all his glory, one hand up another woman's dress, his pants half-undone, and his mouth working like that of a landed fish. She waited for him to say something, to try to apologize…anything. Waited for the space of one breath. Two. Three.

He hadn't even moved. His hand was still up the mage's skirts. His arousal was still painfully evident. He hadn't shown such arousal for her in weeks – or was it months? Pain flowered in her chest, pressing down and at the same time pushing from within until she wasn't sure if she would explode or be crushed.

She shook her head – her throat had closed with emotion, but even if it hadn't there was really nothing to say. It had, after all, been too good to be true. She had known it all along. She had only been lying to herself all these years. Perhaps some part of her had always known.

Unable to look at the pair of them any longer, she turned and fled. Tears blinded her; she had to make her way by instinct and feel. She nearly tumbled headlong down the narrow, twisting stairs several times, but reflex and momentum saved her and she continued to race – where? There was nowhere to go. Their rooms would offer her no refuge. She couldn't bear the thought of anyone else seeing her so distraught. Really, there was only one place she could go; the one place she always had. Blindly, awash in pain and confusion, she turned and ran through the blustering wind towards the stables.

Bane would normally have been out to pasture in the evenings, but with this storm she had sought shelter in the roomy box stall reserved for her among the more common mounts in their stables. In all her life, the mare was the only one who had simply been there through it all. She never left, never wavered, never betrayed her trust. In this storm, she was Tsuga's only rock – her only refuge.

The other horses snorted or whinnied in alarm as she blundered past, but she ignored them. She stumbled into Bane's stall and all but fell against the horse's neck. The steady, quiet strength of the beast kept her from collapsing entirely, but she was in such an emotional state that she couldn't even pin down a coherent train of thought.

So stupid. How could I? How could he? What am I going to do? Where will I-? What about-?

Bane, thankfully, didn't say anything. She simply stood and let Tsuga cry. Ultimately one thought

solidified and began to repeat itself more than the rest.

I can't. Not alone. Not without him; not now.

Bane wouldn't allow it – not if she really thought Tsuga would go through with it. She knew that. So she forced herself to calm her thoughts, quiet her sobs, and pull back.

"I have to talk to him." Her voice was hoarse from prolonged crying, and she had to swallow a lump in her throat before she could go on.

"I have to know why."

As she spoke she sealed herself off – not only from Ramiq, who was still closed to her anyway, but from Bane as well. She couldn't have the horse sense what she planned. Bane would only try to stop her. It was not easy to tell the lie, but it was necessary.

"Alone. I'm sorry."

She gave the horse another tight hug – a last boost for her shattered heart – and fled the stall before she gave herself away. It was only when she was back outside that she paused and looked over her shoulder for a final time.

"I'm sorry. Goodbye."

Even through the mental blocks he had erected, Ramiq could feel his wife's agony. The look on her face broke his heart, but he couldn't bring himself to say anything lest he dig himself a deeper hole. Before his sluggish brain could process what had just happened and decide what to do she had turned and fled.

It took several moments after she had gone for him to come to himself again. At that point he

removed his hand from Pyrena's thigh and gave himself a shake as he took a step back. She didn't say a word; she merely watched him with curiosity and a small, self-satisfied smile curling at the edges of her lips. He turned and fled, unable to face her, needing to find Tsuga. His mind churned as he made his way to their rooms, blindly following the path his feet knew better than his mind in its current state.

How could this happen? How could I let this go so far? Goddess' tits, I have to fix this…

She wasn't in their room. He wasn't particularly surprised; no doubt she had sought refuge somewhere he wasn't likely to go. His shields were still up; his thoughts were chaotic enough without adding the turmoil of Tsuga's mind to the mix. He crossed to their bed and sank down as he ran a hand through his disheveled hair to smooth it. If only his emotions could be so easily tamed.

No sooner had this thought occurred to him than he felt panic – not his own – erupt in his mind. He recognized Bane's mindvoice from long familiarity with the beast, but her speech was so rushed that it took him some moments to decipher it.

She's done it again. In the Southern pasture. I can't stop the blood; I don't have hands. I didn't know she was going to! I'm sorry. I should have suspected! I thought she'd gone to find you! HELP!

"Tsuga?!"

Ramiq leapt to his feet and was out the door before he even realized he'd moved. As he ran down the corridor he tore through the shields and emotional blocks he had so painstakingly maintained.

Tsu, stay with me.

Her presence was weak, and it continued to fade with every step.

Why don't you teleport?

Ramiq shook his head as though irritated by a fly, but didn't slow his headlong flight, even when he reentered the rainstorm. Lyra should know the answer without having to ask.

Have to be calm to transfer. It was all the response he could manage, and indeed, he resented having to divide his attentions even that much. He could feel his wife dying as he raced to reach her.

Don't leave me, Tsu. You can't leave me! You can't!

Chapter 20

Tau sat up in bed, startled awake from a dead sleep by … something. It was fading, now that she was no longer dreaming … getting fainter….

"Momma!"

That's what it was! Tsuga needed help. Needed *her!* She wasn't sure what had happened, but the turmoil of her mother's mind was starting to quiet as her life faded away.

Her life!

Tau didn't wait to puzzle over how she knew her mother lay dying; she knew it with the same instinct that told her to take each breath. She grabbed her dagger from beneath her pillow – Tsuga had instilled in her daughter the importance of keeping a weapon to hand, even in sleep – and belted it around her waist as she swung her feet to the floor and drew on her power through the mage stone set in its pommel. She didn't need to know the location this time; not to find her mother. All she had to do was focus on Tsuga's presence. The bond of their blood was strong enough to pull her to the correct location.

The rain was cold. It hit her in an icy torrent once she made the transfer from her warm, dry room to the south pasture. She knew where she was without having to see her surroundings; fortunate, as even during the flashes of lightning she could scarcely see her own feet.

"Momma!"

She had arrived almost on top of the prone body. The young girl dropped to her knees and drew on her healing magic without hesitation. She knew her mother hated magical healing, but even Tsuga wouldn't be stubborn enough to refuse such help in these circumstances.

"Wrists slashed ... now how under the sun...? Too much blood lost.... Goddess, her heart is so weak! Come on, Mama, come back. Come back!"

The rain was gone. Tau stood in a place with little distinction; light came from everywhere and from nowhere, giving her something to see by, though it seemed to only extend a few feet. Beyond that small distance, she couldn't see a thing.

"Momma?"

"I'm here, Tau."

Sure enough, there she stood. Tau blinked; she would have sworn her mother hadn't been there a moment before.

"Where are we?"

Tsuga's voice shook when she answered.

"I don't know."

"What happened?"

She frowned, but didn't answer.

"Momma, I'm scared. What's gonna happen?"

"I don't know."

"You're not gonna leave us, are you? Da and me? You can't just leave us. Da won't make it without you. And I need you, too."

She could feel the tears sliding down her cheeks, and she swiped at them angrily.

"Oh, Tau...."

"No! I won't let you go! I WON'T!"

Tau flung herself forward and threw her arms around her mother's waist.

"I won't," she sobbed into Tsuga's side.

"Tau?"

Tau lifted her head from where she had buried it in her mother's wet tunic.

"Momma?"

Sure enough, Tsuga's hand reached up to cup her cheek.

"Momma!"

Tau took Tsuga's hand in both of hers and gave it a squeeze. To be certain, Tau delved into her magic again and checked her mother over carefully. The slashes in her wrists were closed and no longer gushing blood. Her pulse was faint, but steady. Her heart was strong, and though her eyes were closed and her body limp with weakness her chest rose and fell with the even regularity of her breath. She would live.

By the time Ramiq arrived on the scene his clothes were clinging to him, and he had fallen so many times that despite the torrential downpour he was splattered quite liberally with mud. He nearly tripped over her body before he saw her lying on the ground and staggered to a halt.

"Oh, Tsuga...."

He sank to his knees, heedless of the mud and rain. He shuddered out a sob when he saw the rise and fall of her chest, and only after he had reassured himself of her condition did he allow himself a moment to take in his surroundings.

"Tau! What are you doing here?"

Sure enough, there was his daughter, kneeling in the mire on the other side of his wife. In her night dress, no less!

"Why aren't you in bed?"

No sooner had Tau established that her mother was in a restful sleep and would not slip away from her the moment her back was turned than her father came blundering in. The emotions roiling off of him were chaotic and raw, and Tau was forced to bend her concentration to redoubling her shields while Ramiq reassured himself. It didn't take long; no sooner had he come to his senses than he began scolding her for being out and about. Tau frowned.

"I *was* in bed! I woke up."

Ramiq rocked back on his heels and blinked in surprise at the vehemence in her voice.

"And where were *you*? What happened to Momma? I had to heal her, Da! *I* had to heal her. Why weren't you here?"

He winced, and Tau could see his expression close against her questions.

"I was working. But come; since you're here, give me a hand. We need to get your mother inside."

Tau considered him for a moment, but ultimately decided to let it go – for now. He was right, after all; Tsuga needed to be moved out of the rain to a place where she could get warm and dry to rest. So she stood and did what she could to help lift Tsuga from the mud.

Chapter 21

$\mathscr{T}$suga was slow in recovering. Ramiq strayed from her side only to relieve himself, both eating and sleeping beside her prone and wasted form. The physical hurts, though grave – she had very nearly died – should have been remedied easily enough. Oh, her strength and energy would take time to return, of course, but after nearly two weeks she should be nearly back to her old self.

As it was, she slept most of the day and woke only to quiet the needs of her body for either nourishment or to make use of the bedpan. In those brief moments of wakefulness Ramiq felt himself shredded to bits by the look of pain and despair haunting her murky brown-green eyes. Her emotional pain was what held her in its clutches and refused to let her go. He often wondered if he would ever get her back. If he ever could.

"Oh, Tsu," he moaned, words muffled by his robes as he buried his head in his hands, "it's all my fault."

Tau stared at her reflection in the fountain with a detached fascination. She looked … *Awful. There's no other word for it. I look like* I'm *the one who should be in that sickbed up there.*

She sighed, her eyes briefly lifting to mark the window of the room her parents shared before her gaze winced away and returned to the sight of herself reflected in the still water, warped slightly as ripples disturbed its surface.

Her hair had never been the curly, vibrant crown some girls boasted, but it had at least always had a gentle gleam of good health. Now it just hung, limp as damp straw, and framed a face pinched and shadowed with worry. She had always been trim, but now even the last traces of baby fat had melted from her angular face, and her cheekbones stood out prominently against the dark circles under her eyes. In fact, she no longer had so much as an ounce of fat to spare on her lean frame.

She had grown taller in the last month, but no one had bothered to re-fit her for clothes, so her robes exposed her ankles instead of floating just above the ground as they should. Even too short for her, they hung limply off her too-thin frame, the bright colors somehow listless and dull. Her eyes, a green that marked her as her father's child, held a haunted, sorrowful look. She, who had always been such an unfailingly vibrant and *happy* child, could no longer muster the energy for so much as a smile. Tau sighed.

Empathy had always been one of her strongest gifts. The first to manifest itself, she had learned to read other's emotions before she was even securely out of diapers. And the emotions around her lately were, well ... depressing. Her mother was bedridden with despair, unable to raise even enough energy to walk from her bed to the necessary unaided. Her father was eaten alive by guilt, and had abandoned everything else to care for his devastated wife.

Everything ... including me.

Oh, the other adults tried to compensate for her parents' relative abandonment. Her mage lessons still continued, as did her weapons' instruction. She still studied history, tactics, and politics, just as she had been doing before. But she missed the proud smiles Ramiq used to boast when she mastered a new ability or asked a particularly insightful question, and the effusive praise of the old soldiers who had taken over her physical training came nowhere close to evoking the same sense of accomplishment she felt from a simple "well done" from her mother's lips.

Under everything – the day-to-day activities, the "normal" routine the entire fort worked to maintain – the strain was palpable. More than that; to a powerful empath, it was unbearable. People walked on eggshells around her, afraid the least wrong word would send her into a depression or rouse her to hysterics. People – right down to the greenest recruits and newest trainees – were worried. They needed their strong, charismatic Queen's Mage, their stoic and unflappable Weaponsmistress.

And you need your parents.

Tau lifted her gaze from the demoralized girl in the fountain to the rooftop where Lilae lounged soaking up the last rays of afternoon sunlight. Even her poor guardian looked faded and dull.

I miss them. I miss how it was.

The sun glinted off of Lilae's copper hide as the dragon lifted her head to peer down into the garden where Tau stood. She had no doubt Lilae could see her; she had paired with her guardian's mind before this and shared her senses often enough to know that

Lilae could probably count the ants that marched in a line across the gravel path at her feet.

It will probably never go back to the way it was. Things change, and there are deep hurts there. Ones that cannot be healed by magic.

Tau's shoulders jerked at that, and her gaze sharpened. They had tried to protect her from what had happened; in her hearing, that night was always referred to as "Tsuga's accident," or "that unfortunate incident." But she had been the first to her mother's side, and though she had not registered all of the facts in the heat of the moment, in the time since she'd had more than ample opportunity to work out for herself what had happened.

Suicide was frowned on in most of the cultures she'd been studying, but it was doubly anathema in Sennor, where it meant the death of not one soul, but two. And for one half of a soul bond to suicide – or attempt to – was horrific beyond imagining.

As an empath as well as the daughter of the two parties involved, Tau was acutely attuned to the pain, guilt, and misery surrounding the whole situation. Ramiq blamed himself. Tsuga was heartbroken, and though she longed for death she lacked the strength of will to seek it a second time. Lilae was right; these kinds of deep-seated emotional hurts could not be healed magically. They may never even heal cleanly, or completely. But things *could not* be allowed to go on this way.

Perhaps not by magic, but getting them to talk will be a good start to a natural healing process.

With a plan of action in mind, Tau steeled herself and set off for the room where her mother lay half-dead.

As she had expected, she found Ramiq in a chair at her mother's bedside, head buried in his hands. The gentle rise and fall of Tsuga's rhythmic breath indicated that her mother slept, but a gentle probe with her healer's senses told her the sleep was feigned.

I wonder how often she's been pretending to sleep with him here. Or if his being here is why she pretends. Interesting. I'm surprised he hasn't noticed – but then, he's so wrapped up in his own guilt that he hasn't even noticed I'm in the doorway. I will have to tread more carefully here than I'd thought.

"Daddy?"

Ramiq's head jerked up, and for one alarming moment there was no recognition in his eyes. Then, as though delayed in rousing, sense flickered across his expression and he frowned slightly.

"Tau? What are you doing here?"

She moved a little further into the room and allowed her gaze to dart to her mother's face and then back to his.

"I came to see her."

"Oh. Oh. Yes, of course you did." His gaze fell to his wife's face, and he heaved a sigh full of such anguish and despair that it made Tau's heart ache with sympathy.

"There's been no change."

Tau bit back a retort – harsh words would do more harm than good, here – and simply nodded.

"She's been through a lot. It will take time. You know that as well as anyone."

"Yes, I know, but...."

Tau smiled with sympathy and moved to her father's side to give him a hug.

"Have you tried talking to her?"

Ramiq winced.

"She doesn't speak at all, even when she wakes to eat."

Tau shook her head slightly.

"No, talking *to* her. Even if she sleeps, the sound of your voice is familiar to her, and comforting. It gives her something outside of herself to concentrate on."

Ramiq tensed, then lifted his gaze from Tsuga's still form to Tau's wan one, and she saw real fear and uncertainty in his eyes. In her Da, who always seemed so confident and self-assured, it was decidedly unsettling. When exactly had their roles reversed? On that night in the rain, she supposed.

"What should I say?"

Tau stepped back until she held only his hand, then took that and placed it over one of her mother's uncharacteristically pale ones.

"Anything that comes to mind. It may help you as much as it could her."

Tau backed away another couple of steps as Ramiq clutched spasmodically at his wife's hand and licked his lips as he searched her face. His daughter had already been forgotten; that much was clear.

As she reached the door and turned to let herself out, she heard her father's voice – shaky and rough with suppressed emotion – and allowed herself a small smile. Perhaps now the healing could begin.

Chapter 22

The days blurred one into the next, minutes stretching until they seemed to take hours to pass. Tsuga existed only on the fringes of herself, floating alone in a sea of bleak misery. She couldn't even muster the will to call for help, let alone try to break to the surface of her own power. What would be the point, after all? Ramiq no longer cared for her; he had proven that by his actions, and though he made a great show of staying at her side at all times his presence served only to arouse a dull ache of loss in her. No doubt he felt guilty for having been caught out, but that hardly meant anything to her any more.

She drifted in and out of wakefulness, scarcely able to separate one from the other save that when she dreamt, the pain stabbed less deeply. The pleasant dreams were the worst; she would wake and remember that Ramiq would never hold her so tenderly again, and lacking the strength even to sob, she would lie awake and let her tears fall silently to moisten her limp and knotted hair.

When, after the first few days, it became obvious that Ramiq had no intention of leaving her side, Tsuga began to feign sleep more and more often. She could not bear to look at him, to see his face and recall what she had lost. People drifted in and out of her rooms: servants, healers, and the occasional visitor. Tsuga roused only when she was forced to in order to eat, drink, take a potion or make use of the bedpan.

She had tried, at first, to refuse the meals, but when the healers had all but force-fed her by spooning a weak broth into her mouth and rubbing her throat like she was a recalcitrant dog, she had given up that notion as fruitless. So now she ate and drank mechanically, never really tasting just what it was she swallowed, so that she would be left alone again.

The healers were baffled by her. There was nothing physically wrong with her, aside from the weakness that was to be expected after such extreme blood loss. But even when she wasn't feigning sleep, real slumber took her under far more often than it should have, and despite the best care Tsuga knew her condition was growing worse, not better. Even the mindhealers had not been able to reach her, despite their best efforts.

That last healer really summed it up, she thought morosely. *I've lost the will to live.*

She sighed, eyes still closed, and rolled onto her back.

"Da?"

She kept her breathing even, but the sound of her daughter's voice caused her a pang of guilt. Tau should not be made to suffer because of her parents' sins. But there was no doubt in Tsuga's mind, as she listened to the limping conversation between father and daughter, that Tau was not holding up well without the support of her parents.

Tsuga didn't pay much attention to the words exchanged, but rather listened to the nuances of the voices as they spoke, and her heart gave another twinge at the pain she heard in Tau's. All too soon her daughter fell silent, and Tsuga sensed that she had left the room. After a moment, Ramiq began speaking again.

Now who is he talking to? There's no one here. With a start she realized, *He's talking to me.* If Ramiq had addressed her directly at all in the time she had lain on this bed, it had been only to coax her to eat or drink. If there had been anything else said, it had been early on, when she was truly too pain- and drug-fogged to register it. Unable to stop herself, she listened.

"This is all my fault. I know it is. Auriga's tits, I'm such an idiot. I don't know what I was thinking. I never meant to hurt you, Tsu. Goddess bless, that was the last thing I ever wanted! You don't hurt someone you love! But I did. Goddess, I'm sorry. I messed up. I know I did. And I don't expect you to forgive me. But I still love you. Auriga help me, I still love you! And I can't stand seeing you like this, feeling you slip away from me this way."

Tsuga felt a stab of white-hot pain jolt through her gut when he said he loved her, and she gasped in involuntary reaction. It dissipated the grey miasma a little, and now she was painfully aware of her every heartbeat. It hurt to breathe, but she forced her breath to flow in and out in a steady rhythm. Her heart, she could not soothe as easily. She heard Ramiq shift as his hand clutched at hers convulsively – almost painfully.

"Tsuga? Can you hear me?"

He waited a few moments, but when she made no response he let out a sigh.

"I don't know what to do. I can't bear the thought of leaving you alone, but that means I am neglecting everything else. The students, the fort, our peace efforts…. Our daughter. Goddess, Tsu, she is suffering. Wasting away. She's worried about you. About us, I suppose." He laughed self-deprecatingly. "She is not used to seeing me so unkempt. I can't even remember the last time I changed clothes or slept in a bed! I must look a sight. But I can't bring myself to care. Not when you're like this. I miss you, Tsu."

Another stab of pain, this time accompanied by a searing warmth that shot through her, making her numb extremities burn with the return of sensation. The shock of feeling almost – *almost* – made her open her eyes.

"You know, I wish sometimes you'd set me on fire, or blow something up the way you used to. At least if you were angry, you'd be talking – well, yelling – and be *doing* something. I've never seen you like this. It's like you've given up. And I did this to you. Goddess, I wish you'd just get *angry* with me. Anything would be better than this!"

Her entire body was throbbing painfully now, as her mind churned. *He says he still loves me. That can't be true, can it? If he loves me, why was he with that other woman? Why do I still* want *him to love me? What's wrong with me that I'm not furious with him? He's right. I should be angry. So why aren't I?*

She had not dropped the mental and emotional barriers she had erected since the night she had woken in her bed feeling crushed by guilt, insane with worry, and realized that these were not her thoughts and feelings, but Ramiq's, as echoed to her through their bond. She had found the flood of emotion unbearable and promptly slammed down her mental defenses. Now for the first time she thinned those shields, tentatively stretching her awareness to sample his emotions.

The torrent nearly overwhelmed her, and before she could be washed away she hastily rebuilt her defenses, redoubling their strength and then doubling them again. Her breathing had become ragged in the scant few heartbeats of time her effort had taken, but she didn't bother to calm it this time. She couldn't manage to think much past what she had read in that brief burst of emotion.

He's ... sincere. He means every word. She felt completely poleaxed by this realization, but gradually her shock melted into wonder. *He still loves me?*

Opening her eyes was an effort, as was turning her head to look at Ramiq where he sat beside her, head lowered and shoulders shaking with emotion. Looking at him hurt – it was as though by allowing herself to feel again, she had walked out of a blizzard and into the heat of a volcano; the heat of her emotions seared her painfully. But she welcomed the pain. Pain had never frightened her the way that numbness had.

"Ramiq?"

Was that her voice, or was there a frog in her throat doing her speaking for her? No matter; he heard her. His head shot up, his entire body taught as a pulled bow string.

He's crying, she noted absently. Then, *Goddess, he looks like death. No doubt I look worse.*

"Tsu?"

His hands clutched hers again, but she scarcely registered the sensation, as it was completely subsumed by the rush of pain and confusion she felt just seeing his face. She winced away from it, and managed to gasp out, "It hurts."

Chapter 23

Her mother's recovery was slow, but at least she was making some measurable progress. Physical strength required little more than time and care to recover; at the end of the week Tsuga was able to bathe and clothe herself before exhaustion chased her, shaking, back to bed.

It was the emotional hurts that healed most slowly. She had begun – haltingly – to speak with Ramiq, and to listen to what he told her. More importantly, she had allowed him back into her heart and mind despite the pain his presence still caused her.

Now that Tsuga was mentally and emotionally present again, Tau began to make a point of visiting each of her parents daily. After a talk with Ramiq she was able to persuade him to leave her alone with her mother while he bathed, and then to have dinner with her in the living area of their suite of rooms, rather than at Tsuga's bedside. During these brief private sessions, Tau exercised her empathic abilities to their fullest, carefully building on the ground work her parents had lain on their own.

Both of her parents longed for the healing of the rift in their relationship, but there was so much pain and guilt between them that without some outside mediation their relationship was more likely to devolve than knit back together. Progress was slow

– very slow – but Tau was both patient and persistent, and progress was indeed being made.

She paused for a moment outside the bedroom door and took a steadying breath.

Fourteen in a couple more months, and here I am holding a marriage together by the skin of my teeth. Ah, well. Nothing doing; if I'm going to fill Da's shoes one day, I have to be able and willing to take on responsibility that I would rather not shoulder. She released her breath in a soft *whoosh* and pushed the door open.

Tsuga was sitting up in bed, her back propped against a pile of plush pillows. She looked up from the stack of papers in her lap – a report on the daily workings of the fort, no doubt – and smiled as her eyes lit on Tau's slender frame.

"Tau! I guess time got away from me. Come on in. You're looking well."

Tau smiled at the lie. She knew she still looked like death's shadow, and was no less stressed now than she had been when her mother lay comatose in this same bed. She crossed the room and seated herself on the chair her father had vacated.

"You're looking quite improved yourself. What's all this?" She gestured at the scattered papers, and Tsuga sighed.

"Progress reports on the trainees. Some are ready to join the ranks, but a few have developed trouble spots that need careful attention. Like this one." Tsuga lifted the sheet she still held and waved it in a gesture of irritation.

"His form with the sword is flawless; he can dance the forms better than me, even. But put him against a live opponent, throw off his rhythm, and he falls apart." She lifted another sheet at random and shook her head.

"This young woman is a fantastic archer; she can hit a target at a hundred paces from the back of a moving wagon. She will make a deadly mounted archer … if we can get her past her fear of horses."

As Tsuga sighed in disgust and scowled at the scattered pages, Tau found a smile tugging at the corners of her mouth. Her mother had not been this animated in a long time. It was good to see.

"Sounds like they need their Weaponsmistress."

Tsuga scowled again.

"I want to be out there. But I'm still barely able to walk without assistance. So," she gestured in irritation at the papers before her, "I read reports and offer advice. It is all I can do, for now."

Tau nodded sympathetically, but an idea had taken root while her mother had been talking. She reached out and took the page about the archer out of the pile and considered how best to proceed for a moment.

"Have you been to see Bane lately?"

Tsuga frowned at her suspiciously for a moment before she answered.

"I have spoken to her, and I can see her from the window when she comes to visit, but no, I have not been down to the stables to see her."

Tau nodded and hid a smile behind a tanned, aristocratic hand.

"As I thought. Come on; it will do you no harm, and likely a world of good."

Lilae? Will you bespeak Erew's guardian, please? Tell her the Weaponsmistress wishes to speak with her in … hmm, in the North pasture, shall we say?

The southern pasture was likely not a good idea; that had been where Tsuga had gone on that fearful night.

A wave of approval from the dragon filled her with warmth as she stood to take her mother's hand.

"It is a good thing you are already dressed. Come on."

Tsuga wore a bemused smile as she pushed papers and blankets aside to stand.

"We are going now?"

"Of course."

"But how? You can hardly carry me all the way to the stables."

Tau allowed herself a mischievous grin.

"You seem to be forgetting the little matter of my heritage."

Tsuga grimaced, and Tau actually laughed at the expression of distaste she wore.

"Try as I might, neither you nor your father will *let* me forget! Very well. Just let me get my –"

"– boots," she finished lamely as Tau lifted her hand from the hilt of her dagger, where her focus stone sparkled in its mount atop the pommel.

"Oops. Sorry."

A light breeze stirred the gauzy outer layers of her robe before it moved on to tease the grass around them. She had transported them with a thought and a small twist of the power stored in her stone without waiting for more than her mother's assent. Tsuga sighed and shook her head, but the sound of rapidly-approaching hoof beats forestalled her from any admonishment she might have been prepared to deliver. She turned to face the sound just as Bane came into sight, galloping towards them at a breakneck speed.

With a small sigh of relief and a smile for the look of radiant joy on her mother's face, Tau stepped back to afford the two a few moments of relative privacy as Bane sat back in an abrupt stop nearly on top of them. Tsuga wobbled forward the few steps that remained between them and all but fell against the horse's neck. Tau turned her back to the pair to save them any embarrassment, and only then noticed the lone figure approaching along the path.

"I see punctuality has not slipped in your absence."

"What?"

Tsuga turned as Erew drew close enough to be identified.

"Erew? What is she doing here?"

"She is here for a lesson in horsemanship."

"A what?"

"A lesson. Who better to show her the potential of a strong partnership between horse and rider and help her move past her fears than the two of you?" Tau turned in time to see understanding dawn on her mother's features.

"Weaponsmistress?"

Erew had halted a few paces away, and Tau inclined her head respectfully to her mother.

"Have Devilsbane summon me when you are ready to return to your rooms, Weaponsmistress."

With a smile and a brief curtsy, Tau took herself away. As she walked towards the path Erew had used to approach, she could hear her mother's voice, growing fainter as the distance between them grew.

"Come on, child. Bane may be a fearsome warhorse, but she is my guardian. Her intelligence is the equal to mine; the better, if she is to be believed. You are as safe with her as with myself. That's it; place your hand there and stroke her cheek. There you are. Now, why don't you tell me a bit more about yourself? Where are you from?"

Chapter 24

Would you sit down?

Tau laughed, head thrown back and hair streaming as she used her outspread arms to balance herself against the peculiar drop-and-rise motion of Lilae's flight.

Why? You won't let me fall.

Terrain spread out below them in a beautiful sun-drenched canvas, the individual features reduced to a blur by their height. She felt the rumble of the dragon's displeasure vibrate up through the soles of her feet.

Of course not. But I would feel better if you would sit.

Oh, very well then. You know, for a dragon, you are terribly cautious.

And for a human, you have a surprising disregard for your own safety.

Tau laughed again as she bent her knees to grasp the straps of Lilae's harness and slid her legs into the stirrups on either side of the immense copper-hued neck. Sitting astride her dragon was something akin to straddling a rather large tree trunk, but the modified saddle she used made for a more secure – and far more comfortable – seat.

It is rather hard to hold a fear of death when I can walk on the other side at will. Even Da says such skill is rare, and understands how it might skew my perceptions a bit.

This is a rather disconcerting conversation for someone whose life has already been reduced from thousands of years to less than a hundred. Mortality is not something dragons usually have to contemplate before they have lived long enough to grow bored with life.

Tau sighed and stroked the supple hide before her with a hand.

I know. Being tied to me means that you will die with me. I am sorry.

I am not. I would not trade what we have for a hundred such lifetimes.

Tau grinned, green eyes shining with the outpouring of love from her guardian, which she returned whole-heartedly. After a few more minutes of peaceful flight, Tau sighed. Reluctance was strong in her mindvoice when she spoke again.

We should head back. I am supposed to sit in on the negotiations this evening. They will expect me to be both punctual and presentable.

And no doubt Amilia will have a fit about your hair. You know how she admonishes you about tangles.

I know. But what use is having all this hair if I can't let it loose once in a while to enjoy the feel of the wind?

A rumble of laughter that vibrated to her very bones was all the answer she received as Lilae dipped a wing to turn and begin the flight back to their home. When Tau had reached the level of Master mage six months ago – at fifteen, she was the youngest Queen's Mage to have ever done so – she had earned the right to be included in the not-infrequent diplomatic and political meetings her parents participated in. Negotiation was a skill almost as critical for a Queen's Mage as any of her magical abilities, and one which, much like her powers, she seemed to pick up with an almost startling ease. A skill she found, oddly enough, she thoroughly enjoyed developing.

It didn't take long to return to the fort – not by dragon-back, at least – and Tau was soon back in her rooms seeking patience as she allowed her maids to help her change clothes and comb the knots from her hair. She seldom made use of the women, but her more formal clothes required some assistance for her to get in and out of them, and her skills with hair styling began and ended with the handful of braids she employed to keep her long locks confined when need be.

Today her maids bustled her into a floor-length gown of a pale golden color slashed through with white along the divided skirts. *Those* had been won only after an uphill battle with both parents and her maids, with Tsuga insisting on practicality (which meant trousers whenever possible, and divided skirts when absolutely necessary to wear a dress), Ramiq set on the importance of first impressions (which meant a showy ensemble, preferably elaborate mage's robes to emphasize her rank), and her Ladies protesting that she was a young woman and should dress appropriately.

Finally, they had settled on something both practical and elegant. Though Tau had been given virtually no say in the matter, she had to admit that she was not altogether displeased with the results.

By the time her hair had been piled atop her head in an elaborate fashion and pinned to within an inch of its life to help it stay in place on the upcoming horseback ride, even Tau had to admit that she cut a rather attractive – if somewhat more severe than she tended to like – figure.

After the addition of her dagger at her hip, a couple of jewels on a necklace and a ring with a large ruby in a simple setting, she was deemed ready. She wished she could have done without the jewels, but she was out of time to argue with her maids. Besides, she knew she would be expected to make a show of her wealth and rank, especially today, on her first diplomatic venture. Perhaps, once she had established herself, she could dress as *she* wished.

After a hurried thanks to her maids she bustled into the hall and downstairs to the courtyard from which they were to leave. Her parents were already there when she arrived, as well as the guards and a handful of other nobles who would be making this trip. With such a large party they would not be able to teleport, so everyone stood holding the reins of a horse. Tau paused a brief moment in the doorway to take a breath and compose herself before striding out to make her courtesies.

"Nice of you to join us, Tau."

She flushed at her father's sardonic tone, but held her tongue as she straightened. When he turned to take up his reins and mount the rest of the party followed suit, leaving Tau to move to the little black mare she rode and swing herself into the saddle. Moments later she was riding beside her parents through the gates in the wall surrounding the fort.

The spring air was brisk but far from cold as the small party made their way into the campsite shortly after noon. The roads were still a bog after last week's rain, but between the lingering puddles the surface had begun to dry again. They had been able to arrive more-or-less free of mud, which was just as well. Ramiq was already in a sour mood from having to ride; if he had ended this trip covered in muck, no doubt any hopes of a peaceful meeting today would have been lost.

Despite hailing from a family of noted horse breeders, he had never been overly fond of the beasts. He was a good rider – he had been plopped down atop his first pony shortly after he had learned to walk – but he certainly never sought out an opportunity to ride. In fact, as she thought about it, she realized he tended to simply teleport over any medium distance when he could get away with it.

Tau smiled to herself as a groom came forward to hold her mare's bridle so that she could dismount.

You might try looking less like you are here to rip the heads off of everyone, and a bit more like we are here to make peace.

Ramiq started, one foot still in his stirrup, and shot her a scathing glance before sliding it free and straightening his robes. Tau had to stifle a laugh at the sudden change in his expression when he turned, though; now he merely looked as though he had a sore tooth. She covered her lapse by reaching up to check that her hair was straight – it was – and then turned to join the party walking to the large tent.

Far from the first such meeting, this was still the first that Tau had attended, and as she walked she had to stifle a nervous flutter that almost made her giggle before she caught herself. She had always known her parents worked to encourage peace between Sennor and Devali. She had spent a great deal of time studying the treaties and contracts that had been agreed upon between the nations over the past few years – the past ten or so, to be precise; her parents had, she'd learned, been the driving force in seeking peace between the two countries.

Tau wasn't precisely clear on when the queen's mentality had shifted enough to allow such negotiations, but she knew that her parents were here today with the monarch's blessing. Today was, in fact, a momentous occasion: they were here to negotiate a visit of state between the king of Devali and Sennor's queen. This would be the first such peaceful meeting in nearly two hundred years.

As the guards dismounted Tau joined the other dignitaries and entered the tent that had been raised to shelter the group from the elements – as well as any prying eyes, as Tau well knew. All but a pair of their guards remained outside the tent, but Tau felt no fear as she left their protection. Even with only her dagger and the pair of throwing knives up her sleeves, she was well equipped to counter any attack, physical or magical. Her parents had taught her well. Even as she strode through the open tent flaps, held aside by a pair of guards in Devalian armor, she was assessing the contents of the tent for potential danger or defensive use.

After years of training under her mother's tutelage this assessment was almost subconscious, and she was able to simultaneously smile and follow the introductions as they were made. There was one face she recognized even before the tall, graying woman was introduced.

"Hello again, Cousin." She could not quite bring herself to say it was good to see the woman; the last time she had seen Ramira, the Adept had held her prisoner in Devali.

"Tau. Your father tells me you have been advancing well. You have certainly grown since I've seen you last."

"Children do tend to grow up, Cousin. And my father has been generous with his praise, it would seem."

Ramira smiled warmly, the expression deepening the fine lines surrounding her eyes. Despite herself, Tau wanted to like the woman.

When she was offered refreshment, Tau accepted a strong tea that smelled of peaches, which she sweetened liberally with honey before sipping. Some of the others accepted wine or other spirits (her mother took water; Tau had never seen her imbibe any form of alcohol, though she wasn't sure why), but Tau wanted her wits about her now. She took careful note of the others who made similar choices.

Once everyone was served the nobles and other representatives moved to take their seats. During the process of getting everyone settled the scribes arranged themselves to one side of the tent to take notes and, if all went well, draft the treaty for review by those gathered before it was approved in their respective monarchs' names. Tau moved to take her own seat to Ramiq's left – her mother sat on his right side – and watched as the rest settled themselves.

The members of her own party were all men and women she already knew and had had previous opportunities to study, but she had been instructed beforehand to make note of her observations and thoughts regarding the Devalian diplomats. She suspected her parents had only made the request to act as another lesson for her, but she intended to surprise them, if she could.

"Well, shall we get down to the business at hand?"

This from her mother, who, although she held little in the way of courtly rank save her status as the wife of Sennor's Queen's Mage, was well known and respected by everyone present, Sennorran and Devalian alike. She had, after all, established herself in both militaries, as well as holding a reputation as a formidable mercenary captain. She had subsequently made friends – and enemies – on both sides of the border.

Certainly none here seemed to object to her presence, nor to her opening of the negotiations. Her blunt nature was widely known, and even the foreigners – no, she must learn to think of them as individuals, not as one like-minded entity; they were as varied and unique as the people she had grown up with – seemed to take it in stride.

"Very well. The king has agreed on a visit of state, but wishes to set down clear parameters. He is prepared to accept the queen and a small party of her choosing, as well as their servants and an armed escort of one hundred. No more than ten of this party, escort included, may be mages above the rank of Journeyman."

This came from a man who, though spry, was obviously past his fighting prime, to judge by his spreading middle and receding hairline. Tau noted the dour expression and sonorous voice. With those traits paired with his overly-opulent clothes and jewel-encrusted sword hilt, she judged him to be a noble, not a general or mage as no few of the others obviously were.

The Sennorran nobles were all shaking their heads before he had finished, but it was her father who spoke, though several of the others looked on the verge of saying something.

"I am afraid you misunderstand. We are here to negotiate safe passage for your king to visit the Sennorran court. Her Majesty has no intention of placing herself at risk, with her heir still in diapers."

The Sennorran queen was very young – only about ten years Tau's senior. Her mother had been killed in an assassination attempt some years back, which was why she had been so hostile towards the Devalians in the past.

"Oh, but it's alright for our king to endanger himself?"

A somberly dressed woman had voiced the question – her dark gray dress was slashed through with a deep blue in the full skirts, and even her gems were subdued. Her expression was schooled to a smooth mask, but Tau caught a gleam of anger in her eye when she adjusted the fall of full skirts twice the volume or more of anything that was currently fashionable in Sennor.

"Danger? Hardly."

This time it was her mother who spoke. The Sennorrans had carefully planned and choreographed their side of this conversation, Tau knew. No doubt the Devalians had done much the same. The only question was how far apart the two countries' goals truly were.

"He will of course be granted safe passage. The queen is prepared to tell off half a legion of her own men to assure it, in addition to the two centuries of his own she is granting him for his honor guard."

Expressions tightened around the room, but the forced smiles stayed in place as Ramira responded. Tau thought it very like watching a sparring match; a feint here, a jab there, neither willing to overextend or commit themselves just yet to anything more serious.

"And just whose safety are five hundred armed Sennorrans really intended to ensure? The king's, or your queen's?"

This time it was one of the generals who spoke for the Sennorrans, a broad-shouldered man with gray spreading from his temples who looked as though he might chew nails for breakfast and wash them down with gravel.

"The queen has no fear of her own safety within our borders. The escort would be as much for the protection of the king and his soldiers as anything. Our country folk have suffered no few casualties and depredations at the hands of your soldiers. Presented with such an opportunity, no few of them may seek to get back a bit of their own. Her Majesty would be appalled if anything untoward were to befall anyone in the king's party on a visit to her."

What was carefully not said, though plainly understood by all present, was that the honor guard would likewise protect the country folk from any further liberties the Devalian soldiers might be tempted to take.

"Not an unreasonable precaution from your queen's point of view, I am sure."

An older man spoke this time, his words slightly muffled behind the hand stroking his long gray moustaches. His appearance gave the impression of a doddering grandfather, but Tau saw a glint of sly intelligence in his pale blue eyes that brought to mind one of the horses she had learned to ride on. The old gelding was docile as a lamb where ground manners were concerned, but he had a habit of taking in air when being saddled, so that an unwary rider would end up dumped in the dirt when the saddle rolled with her weight. More than once, Tau would have sworn the old brute had laughed at her!

"But still," the old man – a mage, Tau knew, though dressed rather more like a military officer than most of the mages she knew, "we would require some guarantee of His Majesty's safety. Some … insurance, if you will."

Tau had to strain to keep a smooth expression; her thick eyebrows wanted nothing more than to join her hairline at such an insult. It was not unheard of for an enemy to be quietly done away with while visiting a hostile – or even supposedly-friendly – court, but to imply so directly that such was likely to happen in the Sennorran countryside was highly insulting.

Ramiq's voice was smooth when he answered, his expression as still as the undisturbed surface of a pond, but outrage practically radiated from him – indeed, from their entire party – to her empathic senses. Well, everyone except her mother; Tsuga seemed to take the accusation in stride. Indeed, she looked almost as though she had counted on it, even nodding to herself as though confirming her own expectations.

"You want us to exchange hostages for the king against our good behavior."

It was not a question. The man could scarcely have meant anything else.

Ramira inclined her head graciously, and Tau felt the mood in the tent shift. Now the Devalians all gave off the air of a hawk preparing to stoop. The Sennorrans, rather than reacting like the rabbit who feels his predator's shadow, felt more like a falconer, waiting for the bird to stoop and knowing that its efforts would bring him what he desired.

What do they desire? No one had bothered to tell her the truth of the matter; she knew only that they were to seek a diplomatic meeting of the rulers. What else they might be looking to gain, she had no idea. At any rate it was a very strange dynamic, and the feelings made her skin crawl as though it were suddenly a size too small for her body. What in the Goddess' name was going on?

"It would help to ease the minds of our people."

Tau noted that Devali's King's Mage very carefully did not say anything about it easing the mind of the king himself.

"Very well." This came from one of the noblewomen that had traveled here with them. Tau could not see her easily from where she sat, but from the cool tone of her voice she could well picture the stern expression on the Lady's too-round face, her dark brown curls swaying as she shifted her weight on the uncomfortable chair.

"We would be open to negotiating the visitation of a few dignitaries, so that your *people* may be at ease."

Ramira was shaking her head even before the woman had finished speaking. Tau had to work again to keep her face smooth when her lower jaw tried to drop open in shock.

"I'm afraid that whomever you appoint, and be assured you may send any additional members of your court you may wish, there is only one person of sufficient rank to justify jeopardizing our king."

Tsuga's voice was sharp when she spoke, and her words cracked through the air like a whip.

"And just who might that be?"

Tau suspected that her mother already had a good idea of where this was going, as she did. The princess and heir to the throne of Sennor was still a young child, and there was only one other person she could think of who would satisfy the Devalians. Certainly neither of the young princes – both older than the heir, one had already been promised to the priesthood, and the other would be joining the military when he grew of age. Neither was terribly important to the future of the country, since they could not inherit the throne.

Her father was out of the question; not only did he have a school to run, but he was an experienced Adept and a skilled politician. They would never be able to restrain him from doing as he wished, and they would have to fret the entire time about what games he might try to play. That left –

"Your daughter."

The reaction of both parties was highly varied – and very immediate. In a small corner of her mind,

Tau noted that the rest of the Devalians seemed as shocked as her own countrymen. Seemed was the key here, though; she sensed a smug satisfaction from almost everyone present. Her father radiated outright denial, and no few of the Devalian nobles – and even a few Sennorrans, who no doubt fretted over the safety of their future Queen's Mage – stank of fear and worry. In fact, the two calmest people present were Ramira, who had to have planned this from the beginning, and Tsuga.

Her mother had spent a great deal of time in Devali. She knew its citizens as people, not as a faceless mass of enemies. And she knew her daughter's capabilities. From this iron-willed woman Tau felt only confidence and one brief, strong surge of pride. Tau took a deep breath and opened her mouth to answer, but Ramiq ran right over anything she might have intended to say.

"Absolutely not. She is still in training, and besides, she is too –"

He broke off when Tsuga lay a hand on his arm and shook her head. Tau shot her mother a grateful look; he had been about to say "too young," she knew.

"Perhaps, Ramiq, you are allowing your feelings as her father to cloud your judgment. There is little more you can teach her; you have told me so yourself. At this stage in her training, she can only benefit from new experiences. If she is to take your place one day, she must learn to conduct herself out from under your watchful eye. She has had the best instruction anyone could give her. Besides which, she is fifteen, and old enough to speak for herself. Tau? What do you think of Ramira's proposal?"

All eyes in the tent shifted to her, and Tau felt heat rising to her face. She looked from her mother, who smiled at her encouragingly, to her father, who appeared as though he had swallowed a live toad which was trying to make its way back up his throat. She took a deep breath before meeting Ramira's eyes.

"Both of my parents raise valid points. This is, more than anyone else's, my decision. But I *do* still have much to learn, both of my magic, and of history, diplomacy, theology, and the like. However, there is only so much I can learn where I am. *If –*" and she emphasized the word slightly, "I agree to this, certain provisions must be made for my continuing edification. I would expect to be instructed in Devalian history, culture, tactics, and so forth. This is not negotiable. I must be allowed to study whatever I wish, without restraint."

To either side of Ramira the dignitaries exchanged worried looks, but the Devalian King's Mage only nodded graciously.

"Of course. In fact, I would be happy to personally oversee your continuing education. It will be nice to have an apprentice at last."

Tau nodded slowly, somewhat dumbstruck. She had not expected immediate agreement, by any means. Hours of arguing and negotiations should have followed her words. She had known Ramira still searched for Devali's next King's Mage – it was common knowledge – but had never anticipated that the woman might insist in taking over as her mentor for the duration of her stay.

There is something deeper here than I thought. But her decision had already been made, and she would not allow herself to go back on it now.

"If these conditions, and any other reasonable requests my fellows may wish to recommend, can be agreed upon, then I see no reason that I cannot join you at court for a short time, in the interest of encouraging peace between our nations."

Triumph oozed from Ramira, but her smug smile promptly slid from her expression when Tau added, as an afterthought, "My guardian will accompany me, of course. I presume you can accommodate a dragon with no trouble?" In fact, Ramira turned an interesting shade of green. Tau smiled innocently at her.

"Surely you do not expect me to leave Lilae behind, any more than you would think to shield me from my magic while I am visiting?"

From the pale faces and furtive glances of Ramira's companions, Tau surmised that they had intended precisely that. She shook her head sadly.

"If we are to have peace, we must learn to trust each other. I place my life in your hands, Cousin, but I will not be stripped and bound like a criminal to be led to the headsman's block."

"No, of course not." Some of Ramira's color had returned, and her voice was steady when she spoke. No doubt it had been the worry of Lilae snatching babes from their cradles to munch as appetizers that had upset her, more than anything.

"Wonderful. And Lilae does not need much. A place to sun and shelter from inclement weather, somewhere to stretch her wings … and to hunt.

Surely a country as rich as Devali can afford to share their game for a brief time."

"Of – of course." Ramira nodded briskly. "I am sure we can arrange something."

Tau inclined her head graciously and settled back into her chair.

"Excellent. Then I shall leave further negotiations to those who know more of such things than I." She gestured vaguely around the gathering, risking a brief glance at her parents as she did so. Her mother looked ready to burst with pride, but Ramiq still looked like someone had hit him in the back of the head with a board.

Well done, Tau, she caught as other voices took up the negotiations.

Thank you, she thought back. *Will he be alright?* It was rare that her mother initiated mindspeech with her – it was not a gift her mother possessed – but Tau knew to always listen for a targeted thought such as this one. It was something she had adapted her shields to let through.

Oh, your father will come around. He is just in shock; in his eyes, you went from the little girl he dandled on his knee and made "pretty lights" for to a grown and competent young woman in a blink.

Tau had to stifle a hysterical giggle at that. Poor Da! She reached over to pat his knee, and his green eyes met hers. She thought at him – very privately, so as not to be inadvertently overheard, *I love you, Daddy. And I will be alright. You and Momma taught me very well.*

He smiled at her weakly, then gave himself a visible shake and returned his attentions with an effort to the negotiation.

Chapter 25

*T*au leaned into the turn as Lilae began gently spiraling towards the courtyard below them. From this height, the castle overlooking the capital city of Devali looked more like the symbols on a map than the imposing structure of wood and stone she knew it to be.

Are you ready?

I suppose I have to be, don't I?

Beneath her, Lilae's chest rumbled with laughter.

Unless you intend to run away to hide in the mountains and have me eat anyone who comes to find us, yes, I suppose you do.

Tau managed a weak chuckle, but her nerves soon drew her back into an anxious silence. After nearly six months, the day of their arrival had finally come. Had it simply been a matter of getting herself here Tau could have arrived moments after the treaty had been signed, but unfortunately a lot more went into a visit of state than merely visiting.

Party members had to be agreed upon and notified, some of whom took months to arrive from their outlying estates. A whole new wardrobe had to be commissioned for her and sewn at her father's insistence, though in truth she hadn't required much persuading. She had, however, made sure that *this* batch of clothing was made to *her* specifications.

Even once they had set off, the armed guard of one hundred and fifty soldiers – ten for her personal bodyguard, fifty additional men to guard the wagons carrying the chests of clothes and supplies, and the bodyguards of the various other dignitaries – had to travel over the ground at the pace set by the draft horses. By the time the servants, ladies' maids, and scribes were factored in, they proceeded at a snail's pace – or so it seemed to her, from her vantage a-dragonback.

Tau had brought the deep-chested hunter she rode, and had even ridden the spirited little mare part of the way. She was not tall, but had great speed over a short distance. Today, though, she intended to make an entrance. Lilae's arrival would cause a great deal of chaos; even with advance warning the arrival of a dragon was an event, and no few people would be terrified by her size alone. By arriving atop her guardian, Tau hoped to quell some of that instinctive fear.

They had been circling high above the castle and city for some small time now, waiting for the rest of the party to arrive. Now the riders were massed before the castle's gates, banners snapping smartly in the breeze, and it was time for her own entrance. The banner signaling for her to land had been raised, and Lilae had begun her descent.

They would take their time to approach, allowing plenty of opportunity for those on the ground to notice them as they drew closer. Unable to resist an opportunity for dramatic flair, Tau drew lightly on her magic to intensify the amount of light reflected from Lilae's gleaming hide until she glittered as though she were made from millions of gleaming copper coins.

When her back feet touched down at last, Lilae backwinged carefully to balance long enough to let out a deafening bugle. It was not the roar of a vengeful dragon intended to strike fear into the hearts of enemies, but rather a joyous trumpeting that rose and fell with a musical lilt. It was not unpleasant, only *loud*. As Lilae settled at last to all fours and flipped her wings neatly to her back, Tau tried to resist the urge to shake her head in an attempt to dispel the ringing in her ears.

You could have given me some warning.

Where would be the fun in that?

Tau shot a sour look at the back of the triangular head as she reached up to unbuckle the leather helmet she wore to keep her hair under control when she flew. She seldom neglected to wear gloves and warm clothing to fly (it grew cold in the thinner air at such high altitudes), but today she had chosen to make a point of demonstrating her power by magically shielding herself from the depredations of temperature.

By making use of her saddle and Lilae's neck ridges, Tau was able to vault with relative ease from her perch and land lightly beside the dragon before calmly turning to address those gathered to greet them. She was somewhat surprised to see Ramira herself step forward, though perhaps she should not have been. It was only fitting, after all, considering Tau's position as Queen's Mage-in-training. No doubt it was a precautionary measure as well; although Ramira was certainly not the only Devalian mage present, she was by far the only one who had a hope of lasting beyond the first few moments if Tau were to take it into her head to attack.

All of this passed through her mind in the time it took her to cover the five steps that freed her from Lilae's shadow and brought her within easy speaking distance.

"Master Tau." She thought she detected strain in the voice of the King's Mage, and sure enough, when she thinned her empathic shields just a hair she caught echoes of stress and nerves from the outwardly-composed woman. Her eyes were tight, her lips somewhat thin and bloodless, but otherwise Ramira was the picture of poise and dignity.

"Welcome to the capitol. We are honored to play host to Sennor's next Queen's Mage, as well as the rest of your party."

Tau inclined her head the precise degree required of Master mage to Adept. If Ramira wished to treat her as a mage first and a noblewoman not at all, Tau would oblige her. Her parents may have raised her away from a formal court, but she had been well schooled in politics from the time she was old enough to speak and think for herself.

"And we are likewise honored to be part of the first visit of state between our two nations in over a century. This is an auspicious day, indeed."

Ramira nodded graciously in acknowledgement, then stepped aside with a gesture to the young man standing immediately behind her. Tau estimated the youth to be near her own age – perhaps two or three years her senior, at most. Though his fine green coat, embroidered with thread-of-gold, and the jewel-encrusted sword at his side indicated some high rank, his eyes sparkled with mischief above his delicate nose. A lopsided grin stretched across his triangular face.

He was the first young Devalian she had seen, and she wondered briefly if all of this country's youth were so … pretty. He was not what she would have imagined to be the Devalian ideal; a broad, burly man with a bushy beard and muscles rippling as he brandished his battle axe, yes. A singularly beautiful young man, slender and refined, who looked more likely to run laughing through a stable yard than to command troops on a battlefield, no.

"Allow me to present the Crown Prince of Devali, the Blade of Glory, His Highness Xanthrall a'Corinin, Hope of the Nation. Highness, this is the Lady Tau Dafrin, Master mage, daughter and apprentice to Ramiq Dafrin, Queen's Mage of Sennor, and her guardian, Lilae." Of course her mother would be left out of the introductions. In Devali a person's rank was determined by one's father, not one's mother. Never mind; it may prove to her advantage if it were not common knowledge just who her mother was.

Tau managed to keep her expression serene with an effort, but her eyebrows wanted to climb up to hide amongst her hair at the introduction – not only because she stood before the heir to the Devalian throne (an honor, indeed), but also at Ramira's inclusion of Lilae in the proceedings. She had never expected a Devalian, who all rumors said feared and mistrusted the guardians, to treat the dragon as the equal member of the party that she was. Tau made her curtsey – again, carefully done to the exact degree proper from one of her station to a crown prince – and rose only when he spoke.

"Lady Dafrin, you and yours are well come to our capitol. Please, rise."

Once she had straightened he strode forward to clasp her shoulders and plant a kiss on either of her cheeks by way of greeting. Her mother had warned her of this – supposedly it was a greeting among good friends, here – but she was unable to keep the flush from her cheeks. His grip on her shoulders was gentle but strong, and his lips against her skin sent a shock right down to her toes. She returned the gesture clumsily, but before she could pull away he leaned in to whisper in her ear, his breath warming her unexpectedly.

"You simply must tell me what it's like to ride a dragon!"

Tau blinked in surprise, then felt her own face stretching into a grin to answer his.

"Perhaps, if it would not be taken amiss, you would like to find out first-hand, Highness?"

His fingers tightened briefly on her shoulders before he released her and stepped back, but the expression on his face was all the answer she needed. There would be no preventing him from taking her up on *that* offer, improper or not.

The rest of the introductions proceeded, but they were all a blur to Tau. No matter; she knew Lilae was paying close attention. She could pick the dragon's brain later. Xanthrall was necessarily absorbed in greeting the remaining dignitaries, but because she couldn't seem to take her eyes off of him she caught each of his not-infrequent glances in her direction. Was it her imagination, or was his smile a little warmer when she caught his eye? She wanted to squeal and clap her hands and dance in place, the way she had when she'd been excited as a little girl.

What has come over me?

You have been smiled at by a pretty face – one who did not used to steal your dolly or pull your hair. It will pass.

Looking at the prince smiling and clasping hands as though he did so every day – he probably did, come to think of it – Tau shook her head slightly. Pass? She wasn't sure she wanted it to.

Chapter 26

Xanthrall stood in his sitting room and looked contemplatively out of his west-facing window. There, a bit to the north of true west, the roof of one of the towers was filled nearly to overflowing by the massive form of the glittering copper dragon. Such a magnificent creature.

He had grown up reading stories of brave knights who fought and killed fearsome dragons, but no bloodlust had stirred in him when the beautiful creature had arrived. It did not now, either. Next to her, the young woman standing at her side and scratching under the massive jaw looked like one of the white birds known for feasting on the insects drawn by cattle. They were too far away for him to make out anything more than the color of the girls' robes, but he caught himself watching her nonetheless.

He had never had one of these spirit guardians, personally – as a Devalian, Ketral had granted him shapeshifting and powerful mindspeech, instead – but he understood the bond to be something like a soul bond between lovers, yet somehow both closer and more intimate. Not that he had ever been soul bonded, either; at eighteen, he had scarcely seen enough of the world to meet more than noble hangers-on and their serving girls. Not that such women – like those in the taverns, as well – didn't have their charms. But after a time the names and faces began to blur; they were all too much the same, interested in him for his rank or his pretty face rather than harboring any true feelings.

What would it be like, he mused, *to be loved for my own sake, and not for my titles?*

Oh, his father loved him, certainly – as his heir, the proof of his virility and his right to the throne. His people loved him – an important thing for a ruler – but they loved him as their future monarch, for the station he held and the future he promised. Even his friends, fond of them though he was, were friends of convenience and mutual social or political standing, not true comrades.

He shook his head, black hair falling into his eyes before he brushed it absently back. He could not even imagine someone feeling genuine fondness for him, let alone the deep love and kinship of a soul bond.

"You seemed quite taken with the young mage."

With reluctance he turned his back to the window and faced Ramira, who sat in one of the plush chairs by the fireplace – currently cold – and watched him with a faint, knowing smile. He flushed slightly, though he did his best to play it off.

"She is bonded with a dragon. Fascinating creatures! I had never seen one so close!"

Ramira chuckled slightly. She had a rich, throaty laugh, rather than the shrill twittering so common among the nobility. Strongest in earth magic, the King's Mage was a very genuine person, well-grounded and unassuming. He valued her company and conversation as much as her intellect and canny insights. Usually.

"Or at all, I'd wager, outside of the picture books."

He cleared his throat and moved further into the room, deliberately keeping his back to that transfixing sight through the window.

"Yes, well. They are creatures practically reduced to legend, after all. See to it that she is seated next to me at dinner tonight."

Ramira tilted her head and arched a questioning eyebrow.

"I hardly think the dinner table is an appropriate place for a dragon, Highness."

He colored again, and his cheeks heated further as he spoke and caught a smugly knowing twinkle in his mentor's eye.

"Of course not. I meant the mage."

"Of course."

"It is only fitting that the leader of the Sennorran delegation dine with the crown prince in the absence of the king, after all."

"Oh, certainly, Highness." Ramira stood and smoothed her deep brown skirts calmly, then turned and walked to the door. She paused there, one hand on the knob, and hesitated with the door partially open.

"In fact, such arrangements have already been made."

Before he could order his thoughts enough to say anything, she had slipped through the door and closed it behind her. He was glad she couldn't see him now; his face must be the same color as the sky over the western wall now as the sun sank lower on the horizon! If she had already made the seating arrangements, why had she let him flounder about so, thinking himself clever? To humiliate him?

No, he admitted to himself reluctantly, *she would not do such a thing.* She was, as he recalled, Tau's distant cousin. Perhaps she thought to further raise the family's standing by playing matchmaker? He shook his head angrily. Nonsense. The world's three most powerful and influential mages in the same family? The only way they could gain any higher standing would be to marry into the royal family itself. *Now,* that *is ridiculous.* Their countries were at war, peace talks or no, and as the future advisor and Queen's Mage of Sennor, the conflict of interest would make such a match impossible.

He sighed and moved back to the window, but Tau was gone. Without her presence, the dragon – glorious though she was – was not enough to hold his attention.

Time to stop daydreaming. His would be a marriage of state, to gain the best advantage for his kingdom. Any wife he had would not bring love to their marriage; it would be a mutually beneficial arrangement, granting her rank and security and him a prized broodmare with sufficient titles and a strong alliance to offer him. He would be lucky if she had a brain in her head; so many of the noble ladies paraded before him as prospects, though attractive, were decidedly lacking in that department. He longed for an intellectual equal, but feared he was fated for something far less fulfilling.

Xanthrall shook his head and turned his back on the window. It was close enough to dinner time for him to change and make his way to the dining hall.

At least Lady Dafrin will offer some interesting conversation for this evening, he mused. Even if he had mistaken that conspiratorial gleam in her eye, she rode a *dragon*! She must at least have something to talk about in that!

Chapter 27

*T*au stood admiring herself in the stand mirror. She had been given a suite of rooms – a luxury which, though demanded by the nature of her visit, she was unaccustomed to – and stood now in her own private dressing room. Not that it was truthfully private, with two ladies' maids twittering about and helping her dress.

The rooms were not overly large, but the opulence threatened to overwhelm her. She had lived most of her life in a fort which, though large, was built more with function in mind than indulgence. Oh, it had its share of unique luxuries – the mages ensured hot and cold running water at the turn of a valve, devices which stored light and released it at a command, and immense cold rooms for food storage – but this was a palace.

Thank Auriga Da insisted on a whole new wardrobe! She'd have felt a beggar at the gates in even the finest of her older gowns.

She could not seem to stop staring at her reflection; she very nearly did not recognize herself. As she'd advanced further into womanhood, her face had lengthened and grown more slender, as had her neck. In recent years her breasts had begun to expand, and now she found that between their fullness and her slender hips and narrower waist she cut a pleasingly feminine figure.

In addition to her magical talents Tau had inherited a strong love of beautiful clothing from her father, and the dress she now wore indulged that passion in a most satisfying manner. She ran one hand reverently along the deep purple silk of her skirt, careful not to let it snag on her roughened skin.

The color brought out tones of red in her hair that she hadn't known were there and made her eyes appear to catch flecks of gold that gleamed within the green irises. Against such a deep colored fabric her sun-tanned skin seemed a few shades lighter, but her cheeks were flushed with excitement.

The sleeveless gown plunged in a deep neckline that would have been scandalous in any other cloth, but the silk draped in such a way that it maintained her modesty admirably. It was fitted with a thin silver cord around her waist, and the skirts clung to leg and hip every time she shifted. The skirt was divided, of course – all of her dresses were, to accommodate spur-of-the-moment rides a-dragonback – but the slit was all but invisible in the soft folds of fabric, even when she walked.

Delicate silver slippers peeked out from beneath the hem of her gown, and as she watched one of the maids wrapped a purple sash to match the dress around her hips below the silver cord. Her dagger hung from it, and Tau adjusted the weapon herself so that it rode comfortably at her left hip before allowing the girl to tie on the sash with an intricate knot.

"My Lady?"

Tau pulled her gaze away from her reflection with an effort and smiled at the maid who had spoken.

"Yes, Amilia?"

"How would you like to wear your hair tonight, My Lady?"

Tau looked back to her reflection and considered. She had taken to wearing her waist-length hair in an intricate-looking but simple-to-execute braid for ease of maintenance during the day and to keep it from tangling wildly when she flew. It was still up from her arrival earlier this afternoon. But this was a special occasion, and she needed to present the best image possible for her country. Perhaps....

"Down," she decided, but then amended, "with the silver clasp to pull the top half back from my face."

Amilia smiled and began unbraiding Tau's hair while the slightly darker and plumper Magla fetched the clip she had indicated. Both of the ladies' maids she had brought – neither truly maids, but in fact very minor nobility – had her own unique talents. Amilia's most notable was hair styling. As Tau watched, the woman carefully ran her fingers under Tau's hair along her scalp to fluff it out of the divided sections of her braid. She pursed her lips a moment in consideration, then shook her head to herself and expertly gathered the top third or so of the hair and combed the upper sections through with her fingers to smooth them over Tau's head and eliminate the part that naturally divided her hair down the middle.

With an expert twist that Tau didn't quite catch the clasp was in, and Amilia was drawing a section of the lightly waved hair – being braided all day always left it so – over Tau's right shoulder. It shone with health, almost seeming to glow with that newfound undercurrent of red against the purple

fabric. It was simple, but no one could call it plain –
not paired with this dress.

Amid breathy declarations of her beauty Tau took
one final, long look at herself in the mirror. She
could see elements of both parents in her features,
blended to make her. Tsuga's prominent nose was
slightly less so on her face, Ramiq's square jaw
somewhat softer and more feminine. His eyes stared
back at her above her mother's wide mouth, the lips
slightly fuller on her own face. Her ears were small
and delicate, almost hidden under her mane of hair.

She had always taken her appearance somewhat
for granted – as a child she had been called "cute,"
and more recently "pretty" and "lovely." But her
reflection now was actually … beautiful. She had
never felt *beautiful* before. Her cheeks colored as
she flushed again.

"Thank you, ladies. That will be all."

Tau was proud that her voice came out normally.
She felt somewhat strangled. The women tittered
some more and made their curtsies, and then Tau
was left alone before the mirror.

**You have always been beautiful, you know.
You just never allowed yourself to see it.**

Tau remained silent, still somewhat in awe. After
a few moments, Lilae spoke again.

**I know you wish to make an entrance, but if
you delay much longer you may be forced to eat
in the kitchens.**

Tau started. It *was* growing late. She took one
final, deep breath to calm her nerves, then turned
from her reflection. It was time.

Chapter 28

Xanthrall usually dreaded dinners with the full court; most of its members spent the meal either jabbering inanely (if they were young women), trying to marry him off if the Lord or Lady had an eligible daughter or two, or talking politics. He generally made it a point to absent himself from such dinners whenever he reasonably could. But tonight, as he mounted the raised platform and took his seat – to the right of his father's empty one, which was bordered on the other side by the one which, had she lived, would have been his mother's – he found himself rather looking forward to the meal. The seat to his right was still empty; Tau had not yet arrived.

Several long minutes passed as the last stragglers wandered in and found their seats. He schooled himself to stillness, though he wanted nothing more than to shift in his heavy chair and crane his neck to strain for a first glimpse of her. He needn't have bothered; it was not his eyes, but his ears which gave first warning of her approach.

The hush began near the main doors, but it spread quickly, so that she advanced in complete silence save for the occasional creaking of benches or quickly-stifled cough. And it didn't take a genius to see why everyone had fallen silent to stare.

She was a vision. Oh, he had seen more beautiful girls, and certainly many who were more voluptuous, but this young foreigner held him – and everyone else, it seemed – transfixed. She was not dressed in the full-skirted gowns favored by the Devalian ladies, but rather in what he presumed was the Sennorran fashion. The fabric gleamed richly in the lantern light, its deep color making her hair almost seem to glow. She appeared to actually float across the floor with the fluid grace of a dancer as she approached.

No, not a dancer, he corrected himself. *A warrior.* He recognized that casual effortlessness of movement, now. She walked with the confidence of someone who knew every capability of her body, who knew her strengths and limitations intimately. The rocking sway to her gait was hypnotizing, and though he could see nervousness in her eyes her face was coolly expressionless. A dagger – her only visible weapon, though as a skilled mage she truly needed none – rode at her hip. She carried it with the air of someone long used to moving with its weight at her side.

His breath caught as she stopped before the platform and curtsied to him. Hastily, he rose and – after disentangling his sword from the chair – descended to lift her from her curtsy with a smile and escort her to her seat. It was well that he was not required to speak at that moment; he rather thought he might be hard-pressed to form a coherent word, let alone a proper speech.

Once the two of them were properly seated, he was spared for a few moments more as servants emerged from the kitchens with the first course and the wine was poured. Once everything had been arranged, however, he felt the pressure to converse, and cast around desperately for something to say. Before he could settle on anything acceptable, she took matters into her own hands.

"Forgive my tardiness, Highness. I'm afraid I am not accustomed to such formal meals. It was never my intention to keep everyone waiting on my account."

Bless the girl! He exhaled in relief and managed a warm smile – not so hard after all, with her seated beside him.

"Nonsense. *You* are our guest of honor! You are entitled to make an entrance."

He looked to her sharply when she spluttered into her drink, but she recovered quickly by dabbing her mouth with the linen napkin and setting the cup down.

"You are too kind, Highness."

"No doubt you needed the extra time to settle into your rooms. I trust you found everything to your liking? Your dragon certainly seems to have made herself at home."

Tau colored slightly but didn't look directly at him, making it difficult for him to read her expression.

"She is not my dragon."

She spoke so softly that he wasn't sure he'd heard her right.

"Forgive me, Lady, but the noise in here is quite overwhelming. What was that?"

She did look at him now, with a slight frown pursing her full lips and a gleam to her eye that spoke of strong emotion – though which, he could not have said until she spoke.

"Lilae does not *belong* to me. I beg your pardon, Highness, but she is my guardian. A partner, not a pet."

He felt himself color, but forced himself to meet her steady gaze. He was as unaccustomed to such boldness as he was to being corrected – well, by any but his tutors, at least.

Ketral's balls. I knew that. Blood and war, but I've gone and put my foot in my mouth!

"Of course. I meant no offense. Forgive an ignorant princeling his errant tongue."

This time she flushed and looked away, attempting to cover her discomfiture by slicing a piece off of the roast vegetables with the small dinner knife and taking a bite.

"It is I who should apologize, Highness. It is not my place to correct you." She smiled ruefully as she raised her eyes to his again. "We Sennorrans can be admittedly touchy about our guardians."

He felt some of the tension bleed out of him at her smile, and was even able to raise one of his own in answer.

"We are of two very different peoples. But is that not the point of your time here? By learning from each other, perhaps we can begin to bridge these gaps."

Now her smile stretched, and her eyes shone with pleasure at his words. He felt himself warming again and had to look away – to take a bite of his own food, of course.

"Very well put, Highness."

Xanthrall sighed and set down the fork that had only made it half way to his mouth.

"Please stop that."

"Highness?"

"*That.*" He shook his head. "That 'Highness' business. If we are to be both student and teacher together, my already-tedious title will only grow more so. Call me Xanthrall, please. Or better yet, Xan. That is what my friends call me."

She arched an eyebrow at him, but her eyes danced merrily when she spoke.

"Oh? And are we to be friends, then?"

He found himself grinning in answer to the laughter she seemed on the verge of loosing.

"If you will accept my offer of friendship, yes. I would like that very much."

She pretended to consider for a moment, a smile twitching at the corners of her mouth, and then nodded gravely and extended her hand.

"Very well. I will accept this most humble offer. But only –" she forestalled him by holding up a slender finger when he reached to take her hand – "if you likewise drop the 'Lady' nonsense. I may be entitled to it by virtue of my blood, but my *friends* do not call me 'Lady.' I am Tau."

"Tau, then."

Her name sounded somehow special, coming from him. She shivered slightly.

"Xan."

He smiled and took her hand, but where she expected him to clasp it as though to seal a bargain, he raised it to his lips – those soft lips again! – and kissed it. Heat instantly flooded her from head to toe, and she knew her face must be quite red. Thank the Goddess that she was experienced enough with her magic to separate it from her emotions, or she might have lit the entire table on fire! Her father still told stories of Tsuga doing such things before she had learned true control.

His eyes, the gray of an overcast sky, watched her intently as she withdrew her hand and reached hurriedly for her drink. The water (wine was the *last* thing she needed, when she already felt slightly drunk just from his presence) sloshed as she brought it hurriedly to her lips, and without thinking she caught it with a tendril of magic and moved the droplets to splash harmlessly on the floor, rather than her dress.

When she lowered her glass she found him staring at her, wide-eyed as a child who has just seen a marvelous trick. She cleared her throat and shifted self-consciously.

"I'm sorry. I didn't think; I just reacted. Reflex, I suppose. I forgot that magic is not so readily accepted here as it is back home."

Xan shook his head and licked his lips – twice – before he managed to speak in a decidedly awestruck voice.

"It's not that. It's just … you were so casual about it. You made it look so … easy. I suppose I am not used to seeing magic used so … so…."

"Wastefully?" That was what her mother would call it. Ramiq would feel her totally justified, however, in saving the gown.

"Simply. Magic here always seems to be such a production. I have never seen a mage use her power for anything less than some grand purpose – moving boulders, calming a stampede, and the like. There is something truly enchanting in seeing it used with finesse like that."

Tau flushed with pleasure again, but shook her head.

"In Sennor – at least, in the fort where I live – magic is no longer so wondrous. Using it for mundane things like heating bath water and building walls takes much of the mysticism out of it. Most have come to view it as just another tool."

"But not you?"

She smiled at his perceptiveness.

"Not me. Magic is an art, as pleasing as any painting, as intricate as any symphony. It is both chisel and sculpture, both dance and dancer. It is a tool, yes – but the tool is beautiful and admirable in and of itself."

"You make it sound truly wonderful," he breathed.

You make it sound truly pompous.

Her eyes narrowed at the dragon's words, but she hastily dismissed them from her mind to explain when she caught Xanthrall's look of confusion at her scowl.

"Lilae thinks my wording is a bit heavy-handed, but I don't know of a better way to say it."

At the mention of the dragon's name, the excited youth from their first encounter reclaimed his expression – wide grin, earnest eyes – and she found herself smiling in answer to his obvious excitement.

"She is speaking to you? Is she listening now?"

"She is always listening in on my thoughts, unless I actively block her from them."

"But why would you ever want to do that?" He sounded appalled at such a thought.

"Well, there are times when it is preferable to be alone in my own head."

He still looked confused, so she went on.

"Imagine having your best friend – with all of his jokes at your expense, comments, and concerns constantly in your head. During meetings with your council, while taking a ride, or a bath. While taking a sound beating around the salle from your Armsmaster. Out carousing in the taverns. While trying to seduce –"

He held up a hand to stop her, laughing as he shook his head.

"Stop! I see your point."

She grinned at him, unable to resist finishing, "a woman."

He groaned and shook his head again.

"Alright, alright! I give. You're right. But still," he continued, his voice decidedly wistful, "it must be wonderful to have such a bond."

"Oh, it is." She nodded. "I would give my own life before I would even consider living it without that beast – and any Sennorran would feel the same, as I'm sure you know. Your armies have targeted our guardians as a way to get at us no few times."

He winced, and she berated herself inwardly.

You are here to foster peace, not poke at barely-scabbed wounds!

"But of course, if – no, when – peace does truly come, all of that will be behind us."

"Of course. To peace." He raised his glass, and then pushed his chair back to stand and spoke more loudly, so that his voice carried over the din of other diners – other diners who she had all but forgotten were there!

"To peace!"

Cheers answered his words, and she clinked her glass against his to toast him before taking a sip. She wondered absently if those cheers were sincere; she had no way of knowing, having not even been here a full day.

Chapter 29

When dinner was over and everyone began to trickle away – to walk in the gardens, listen to music in the ballroom, or enjoy some other evening entertainment – Tau begged exhaustion from her journey and excused herself to (presumably) ready herself for bed. And just like that, Xan found himself at loose ends.

He circulated for a time among his nobles, as was his duty. Most wanted to know what he thought of the foreign mage – some with an eye to politics, some (of course) jockeying to court her. She would be a prize for any man who could win her hand; as Sennor's next Queen's Mage – and member of a prestigious noble family besides – her rank very nearly put her on an equal footing with the queen herself – or would, once she stepped into her role fully.

As the evening wore on, Xan found himself more and more bothered by those who came to him seeking to use the girl for their own ends. Finally, he had enough and slipped away to his own room before he lost his temper. Once there, he did not bother to summon his manservant – Lyle would be out enjoying himself at the servants' festivities – but instead removed his own coat, rolling his shoulders in relief as its heavy weight was dropped. Next he kicked off his boots, then unbuckled his sword belt as he strode across the room, leaving a trail of discarded clothing in his wake.

"Servants like to feel needed," his father had told him once, when Xan had commented on the king's similar actions. *"I could clean up after myself, fetch my own breakfast, polish my own armor – but then what would my servants have left? No, son – a man with a purpose is a man secure in his place. As king, it is my duty to see to it that theirs is not usurped. Do not take your men for granted, but do not fail to give them a clear purpose, either."*

Wise words. Xan followed that advice, though he did carefully wrap his sword belt around the scabbard of his sword of office before laying it down on a side table. He grunted at the thing disgustedly. The blade he wore into battle was a plain one, though finely crafted; this ornate monstrosity was purely for show.

He pulled his loose tunic free from the waistband of his trousers and stopped before the window that looked out on the dragon where she lay. He had thought her asleep, but as he watched she lifted her great head and craned her neck about to look at something behind her. After a moment a light appeared as the door to the stairway swung open, and Xan caught his breath.

The distance was too great and the light too faint for him to make out who it was by sight, but that illumination was far too steady to be a candle, or even a lantern.

Tau.

Who else would be visiting the dragon this time of night? He continued to watch them for a while longer as the light – and presumably Tau – moved

around to the front of the dragon, who lowered her head as though for a caress. He sighed. Had Tau gone to her to seek comfort, or merely to say good night? What were they saying to each other? Did they speak of him?

Arrogant. Why should they speak of me? He shook his head, an argumentative voice in his thoughts answering his own question.

I am *the prince. She was sent here as a diplomat. Why* shouldn't *she be thinking of me?*

He might have continued the argument with himself for quite some time, but just then the light vanished. It had not been cut off by the door; he had last seen it by the dragon's shoulder. It had simply winked out. He sighed regretfully and turned away; he could no longer see anything more than a hulking black shadow on the rooftop.

He finished undressing and made his way to bed. His thoughts may have been active, but his body cried out for rest. It had been a long day for him, beginning well before dawn with his review of the guard.

Once in bed he found himself unable to resist the siren song of sleep. As his eyes drifted closed, he had one last, somewhat disjointed thought.

Lovely girl. Let me ride the dragon. Fly....

Chapter 30

"So this is where you are."

Tau came awake with a start, her hand automatically seeking her dagger where it rested on the ground beside her even as she opened herself to the power around her – through the focus stone set in its pommel, of course – and she cast about for the source of the voice as she stood. Before she had even made it to her feet, memory returned.

She had been unable to sleep, restless and still excited from the events of the day. She had sought out Lilae's steadying presence, and then fallen asleep cradled in the copper dragon's forearms. From the angle of the sun, it was now mid-morning – she truly must have been tired, to have slept so late! – and the source of the voice stood before her, expression unreadable.

"Ramira. My apologies. I came to see that Lilae was settled for the night, and … well, I fell asleep."

"So I see."

The older woman's gaze swept her from head to toe, and Tau realized she stood before the King's Mage barefoot in a thin night dress. Its warmth had been sufficient for the late summer night, especially when coupled with the comforting heat her guardian radiated like a sun-warmed stone. But it was certainly not appropriate for anything save sleeping. Abashed, she hastily wove light around herself in an illusion of clothing, so that at least anyone who looked at her without the benefit of mage sight would see her decently clothed. Ramira merely arched an eyebrow at her altered appearance.

"Was there something you needed of me, Lady Ramira?"

"Well, as I promised your father that your education would continue while you are here, I thought to spend the morning establishing just where you stand, and what you have yet to learn. Magically speaking, of course. There are others who will be seeking you out for your lessons in other subjects. Our time will be somewhat shorter than I had hoped today, it would seem; I believe you are slated for a similar evaluation with the Armsmaster after lunch, with lessons in Devalian politics and customs after dinner."

Tau felt her shoulders slump slightly. She had hoped for at least a little free time to explore the castle and city, to fly with Lilae over the countryside and to generally enjoy herself, but it seemed as though Ramira truly did intend to keep her just as busy as her parents ever had!

She drew herself back up quickly and stiffened her spine. She was not here for pleasure; this was a job, and she had agreed to this knowing it would be hard work. Her country's future rested largely on her presence here and how much she could learn of their neighbors. Besides, it wasn't as though she was used to a *light* work load.

"As you say, Lady. May I take time to dress myself and eat before we begin today?"

Was that a hint of a smile she saw? It was gone as quickly as it came.

"I would highly recommend that you do so."

Tau nodded respectfully.

"I will not be long. Should I meet you – well, I apologize, but I am not yet familiar with the castle. Where are the mages' training grounds?"

Ramira actually looked surprised for a moment.

"Training grounds? My dear girl, our training is conducted in workrooms, where proper shields can be maintained. Once you have eaten and dressed have one of the servants bring you to my chambers; I have a room set aside for magical exams that is sufficiently shielded for our purposes."

Now it was Tau who was confused. How could a *room* be shielded? Shields were set by a person, and moved relative to that person, or the person they were set on, in the case of a captive mage shielded from using his or her magic. It seemed she would have more to learn here than she had anticipated. And to think, she had expected magic to be the one thing she had an advantage in!

"As you say, then. With your permission?"

She scarcely waited for the Adept's gesture of consent before fleeing through the door and down the stairs. She could have simply teleported, but she had a sinking feeling that she would need every drop of energy she could muster to see her through whatever "test" Ramira had in store.

She reached her rooms without incident aside from a few startled glances scarcely registered as she hurried by and found a plate of breakfast foods set out against her return, but no lady's maids in sight. Just as well; she was in a hurry, and it would be faster and easier to simply dress herself.

She selected a large muffin with coarse sugar on top and the telltale purple speckles that told her it had been baked with blueberries in the batter and took a large bite, silently thanking Magla for her foresight. The plate held mostly fruits and muffins, with only a few cheese spreads and a bowl of nuts. Exactly what she would need to see her through a vigorous lesson in magic.

She took another bite of the muffin – soft and sweet, it was really a shame she had to wolf it down this way rather than enjoy it. As she chewed she strode to the wardrobe where the maids had carefully stored her clothes.

Likely no time to change between lessons, since I'm so late.

She passed over the fine dresses and elaborate mage's robes and selected a pair of tan breeches and a fitted tunic – fawn-colored cotton, since she expected to be working up quite a sweat this afternoon – and threw them over the back of a chair while she stripped off the nightdress and shifted the muffin to her mouth, where she held it in her teeth to free both hands so that she could pull on the pants and lace them around her waist. They would be loose enough to allow movement, but not baggy, which would only serve to get in her way. The same with the shirt, which would move with her, rather than restricting her.

She hastily wound the fabric that would hold her breasts in place around her chest and fastened it so that it would stay between bites, then slid into the shirt and plopped down in the chair to pull on the soft, mid-calf boots she wore for arms training. They were scuffed and well-worn, but showed the muted sheen of oil and care.

Finished with the muffin, she poured herself a glass of the orange juice she found chilling in a pitcher and drank half of it before retrieving her dagger and belting it on. She popped a strawberry in her mouth and took up her brush, which she pulled ruthlessly through her long hair, wincing each time she hit a snarl.

She took another of the ripe red berries and separated her hair into sections before braiding it with the deft motions of long practice. After a moment of consideration, she took the long braided tail and wound it about itself so that she could fix it into a tight, low bun. She remembered all too well the training session in which her mother had grabbed onto her long braid and yanked her to the ground.

"Long hair is your choice," she had said, *"but if you wish to keep it – and your head – I suggest you do not make of it such a convenient handle for an enemy."*

Tsuga had always worn her hair short, but Tau was somewhat vain of her long tresses. She had not failed to bind it close to her head for sessions with her mother after that incident, though.

Dressed, Tau snatched up a slice of the sweet pink melon and crossed to her small desk, where she located paper and pen.

Lessons all day. She wrote quickly, but neatly; her father had not failed to emphasize the importance of legible handwriting. *Not sure when I will take lunch, but I'll need to have plenty of fruits and nuts. Nothing too heavy; arms practice immediately after lunch. I will want a hot bath before dressing for dinner. The rest of the day is yours. Enjoy it. And thank you for the breakfast.*

She added the last almost as an afterthought, then signed her name and placed the note next to the half-eaten meal. She selected another muffin and headed for the door to find someone who could tell her where to go.

Tau paused for a moment outside Ramira's rooms – just a few seconds to catch her breath and settle her thoughts – but before she could raise a hand to knock the mage's voice came from within, somewhat muffled by the thick wood of the door.

"Come on then, child. You are already late; let us not waste any more time."

Tau had to smile at that. No doubt Ramira thought to unsettle her, either by greeting her before Tau made her presence known or through the barb about her tardiness. The effort had much the opposite effect, though; of course Ramira could sense her presence, just as Tau could sense the older mage, this close. Each was a purely unique beacon of power to the other – or indeed, to any mage who knew what to look for. And the brusque comment on her punctuality (or lack thereof, in truth) sounded so much like something her mother would say that she nearly laughed aloud as she opened the door and let herself in. The smile faded, though, when she found the sitting room empty.

"Well, come on! We don't have all day!"

Tau shook her head and followed the sound of the voice through an open doorway to her left – where, now that she was paying closer attention, she could sense the other woman waiting. Her skin tingled as she crossed the threshold, and she slipped into mage sight to examine what was around her. Her breath escaped in an awestruck "Oh!" as she looked about the room.

To the naked eye it was simply a largish round room walled in stone. There was no furniture save a single wooden chair, which Ramira occupied near the center of the room. None of this was what gave her pause, however.

Everywhere she looked the stone swirled with a hundred different colors to her mage sight. The floors, walls, ceiling – even the door behind her – seemed almost alive with moving, shifting power. Intellectually she knew it must be some type of shield, but looking at it she could not begin to say how it worked, let alone how it had been created.

"Close the door."

The no-nonsense tone jolted Tau out of her shock and she did so quickly, watching in amazement as, with its closing, the colors seemed to pulse brighter for a moment before they all settled into place in the single-most intricate set of shielding she had ever seen. Layer upon layer swirled about the room, only a few of which she recognized.

Here was one to absorb any physical force directed at it. There was one to contain and convert magical energies. This one blocked the thoughts and emotions of anyone outside the room from getting in, while one that looked like its mirror image prevented any rogue mental energy from getting *out*.

"Incredible."

Ramira's gaze flickered over the spells briefly, and she shrugged.

"Basic shield layering, built upon and perfected."

"I've never seen anything quite like it."

Ramira arched an eyebrow in incredulous surprise.

"Your mages do not use work rooms in Sennor?"

"Oh, we do, of course, but not like this. We set the shields anew each time, and they are never this elaborate."

The King's Mage frowned slightly in puzzlement.

"But why? The shields you see here are added to periodically – it is one of the final tests for my students, to build upon the set-spell with a shield of their own. But it is always in place, activated when the circle is completed by the closed door."

"Set spell?" Tau tilted her head to the side and looked again at the shields.

"Yes, a spell that is set into an object instead of tied to a person. Surely you are familiar with them; they are part of the testing to rise to Journeyman."

Tau shook her head.

"We have set-spells for things like lighting and heating, but they are relatively new, only coming into common use in the last few years. No one has discovered how to use the process for anything more complex, yet. To my knowledge, I am the only one to figure out a spell for teleportation – it uses a fraction of the power – but even it still requires a mage to be functional."

Ramira pursed her lips thoughtfully. "It would seem we each have something to learn from the other. But for today, I would like to begin evaluating just what you *do* know. We will start at the Apprentice level, with the elemental magicks."

Tau nodded. This, she was confident in.

"Which element shall we begin with?"

"My dear girl, I don't know how they do things in Sennor, but in Devali the Apprentice testing for a King's Mage is a bit different than that for anyone else. Begin by manifesting a representation of each major element – earth, air, fire, and water – and then add the minor elements as well – light, metal, stone, lightning and ice – and maintain them until you are instructed to do otherwise.

Tau's eyes widened. The Apprentice testing she had undergone had consisted of successive manifestations of each element, one following the next, not all of them at once. She took a deep breath. *I am a Master mage. More complex or not, this is an Apprentice-level exam!* She gathered her magic like a rider gathering the reins in anticipation of a wild gallop and began.

Chapter 31

"That's it child; small sips."

The fruit juice was cool and sweet, and it took a great exertion of willpower for Tau to keep from gulping it as she wanted to do. She now sat in a comfortably padded chair in Ramira's sizeable sitting room, with the King's Mage herself holding a cup to her lips and helping her drink. It was a good thing she was; Tau's hands shook so badly from exhaustion that, had she been forced to try on her own, she would likely have been *wearing* the juice rather than drinking it.

"Thank you," she managed at last, and Ramira set the cup down and looked at her concernedly.

"You should have said something, dear. Using magic when you are this fatigued is very dangerous."

As though she didn't know! She had not anticipated the room's shielding blocking her off from Lilae's magical support, though in retrospect she should have. She'd continued to push herself well past the point she knew she should have stopped, expecting to be able to draw on the dragon's strength when her own failed. When that had proven impossible, she had pushed on stubbornly, refusing to show incompetence in front of the imposing King's Mage.

She said nothing for a moment as she took a bite of a fruit-filled pastry covered with icing, and Ramira sighed.

"I don't know why I'm surprised. No doubt you inherited that stubbornness from both your parents. Neither of them ever has known when to admit defeat."

Normally Tau would have bristled at the jab to her parents, but she was too tired to do more than frown at the older woman.

"How did I do?"

Ramira made a sound of disgust and threw up her hands.

"Why am I surprised?"

Tau waited quietly, chewing on her pastry and mentally coaxing it to grant her energy more quickly. Now that her bond with Lilae was once again open, the dragon was steadily feeding her strength. While it was helping tremendously, she had used a great deal of power, and that exhausted a persons' reserves as surely as any physical exertions she had ever endured.

The Devalian mage sighed and shook her head.

"You passed the Apprentice's test, though how in such a state is beyond me. That test usually takes four days for a King's Mage: one for elemental testing, one for mental, one for spiritual and shielding, and one for basic spell-casting. *How* you managed all four in one morning –"

Tau's eyes widened, and she broke in to Ramira's sentence abruptly.

"Four days?! But you never once mentioned that! You only asked if I was alright to continue!"

Ramira hissed through her teeth, but her response was not the reprimand Tau had expected.

"I thought you must have a similar timeline in Sennor. And I trusted you to know your own limits."

The sour note to her voice and pinched expression spoke clearly of what she now thought of Tau's judgement in that area. Tau could only shake her head dazedly.

"In Sennor each power is tested separately, but far more extensively. And each test must be completed, start to finish, without stopping. I wrongly assumed this test would be the same." She shook her head ruefully.

Ramira chuckled softly, her expression one of dazed amazement.

"What you have done is unheard-of, even for a regular mage. Occasionally the testing for one of our Apprentices – those not in the King's Mage training only undergo a three-day test – will complete the trials in two days, but to my knowledge no one has ever done it in one."

Tau could not hide her smile at that. So she had impressed the woman, had she? All to the good, though she was now so tired that she feared for what an afternoon with the Armsmaster would do to her. All she could do was eat, take advantage of what few moments she had to rest, and pray to the Lady above to see her through this day.

There likely were those who envied a mage's ability to eat sweets with the relish of a child on a feast day without gaining weight or rotting their teeth, Tau mused as she hastened across the paved courtyard to the salle. For her, it had lost all sense of pleasure long ago. Food was fuel, and different exertions required different kinds of fuel.

Most people only ever had to deal with hunger brought on by day-to-day life. Moderate amounts of meats, breads, and sweets were enough to supplement their largely vegetable-based diets. Those who exerted more physical effort – laborers, farmers, and warriors, mostly – needed more meats and broths to sustain their muscles, and more bread and root vegetables to maintain their energy throughout the day.

But mages worked themselves in an entirely different fashion, and the most efficient way for them to refuel was with sweets and fats. Cakes, pies, pastries, fruits, cheeses, creams, and syrups were all delicacies – to anyone but a mage. To Tau, they were no longer anything but necessary sustenance. She considered this phenomenon as she licked the last of some powdered sugar from her fingers and entered through the open door of the salle.

At last, something that was exactly what she expected it to be! Racks of weapons and stands of armor and padding lined one wall of the massive open room. The floor was packed dirt, and one of the long walls boasted floor-to-ceiling mirrors where even now a handful of young men practiced their forms.

She inhaled deeply the familiar scents of old sweat, oiled leather, and dirt as she cast about in search of the Armsmaster. He was not hard to find; a shorter, broad man, he stood off to one side of the room watching a pair of young men circle each other with practice swords. They were metal, not wood, but Tau could see that their edges had been ground to a harmless dullness.

"Someone's got to make the first strike, lads! Have at it!"

Both of the combatants started at his booming voice, and one nearly dropped his sword. The squat man – he was built like a barrel, though it was obvious his bulk was muscle, and not fat – threw up his hands in exasperation.

"Enough! To the mirrors with you! You both look ready to fall over at a gust of wind! Have Mattìn show you the proper stance – *again* – and, by Ketral's balls, *listen* to him! He may not have noble blood, but he's a bloody good swordsman. Knows what he's talking about. Well? Off with you!"

The two boys – young lordlings, she gathered from the Armsmaster's words – hastened to do as they were told, expressions sour, and their instructor caught sight of her and sighed.

"You must be her, then." He shook his head. "Wantin' me to train a girl, and a little slip of a thing like you, at that! Oh well. King's orders. The name's Cleo." He looked her over disparagingly and sighed.

"At least you had the sense not to show up in a dress. I don't suppose you know how to use that pretty little dagger of yours?"

Tau's spine stiffened, and she was unable to keep the heat from her voice when she answered.

"I will not pretend to expertise I do not have, Armsmaster Cleo, but I have been trained by one of the best Weaponsmistresses in Sennor. I know which end of a blade to stab with, and have been drilled in basic proficiency with all weapons to which I have been exposed. My main focus has always been my magic, but my arms training was not neglected, I can assure you."

He snorted, and Tau's face heated under his scrutiny.

"Well, I can't just throw you into a match without seeing something of your skill level. Don't bother with the padding; I doubt you'll be fending off any blows today. We will see just what this great Weaponsmistress of yours actually managed to teach you. Select a sword from the racks, and return to me."

Tau nodded stiffly. It was obvious that in his opinion no woman could possibly be a reliable teacher in the arts of war. She wondered idly how he would react to meeting her mother as she walked to the rack and perused the weapons there.

The sword was not her best weapon – not as it was her mother's, certainly – but she knew the basic forms of attack and defense. Enough to buy her time and space to counter with something else, at least. And she *had* been taught how to select a weapon suited to her size and strength.

Lined up tidily along the wall was an array of swords that would have been impressive had she not seen a similar collection nearly every day of her life. Tau passed over the greatswords; their weight and two-handed grip was too much for her. She also spared the longswords and the hand-and-a-halfs little more than a glance. The last, also known as a bastard, was the weapon her mother tended to favor, but the length of the blade was unwieldy in Tau's hands.

She began to worry that nothing here would suit her – surely he did not intend her to choose a rapier;

fine for courtly dueling, the light, thin blade was never intended for a melee-type battle. But at last, she came to the short swords.

A one-handed weapon, the short sword was only about the length of her arm from point to pommel, the blade wide for its height in comparison to some of the other styles. It was made to be used with a shield on the opposite arm; a weapon for the foot soldier, useful on a battlefield where there was not always adequate room to maneuver. She tested the balance of three such swords before she found one weighted to suit her. A brief moment of self-debate convinced her to select a light, round shield as well. It was a customary pairing, and she would frankly be surprised if she was not asked to demonstrate with a shield, based on her selection.

She returned to the Armsmaster to see him considering her with a frown.

"Well, it seems you know how to suit your weapon to yourself. Why the shield?"

He did not tell her to put it away, so Tau surmised the question was intended to act as some sort of test. She gave the answer she had gleaned not only from Tsuga's teaching, but also from her own experience sparring against other trainees.

"There is a good reason the shield is frequently paired with the short sword for combat. Defense is the obvious reason, as it will effectively block a variety of blows. While the small shield is not particularly effective against arrows it is highly mobile, allowing a fighter greater range of motion and more options than many of the larger, heavier shields. It can be used to bash, smash, or throw an opponent off-balance. It's useful as a counterweight to balance the heft and movement of the sword. And it does offer some protection, especially in a melee situation where there is little room to maneuver and most blows you face with be the hack-and-bash type, rather than precise and well-aimed strikes such as one tends to face in individual combat."

By the time she finished speaking Cleo's eyes had widened slightly and his scowl had morphed into a thoughtful furrowing of his brow.

"A knowledgeable response. But knowledge and proficiency do not always march in line. Take up your ready stance. I will name a form, and you will execute it. If you do not know, do not guess; return to ready and wait for the next. Understand?"

Tau nodded and lifted her sword and shield into place, ready for anything. Thank Auriga Tsuga had taught her Devalian names and forms as well as those known in Sennor. Perhaps this would go well, after all.

She had no more time for thought after that, though – the first command came, and she performed The Cobra Strikes almost reflexively. The lesson had begun.

Chapter 32

Bless them, Tau thought of her maids as she luxuriated in the tub of gently steaming water, submerged up to her knees in the scented bath. They had heated the water for her and filled the tub, then provided an array of soaps and oils in all of her favorite scents for her to choose from. Her magic was so depleted she could not have heated the bath with it had her life been on the line, but the women had chattered away happily while they stoked a fire and warmed water the mundane way.

Magla had waited for Tau to relax a bit in the steaming tub before plying her tired neck and shoulder muscles with pressure and scented oils. Now Tau simply luxuriated in the water, postponing the moment she knew she must scrub away the dirt and sweat and sluice herself off. She smothered a yawn behind her hand and shook her head ruefully.

If you drown in your bath, I will never forgive you.

Tau smiled to herself and picked up a loofa sponge from the small table beside the tub.

Amilia and Magla would rescue me before I drowned.

The two women were still bustling about, preparing her clothes for the night's meal and tidying the already-pristine rooms. For answer Lilae only sent a wave of reproach, and Tau found herself rolling her eyes.

Before long she was thoroughly scrubbed, and when she stood in the tub Magla appeared to sluice her off with clean water before offering her a soft, over-sized towel, which she stepped into gratefully. Too tired to admire her reflection tonight, Tau endured the dressing process with quiet good humor. She even allowed Amilia to use the flat iron to help dry her hair. It left her locks board-straight, like a sheet of spun silk, and though the sizzle of evaporating water made her wince, she knew her hair was safe from scorching.

When the women finished with her, Tau paused only a moment to check her reflection and make sure that everything was in its place before she thanked them and strode from the room.

Her entrance from the previous night was almost perfectly duplicated now, with a hush falling over those assembled as she made her way to her seat.

Is this to happen every night while I am here? she wondered.

I suspect you will lose some of your novelty over time. Right now, you are still something new and unknown. You are a spectacle.

Lovely. A spectacle.

Once again she scarcely had time to settle herself before the servants brought forth the first course. Her stomach growled insistently as she caught the smell of roasted fowl, and she realized with some embarrassment just how hungry she was. She detained the young boy serving her with a gentle hand on his arm.

"I am very hungry tonight. Do you think you could arrange with the cook to bring me a double portion of the rest of the meal?"

She spoke softly enough that she didn't think anyone else could hear her, but the boy nodded eagerly. In Sennor the servants ate before the main meal was served – usually simple fare made from the trimmings of what was prepared for the nobility – but in Devali, she knew, the pages that served at table would not eat until after the last dish was cleared away. It was simply understood that one left some of each course behind on her plate for the children to have, to help them make it to the end of the night.

Tau knew there would be none of this first course left on her plate, but she didn't want to deprive the boy of his morsels. A double portion would ensure that she could eat her fill and still keep with custom. Conscience appeased, she tucked in to her first course with gusto.

"That was very kindly done."

Tau looked up from her plate, mouth full of food, and found Xanthrall smiling at her. She flushed and swallowed hurriedly.

"What do you mean?"

"The extra portions. The lad will appreciate your thoughtfulness. You've likely just won his loyalty for life."

Her blush deepened and Tau shook her head.

"I had no thought of winning loyalty from him, only of filling my belly – and his."

Xan laughed. The sound was rich and musical, much like his voice, an animated alto that seemed to tease extra life from each word he spoke.

"And that is precisely how you've done it. At that age, a boy's first thought is *always* for his belly."

Tau managed a small smile as she cast a slanted look at him through her lowered lashes.

"In Sennor, the women have a saying. 'Some men think with their muscles, others with their manhood. The good ones think with their heads and their hearts. But none with an empty stomach will think far past his next meal!'"

He looked at her in shock for a moment, then her colloquialism had its desired effect: he laughed again. She grinned in answer. It was hard not to, with the music of his mirth teasing her ears.

"Terribly accurate, I'm afraid!" He shook his head and sobered slightly, his gray eyes considering her. "You are not at all what I expected."

Tau quirked an eyebrow at him, not quite certain how she should take this revelation.

"Oh? And just what, pray tell, *did* you expect?"

Xanthrall offered up what he hoped was a nonchalant shrug and shook his head.

"We don't see many Sennoran women, this far from the border. You're painted as barbarians who dress like men and don't know your proper place, and –"

She held up a hand to forestall him and he cut off mid-sentence, painfully aware that he had blundered somehow.

"Let me stop you right there. What, precisely, is my 'proper place?'"

The phrase dripped scorn coming from her lips, and it was all he could do not to wince at the flash of anger in her green eyes.

Idiot! Was he forever doomed to misspeak in the presence of this young woman? How to recover?

"That is not to say that *you* are out of place in any way!"

Her voice was cold when she spoke again.

"I see. So I am not bound by the restraints that should rightly hold other women, is that it?"

He groaned inwardly. *From bad to worse!* What had become of his courtly grace? He had been reduced to a stammering fool!

"No! I only meant that it is our custom to –"

"Oh, I know your *customs*, Highness. No land, no power, no freedom for women. A woman cannot inherit, has no money save that given her by the men in her life. If she doesn't look the way she is expected to, speak the way you say she should, *behave* as custom mandates, she is seen to be shameful and somehow inferior. It is disgusting!"

Xanthrall was left with his mouth hanging open and nothing to say in the face of her tirade. Truthfully, he had never thought twice about Devalian customs when it came to women. They were expected to run the household and oversee the servants (if noble) or the children (if common). A common wife was in charge of the cooking, cleaning, and mending for her husband. She lived to please him, and in return the man protected her, their home, and their children. He worked to provide for them, saw to their material needs, stood as a rock to shelter his family from life's storms. That was simply the way it was.

Not everywhere. That much was obvious. Tau plainly felt affronted by the place women held in

Devalian society, and he had only the smallest inkling why.

Here beside him sat a woman who turned everything he had ever known about the fairer sex on its head! However they may be in private, in public a woman was quiet and demure, always deferred to a man's wishes, and had little concern for the world beyond her door if it did not seem likely to affect her or her household.

But here was a woman who disagreed with him – frequently and heatedly! One who spoke her mind, thought beyond the end of her nose, and had a head for politics – obviously, or she would have been sent to court him, not to act as envoy and diplomat! She could fight her own battles (he had heard of her impressive showing in the salle this afternoon, and had vowed to find time tomorrow to watch her in person).

She was, quite simply, the most fascinating – and confusing! – young woman he had ever met. And right now, she was looking at him as she would a pile of excrement she had unwittingly stepped in.

"I know only what I have seen, Lady. Women in Devali are nothing like you. I meant no offense! I am too used to noble women who titter behind their fans and swirl their skirts or bat their lashes to capture my attention. I had never expected there could exist a woman as intelligent, willful, and fascinating as yourself. I am but a humble prince who has seen little of the world outside of his own borders, ignorant of what wonders may exist on the other side."

She looked at him now with narrowed eyes, but she was not snapping at him, which he took as a good sign, so he plowed on.

"I sincerely hope my misconceptions and bumbling will not cost me the opportunity to continue to learn more about you – and from you."

Was he mocking her? Tau couldn't be certain, but she felt sure that he truly had not meant to offend her. She nodded stiffly and moved to take another bite – only to find her plate already empty. She looked at it with regret, wondering how long it would be until the next course was served. Xanthrall must have sensed her shift in focus, because he promptly changed the subject to safer ground.

"I hear that you have made quite a showing for yourself on your first official day here."

She flushed slightly. Of course he would receive reports on her progress; everything she said and did while she was here would be under close scrutiny. She would do well to remember that.

"I survived. I suppose that could be considered an accomplishment."

"Oh, from what I hear you did more than survive."

He shifted on his seat, and the movement drew her eye. He wasn't dressed quite as richly tonight as he had been the previous evening. The fabrics he wore were just as fine, and cut well to suit him, but there was no thread-of-gold decorating his coat tonight. The deep red fabric was embroidered with white thread in an abstract design, instead. His sword, she had noted, was not the jewel-encrusted monstrosity he had worn yesterday, but a rather more plain weapon. No doubt it was finely made, but this was obviously a blade made to use, not to look at.

He was still speaking.

"There is something to be said for anyone who can make it through an entire afternoon with our Armsmaster without being sent off in shame. And Ramira was quite vocal about your magical prowess … though I do believe the phrase 'just like that stubborn old goat of a father' was used more than once."

Tau met his eyes in surprise – those expressive, slate gray eyes could hold her transfixed, if she'd let them – and found him grinning at her mischievously. She relaxed slightly and lifted her shoulders in a shrug that felt surprisingly good; her muscles had cooled after the hot bath, and she could already feel the tension and stiffness that heralded soreness settling in.

"I suppose that may have been part of it, but this morning was mostly due to a miscommunication." She smiled slightly. "Your testing process for mages is vastly different from what I am used to." She allowed herself a slight chuckle. "It's a bit ironic; Devali is not thought of as a magically-advanced nation by most Sennorran mages. You are known for your prowess in physical combat; that is where I expected the greater difficulty of the two. But all of those expectations were stood on their heads today!"

He laughed with her, and as their mirth faded the dishes from the previous course were swapped for platters full of food – Tau's doubly so. She smiled her thanks to the young page and picked up her fork.

"You continue to surprise me, Tau."

Her own name had no business sending that little thrill up her spine, but every time he voiced it, she wanted to shiver in delight.

"How so?"

"A woman who rides a dragon. A mage who carries a dagger and knows her way around a sword. What will you reveal next?"

Tau looked at him soberly for a moment before answering.

"I have eleven toes."

He looked as though he had just swallowed a live roach; in the face of his expression, Tau was unable to hold her composure more than a moment before she burst into laughter.

"Oh, come now, Xan! Where is your sense of humor?"

The rest of dinner passed more smoothly, and before long it was time for her to push away from the table and dismiss herself. Xan rose with her and graciously offered his arm.

"May I escort you?"

They had just finished talking about the lesson she still had to attend this evening, but she was still mildly surprised at his offer.

"Thank you, but I was actually hoping to steal a few moments with Lilae beforehand."

"Ah. Of course."

Was it only her wishful thinking, or was that genuine disappointment on his face?

"Would you…?" She hesitated for a moment, then plunged ahead before she could overthink it. "Would you like to meet her? Without all the formalities and the fanfare?"

Her gamble paid off when his face lit up, and she found herself smiling in response to his eagerness.

"Really? Could I?"

Tau laughed and extended her arm to him so that he could take her hand, which he did eagerly as she moved around the chairs and came to join him.

"Come on. She's on the rooftop."

Normally Xan would have tried to persuade a pretty woman to detour through the gardens with him, lesson or no, but he was so anxious for the chance to see the magnificent dragon that it was all he could do to keep his stride in check. He must have been fairly transparent, though, because Tau laughed and gave his arm a gentle squeeze.

"Do you think your princely decorum could withstand a race?"

He cut his eyes to her and found her grinning at him in challenge.

"You think you can keep up with me?"

"Oh I'm a bit tired, true, but I think I can manage. Come on!"

She dropped his arm and took off, leaving him to gape after her in bemused surprise before he realized that she had meant the race to start immediately.

"Hey! Not fair!"

He took off after her, legs pumping as he pushed himself in an effort to catch her. He was surprised to find himself unable to close the gap by any significant amount.

By the time he had chased her across the courtyard and up the narrow staircase that spiraled around the outside of the tower, he was breathing heavily and his thin tunic was stuck to his skin by a slick of sweat.

"How is it," he panted, "that you're not even breathing hard?"

Tau laughed and gave him a once-over from where she stood by the dragon's muscular copper shoulder. She filled her lungs deeply – he did his best to ignore the way it made the fabric of her dress stretch across her chest – and exhaled with a chuckle.

"I have been running almost since I learned to walk. Besides, when you spend so much time a-dragonback you have to build up lungpower. The air is much thinner the higher up you fly. I suppose my body has adjusted to it."

He shook his head and moved away from the stairs, hands on hips as he fought to get his breathing back under control.

"Well, you certainly put me to shame!"

She smiled, and between being alone with her – sweat-dampened hair and flushed cheeks only added to her beauty by emphasizing the life and energy she exuded – and being next to her dragon, he began to wonder if the run was the only thing stealing his breath.

He caught himself staring at her, thinking about the spirit he saw sparkling in her green eyes, and with an effort he pulled his gaze away and cleared his throat.

"And a good evening to you, Lady Lilae." He bowed to her respectfully, and the rumble he received in response as she lowered her head to regard him vibrated through the roof and up into his very bones.

**If Tau counts you as a friend, so do I,
Princeling. Just Lilae, please.**

He smiled and straightened once more to his full
height.

"Lilae, then. It is quite an honor to be counted
among your friends."

I like this one.

Tau smiled, more breathless than she was willing
to let on. He looked more disheveled than she had
yet seen him, but still he carried himself with an air
of graciousness that was undeniably sincere.

He is well-spoken.

He should be, silly; he's heir to the throne! Aloud,
she said, "Would you like to touch her?"

His eyes widened as he shifted his gaze to her,
then back to the dragon.

"She would be alright with that?"

Tau laughed, reaching out to slap Lilae's powerful
shoulder affectionately. "Of course!"

Lilae lowered her head to the roof in front of him
and regarded him hopefully. **The ridge above my
eye itches terribly.**

He looked to Tau in amazement, and when she
gestured for him to proceed he reached out a
tentative hand to oblige the immense beast, careful
to avoid the sharp-looking spines that lined her brow
ridge.

**A little to your right – yes, that's it. Ooh, that
feels *good!***

"She likes it!"

Tau laughed merrily as she moved to stand next to
him and scratch the soft skin at the hinge of Lilae's
jaw. The dragon's eyelid drooped in pleasure, and

she let out a contented sigh that stirred their hair and clothing in a meat-scented wind.

"Of course she does. She is like most animals that way; she loves to be doted on."

I am more than a mere animal!

Of course you are, Love. But you are *a glutton for attention.* Lilae snorted in response and Xanthrall withdrew his hand hastily. On impulse, Tau grasped it and guided his hand to the dragon's neck. He gasped as he stroked upwards along her neck towards her head.

"Ouch!"

Tau *tsked* and reached out for his hand again. Sure enough, though the cuts were shallow, his skin was thoroughly lacerated.

"I should have warned you," she muttered as she drew on her magic, pushing past the fatigue and stubbornly resisting the urge to sway with the effort. "Always go with the grain of her scales; they are razor-sharp."

She concentrated briefly as she healed him, then gently wiped off the blood with the kerchief she carried in her belt pouch. "There."

Xan stared at his hand in wonder. "Simply marvelous."

Tau flushed slightly at his words and, to cover her discomfiture, moved his hand back to the dragon, this time guiding him with her hand atop his.

"Oh," he breathed in amazement, "it's soft."

Tau nodded and smiled. "And tough. Her scales are very small, but they are tougher than chain mail – in most places." She moved her hand to Lilae's belly, bringing his with her and reversing the direction of her stroke. "They grow the opposite direction on her underbelly."

"Incredible." His voice was thick with wonder. Tau could not keep the proprietary pride from her voice when she responded.

"Yes, she is."

"No, that's not what I meant." Tau arched an eyebrow at him, and he hastily backtracked. "She *is* amazing." He took Tau's free hand in his and squeezed it lightly, causing her stomach to clench uncertainly. "You both are."

She swooned slightly at his words before her knees locked and her sensibility took over. She gently extricated her hands from his.

"I … should be getting to my lesson."

She hesitated a moment, then turned and fled down the stairs. He was a prince! What was she thinking?!

Chapter 33

"But, I –"

Xanthrall let the words die on his tongue. She was already gone. He watched her descent with a little sigh. It was the sound of the dragon's tail rasping across the stone of the roof that brought him back to himself with a little start. He bowed to the dragon again, still in awe of the incredible animal.

"By your leave, Lilae."

The dragon rumbled her amusement.

Go, Princeling.

He nodded absently and moved to begin his own descent. He had never gotten the chance to tell Tau about her teacher for the evening's lesson, so he lengthened his stride and cut across the courtyard to take the servants' staircase to reach the castle's library; it was faster. He received a few startled glances from those he passed, but he moved so quickly that the belated bows and curtsies rippled behind him unseen.

The immense room was mostly empty when he arrived; a couple of scholars worked at desks here and there, and a handful of librarians made their way through the rows of shelves replacing books. He let out a sigh of relief and ran a hand through his still-damp hair to push it back from his forehead.

"Xan?"

The voice behind him was surprised, and he forced himself to turn slowly and take a moment to school his own expression.

"Tau."

"How did you beat me here?"

He raised an eyebrow and smiled slightly at the question.

"You may be the faster runner, but this castle has been my home my whole life."

"You took a shortcut!"

Her voice was accusatory, but her expression held a grudging respect. He allowed himself a little chuckle.

"Guilty."

She shook her head bemusedly. "But why? I'm supposed to have my –"

"Lesson, I know. You ran off before I could tell you."

The confusion lifted from her expression as realization dawned. "You're my political tutor?"

He grinned and gestured broadly. "And who better to teach you the history and politics of this great land than one who has lived and breathed it from birth?"

Her lips twitched upwards in an answering smile, causing his heart to thump more loudly in his chest under her regard.

"Well then, Master Xanthrall, where do we begin?"

Tau was unaccustomed to the way her stomach churned in his presence. She felt excited and nervous all at once. The emotional turmoil made it difficult for her to concentrate on anything.

Lady, don't let me make a fool of myself!

Her heart fluttered when he offered his arm again, and she placed her hand in the crook of his elbow, quietly grateful that his shirt was still damp enough to disguise the sweatiness of her palms.

"Shall we?"

She nodded mutely and allowed him to lead her at a leisurely pace through the aisles between the towering shelves of books.

"What do you know of Devalian history?"

She shook her head, determinedly keeping her eyes on their surroundings, rather than her feet.

"Very little, after the division. I know the successive kings, and the various branchings of your royal line. Well, most of them, at least. Aside from that, my knowledge is only that of an outsider looking in. I have seen and read of things, but have not had the opportunity to learn the 'why' behind any of them."

Xan nodded; she caught the movement from the corner of her eye as she reached up to tuck an escaped lock of hair behind her ear.

"The why of things is often more convoluted than a maze, and follows less logic. Why don't we begin by answering the questions I am sure you have? If it is something I can answer, I will."

Tau nibbled her lower lip pensively as she ordered her thoughts. She did indeed have many questions, but where should she begin?

"Why does your succession follow the male line? Is it only because your nation worships a God, rather than the Goddess, or is there another reason behind it?"

Xanthrall was silent for a long moment as they strolled among the books, and Tau was content to

simply walk beside him and breathe in the scents of paper, leather, and ink. As they passed a stand lamp, she also caught a whiff of the oil it burned.

She very nearly jumped when he finally answered; she had begun to let her thoughts wander, and it took some effort to bring her focus back to their conversation.

"I never really considered that it might have something to do with Ketral, but I suppose that may have played a part when the tradition was established. But in Devali, it is believed that it is a man's role to protect those who depend on him. I suppose that is what it boils down to, in its simplest sense. The king has to be stronger even than any other man, because every man, woman, and child is his subject and his to protect."

"Not because women are considered inferior here?"

Xan shook his head adamantly.

"Oh, no! Women are our greatest treasure. They are not allowed to fight in our armies because they are far too valuable to be risked."

"Of course," she scoffed, her voice dripping with sickly-sweet sarcasm. "If all of your women fought and died, who would give you sons to fight and die in the next battle?"

He chuckled, and her lips thinned in irritation.

"That is a part of it, yes. But not all. A man's wife is his greatest strength; she supports him where he is weakest, and does such things as he cannot. Noble ladies manage their husband's estates so that he may concentrate on what needs doing when he is away. The same for the poor, I suppose; the women tend the fields and mind the children so the men can march to war to protect their ability to do so."

Tau shook her head in amazement. "But I always thought –"

"Most outsiders do. They see our women toiling in the fields or kept away from the front lines, and presume to know why. They assume we treat women as little better than indentured servants, when in fact the opposite is true. Our women take great pride in their duties and in knowing that it is their labor that allows our land to thrive."

"Incredible. So you have kings because –"

"Because a king leads his men in battle. His consort minds the everyday workings of the country, so that the king may see to the safety of his people."

"I … see."

He grinned at her. "You thought we kept women from battle because we view them as incapable? It's because you are far too precious!"

Tau didn't know how to respond to that, so she steered the conversation to something easier for her to contemplate instead.

"But the line of succession has changed –"

"Several times, yes. Four, to be exact."

"Why?"

"Well, if it is assumed that the king must be the strongest and most fit to lead, what is to be done when it is found that he is not?"

Tau's eyes widened in shock.

"But that's regicide!"

Xan shook his head. "Yes, but here it's the greatest show of loyalty to the crown. If a king is unfit to rule, it is the citizens' duty to see a fit man raised in his place."

Tau could not quite wrap her head around this. "So what, then, is the point of having an heir or a royal line at all?"

"Well, a man hopes to pass his skills and knowledge on to his sons. But if he is unable to do so for whatever reason, he does not expect his people to blindly follow a fool."

"So, *you* ...?"

"Have been judged by my father to be worthy to succeed him. If when the time comes I am not, then...."

Tau's eyes widened in alarm. "Oh, but you will be! You must be! I mean –"

He pulled her to a stop beside him, and she turned to look up into his eyes breathlessly.

"That is kind of you, Tau. I am glad you hold me in such high regard. But if I am found wanting, it is as much my duty to accept that as it is their duty to remove me."

His expression was peaceful, and Tau found herself unable to grasp how he could speak so calmly of the possibility of his own murder. These Devalians were both more similar to what she knew than she had expected and far more different than she could have ever imagined.

Xan could tell the turn their conversation had taken made her uncomfortable. Could it be possible that she felt genuine concern for his well-being? No; that was his ego coloring his perceptions again. No doubt she was simply horrified at the thought of something that, in her eyes, amounted to treason.

This certainly wasn't having the effect he had hoped for; what had happened to the laughing,

carefree spirit she'd displayed on the rooftop? This Tau was pensive and soft-spoken, not at all what he had come to expect from her. Perhaps he could steer the conversation to less troubling ground.

"And what of Sennor? Have you no separation of duties for men and women?"

Tau shook her head slowly, causing a wisp of hair to escape from behind her ear again. She pushed it back absently, and his eyes followed the movement, lingering on the nape of her neck where it peeked from behind the concealing red-brown curtain of her hair.

"I suppose we do." As she spoke she turned to resume walking, and he perforce fell into step beside her.

"For the most part women hold many of the same roles back home as they do here. But in Sennor, it is a *choice*. It is more traditional for a woman to tend hearth and home, yes, but if she chooses to become a scholar or a musician, she has that option. If her feet itch, she is free to wander; if, like my mother, she finds herself possessed of a talent for tactics and battle, she can not only fight, but she can aspire to gaining rank in the military."

Xan could only shake his head; the concept of a woman – a mother, no less! – marching to battle was entirely beyond his scope. Then, something he'd heard and dismissed as inconsequential occurred to him.

"Your mother? Isn't she the Armsmaster in Sennor?"

Tau flushed slightly – and why should such an admission embarrass her? – and nodded slowly.

"Weaponsmistress, yes."

Xan barked a laugh, causing Tau to look at him in surprise. He couldn't stop the grin that spread across his face as he spoke.

"No wonder Cleo was so impressed with you! You've been taught by the master! Tsuga Dafrin, citizen of Sennor, soldier of Devali, mercenary captain, fire mage, wife to the Queen's Mage, and Weaponsmistress!"

She was blushing in earnest now. Why should her lineage embarrass her? She should be proud to call such notables her parents! He shook his head in wonder.

"You truly are a marvel, Tau Dafrin."

She shook her head, her look pleading with him.

"You won't tell him, will you?"

He quirked an eyebrow questioningly. "Tell who?"

"The Armsmaster," she said miserably. Xan was confused.

"Cleo? But why not?"

Tau sighed and shook her head.

"My parentage is no secret from anyone who knows the slightest bit about Sennorran court. But my parents are so well-known…. I simply hoped to live for a while as myself, out of their shadow. To be just Tau, not Tau-daughter-of-Ramiq-and-Tsuga." She sighed again. "Perhaps you wouldn't understand."

Xan stopped, thus forcing her to either stop with him again or else extricate her arm from his and continue on. She stopped.

"I wouldn't understand? Tau, I am the crown prince. Heir to the throne of Devali. My father is the king! You talk to me of living in the shadow of a

parent, of unfair expectations heaped upon you because of their accomplishments? Everything I *do* is weighed against the deeds of my father. I learn to ride at seven? Father was five. I master the sword at twelve? By fourteen, he was riding to his first battle! I'm wearing a blue tunic? He would have chosen green!"

He shook his head. "Tau, of all the people in this castle, I suspect I understand your sentiments the best."

She let out her breath in a *whoosh* as relief stole across her features.

"So you won't tell him?"

He smiled and gave her hand a little squeeze.

"I promise. Now," he went on as they resumed walking, "perhaps you can explain to me why the Sennorran crown passes through the maternal line?"

Tau fell into step beside him once more, still marveling over his words. No doubt he was right; if anyone could understand what it was like for her to live in the shadow of her parents' greatness, it was this man. It seemed he had no end of surprises for her. His next question was no exception; shouldn't the answer be obvious?

"Legitimacy."

He quirked a dark eyebrow above one steel gray eye and looked at her dubiously, so she expounded.

"The maternal line is the only way to track heritage and legitimacy that is above question."

"Oh? And how do you figure that?" He sounded unconvinced, but to her it was simple good sense. Why would anyone choose to do things differently?

"Well, think about it. A man can lie with a woman. She gets with child. But how can that man ever know for certain the child is his? Could she not have already been pregnant when she lay with him? Or perhaps she slept with another man after him, and the child in truth belongs to the latter."

She shook her head.

"But a woman's part in childbirth is unmistakable and undeniable. The child grows within her. Her body changes visibly to accommodate the new life. Witnesses can see the babe expelled from her very body, and so know without question the child is hers. The female line is the only sensible way to trace legitimacy."

When she cut her eyes to look at him, Tau had to hide a bemused smile. He looked positively flummoxed.

"I … I suppose I never thought of it that way." He shook his head. "It does make a certain kind of sense. I doubt it would go over very well here, though," he finished with a chuckle.

Tau shook her head bemusedly. "I suspect you're right."

They came to a stop in a secluded corner of the library inhabited by a few plush chairs and a comfortable-looking couch. They were alone, surrounded by towering shelves of dusty tomes. Not even the low hum of conversation elsewhere in the large room reached them here.

Xan gestured for her to choose a seat, and after a moment of consideration she moved to perch on the couch a little left of center. She suppressed a flutter of butterflies in her stomach as he sat beside her, close enough that she could feel the heat radiating from him.

She had to swallow around a lump in her throat before she could manage to speak again.

"Now it's my turn for a question." Xanthrall nodded graciously, so she continued. "Shapeshifting is something unique to Devalians; there is no magical equivalent. How does it work?"

He tilted his head to the side and considered her for a moment.

"That may be a difficult one for me to answer; I don't know how it works for everyone. But I can," he went on when she opened her mouth to respond, "tell you what it's like for me."

She closed her mouth promptly and nodded. "Please, do."

Xan shifted slightly on the couch, and his knee bumped hers when he moved to see her better. How to explain? He'd never tried before.

"Well, aside from mindspeech I don't have any conventional magic, so I don't know if any of it is similar. I've heard mages talk about having to ground and center, but none of that is necessary for me. I just … concentrate, and it kind of happens on its own."

Tau was frowning in thought, a small crease between her brows.

"So you don't have to *do* anything?"

He shifted uncomfortably as he felt heat rising to his face. With his fair skin, the color change was marked.

"Well, there is one thing...." She quirked an eyebrow at him questioningly and his flush deepened. He cleared his throat.

"My clothes don't change when I do."

He felt sure his hair was about to catch fire from the heat of his blush, and though he didn't think it possible, his discomfiture deepened as Tau's eyes widened and she colored slightly in response.

"Oh. You mean...?" He nodded, feeling strangled.

"I'll just say that if I plan on shifting back to my human form, I have to do so within easy reach of clothing."

"Oh, I see." More color rose to her cheeks, and he smiled sheepishly at her.

"So I guess there is some preparation involved." He managed a lopsided grin when his comment elicited a laugh.

"I suppose so." She paused a moment as she dropped her eyes to her hands where they rested in her lap before she looked up to meet his gaze again.

"So, if your father's wife handles the actual running of the kingdom – as I must assume your future wife will do for you, once you take the throne – why don't you go with him when he marches with the army?"

Xan shrugged, not quite ready to explain the odd situation caused by his mother's passing. At least they were off the subject of his nudity.

"I do, sometimes. Not on the most dangerous campaigns – he has this thing about keeping his heir alive – but if he feels the risk is worth it, I ride along. I always sit in on the war councils and strategy meetings, though."

Tau nodded slowly. "I suppose that makes sense. There has to be a line drawn somewhere between grooming you to be a ruthless war leader and keeping you safe as the protected heir."

He smiled. "I suppose so. Now," he went on with a lopsided grin, "by my count, that was two questions."

When Tau smiled in response to this gentle teasing, Xan felt his heart rise in answer. Her green eyes sparkled with amusement as she gestured for him to proceed.

"Your parents are married, are they not?"

She nodded, obviously uncertain as to what he was driving at.

"Of course."

"But your mother did not take your father's name, and you do not go by his name, either."

Now Tau looked positively perplexed.

"Why would we?"

He looks as though I just asked him why he can't breathe underwater, Tau observed, confused by his reaction.

"Because she's his wife! You're his daughter!"

Tau still had no idea what he was driving at. "Yes...." She trailed off, her eyebrows knit together as she considered him. "And when they married he took her name, as is traditional. The same when I was born."

She couldn't quite decide if his expression at that point was more confused or horrified. She was still perplexed, and his next words only served to confound her further.

"*He* took *her* name?"

Tau nodded and waved one hand in exasperation. How many times must she repeat herself?

"Yes, of course. Just like every other marriage. The husband takes on the wife's name, and –"

"But that's wrong!"

Tau broke off when he interrupted her and frowned at the outburst.

"Excuse me?"

Xan flushed and quickly tried to backtrack, but Tau was having none of it.

"What do you mean, it's 'wrong?' It is the way things have been done in Sennor for generations!"

"But – but a man's name is his legacy! How is he to pass that on to his children if he must give it up when he marries?"

Tau scoffed. "A man *has* no legacy in Sennor. It is an honor to take on his wife's name and to sire her children. A man has little right to inheritance in Sennor; the only way land or wealth passes on to the male line is if all of the female line is exhausted. What need has a man for his own name when he is without his own estates?"

Xanthrall simply couldn't wrap his head around this new information. He had known that men in Sennor had little in the way of property save that which they bought for themselves, and that alone was strange enough. But this! When a man had nothing else, still he always had his name!

He shuddered slightly. To have even that stripped from him was more than he could even imagine. How did their men tolerate it? He shook his head in befuddlement.

"I can't even begin to comprehend...." He groaned, suddenly acutely aware of the headache blossoming between his eyes. Tau was watching him consideringly.

"I gather from your reaction that you do things a bit differently here in Devali?"

Xanthrall nodded slowly. "You could say that. Here, the wife takes the husband's name."

Tau's eyebrows arched at this, and incredulity was thick in her voice when she spoke.

"You still hold to that archaic tradition? From the strength of your reaction, I had assumed that you had moved beyond the practice completely. Ever since Sennor was divided all those years ago and the line of succession was cemented as following the female descendants, no woman in Sennor has taken her husband's name. As the queen, so her people."

Xanthrall could only shake his head.

"I cannot even begin to comprehend a culture so vastly different than ours in one night." He managed a small smile. "I'm afraid I must beg an end to this evening's lesson. Perhaps a night to mull over this new information will help me to absorb what you have said and approach this with a new outlook tomorrow."

Tau smiled at him crookedly as he rose and offered her a hand to help her to her feet.

"It is rather a lot to take in all at once, isn't it?" She shrugged. "I think time to absorb everything is a very good idea," she added as she accepted his help and stood.

Xan's smile was more sincere this time; now that their lesson was officially over for the evening, he found himself relaxing again and enjoying the simple pleasure of Tau's company once more.

"May I escort you to your chambers?"

Tau nodded graciously, the aloof gesture spoiled by her warm smile.

"I would like that."

Tau leaned against the closed door, breathing deeply. The two of them had lingered over their walk, keeping the conversation to less serious topics as they made their way back to her rooms. When Xanthrall had paused outside her door after bidding her good night, she had almost thought….

No, that is ridiculous. He has his pick of any woman in the kingdom. He has no reason to find me any more interesting than any of them.

She sighed and pushed away from the door. She briefly considered waking one of her maids to help her undress – it was late enough that the girls were likely asleep – but decided against it. The dress was easy enough for her to loosen and shimmy out of on her own, and it wasn't as though her hair was in some kind of intricate up-do that she would require help to sort out.

It wasn't long at all before Tau was sliding under the warmth of her thick blankets and sinking blissfully into the large, overstuffed bed. She sighed with delight and rolled onto her side to pillow her head on her arm and closed her eyes. Though her mind still raced, her tired body soon ensured that she fell sound asleep.

Chapter 34

Ramira sat at the stone table in her workroom, bent close over her mage stone. Lines of concentration creased her sweat-beaded brow as she muttered to herself. She was on the verge of something here; she could feel it!

"There *must* be a way.... I'm missing something. I know I am. But what?"

Experimentally, she pulled on the threads of the spell she had set on her stone and watched as the magic stretched and pulled oddly. For a moment she held her breath; had she finally succeeded? It looked as though it might –

She let out her breath in a disappointed *whoosh* as the spell unraveled, shaking her head at the minor backlash it caused.

"Damn."

She had been so close – so *close*. If she could puzzle out a way to make her mage stone self-charging, so that it constantly replenished its own stores of power without her having to do so consciously, it would be only a small step for her to adapt such a spell for other uses. Ideas of self-warming cook pots and permanent mage lights danced briefly through her mind.

In the weeks that Tau had been here the girl had told her of many magical marvels. Ramira had learned how to implement a few of them; the hot and cold running water was truly amazing! Now, she had an idea for how to take such conveniences one step further. If she could just puzzle this out, she'd be able to make magical items that any commoner could use!

She allowed herself a brief moment to fantasize about self-warming blankets for the poor and fires that did not need wood to burn. The possibilities were endless!

As Ramira bent over her stone to begin again, she felt her magic strain against her control. With a sigh of regret, she pushed back from the table and rose as she loosened her hold on her power until she had released it completely. She wavered slightly on her feet, forced to catch herself on the table to stay upright.

I can't do any more tonight, she realized.

She gazed at her mage stone regretfully. Tomorrow would have to be soon enough for her to try.

Chapter 35

"No."

Ramira looked as though Tau had just doused her with water. She spluttered indignantly for a moment, but – miracle of miracles – stopped when Tau held up a hand to forestall her.

"I know I am supposed to continue my training while I am here. And I have been. But even at home I am allowed an occasional day off. It has been *weeks* since I've been out of the castle, and Lilae needs to stretch her wings. I *am* taking the morning off."

Ramira seemed to deflate slightly in the face of Tau's quiet determination, and at length she nodded.

"Very well. I suppose I can't force you. But do keep in mind, child, that you have a duty to your country."

Tau's eyes narrowed. She disliked being coerced, and Ramira was treading dangerously close to trying to do just that.

You would think the King's Mage would know better than to try to manipulate an empath.

She does, Lilae commented bemusedly, **but logic seldom takes much part in pride. She feels she is in the right, and wishes you to acknowledge that.**

Well, she's not right. She isn't Sennorran; she can't possibly understand how badly you and I need to have time together.

Then help her understand.

Tau let out a sigh. The dragon was right; she was here to do more than learn. She was also here to educate. How could she expect these Devalians to understand such a purely Sennorran urge if she did not at least *try* to explain it to them?

"I am fully aware of the duty I owe my country, Ramira. And may *I* remind *you* that my duty extends beyond mage training. I am here as a diplomat, and one of my foremost duties is to act as a bridge between our nations. So, I beg you, permit me to offer you a bit of enlightenment.

"The bond between a Sennorran and her guardian is deep and strong, but it is something that requires nurturing nonetheless. Even the sturdiest oak cannot thrive in an extended drought. Our bond is parched, with our time together so limited lately. I will not deny my guardian any longer.

"I can assure you that I will resume our normal schedule tomorrow, and you will be all the happier with my abilities for the time off to recharge."

Tau could see it in the woman's eyes; she still did not fully understand. Perhaps she never would. Could any Devalian ever hope to comprehend the soul-deep bond between human and guardian? Somehow, Tau doubted it.

Luckily she was spared from the need to struggle through a further explanation by the arrival of her passenger.

Xanthrall had done his best to keep from pestering Tau about the promise she'd made him. She had been at court for over a month now, and in that time they had come to understand each other increasingly well. He would even venture so far as to call her a friend, and he thought she might feel the same. But in all the time she'd been here and all the hours they had spent together discussing politics and traditions she had never once tried to make good on her promise to take him flying. The fact that she had not taken her great copper beast for a flight alone either was but small consolation.

As he crested the stairs to the tower where the dragon perched, an interesting tableau greeted him. Tau and Ramira stood facing each other, the tension between them palpable.

He would have been perfectly content to wait unobtrusively for them to resolve whatever it was that held the two women thus – in the interest of self-preservation, he tended not to get involved in the machinations of women, let alone two of the world's most powerful mages – but Tau spotted him immediately and waved him over.

He made a carefully-precise bow aimed between the two women, and then a lower one in the direction of the massive dragon.

"Ladies. Lady Lilae. Good morning."

Ramira only nodded an acknowledgement to his greeting – as King's Mage, she was basically his equal, and so not required to show him any particular courtesy – but Tau made a shallow bow in response. That had taken some getting used to; when Tau wasn't dressed for court, the young woman was in breeches as often as not. He was not at all used to a woman who dressed so; her bowing instead of curtsying only served to heighten his sense of peculiarity. Now, though, he found it all far less absurd than he had in the beginning, and so was able to take the gesture in stride as she straightened and smiled at him.

"Your Highness. Good morning. Your timing is impeccable. I trust you are ready?"

When she gestured behind herself to Lilae, who he only now noticed was wearing some manner of saddle-like contraption, his breath caught. He had scarcely dared hope that this had been the reason she'd invited him to the rooftop this morning. His heart flip-flopped excitedly as he nodded.

"Certainly, Lady Dafrin."

She eyed him critically, and he had to resist the urge to squirm under her measuring gaze.

"You may get a little cold; the air is thinner up high, and there is a marked temperature difference."

He glanced down at himself self-consciously. He was dressed appropriately for the warm day in lightweight fabrics and a sleeveless tunic. Tau was bundled warmly in leathers, and even wore a pair of leather gloves to protect her hands, he saw. He flushed slightly. The last thing he wanted was to be denied this chance because he had failed to dress appropriately.

"I can fetch something warmer. It will only –" He broke off when Tau held up a hand.

"There is no need. I have asked Magla to send your things for you."

Xanthrall flushed. He truly was flustered; it should have occurred to him to use mindspeech to have one of the servants bring his things. Several of them were strong enough to hear his summons. And they all knew to listen for him. He was still berating himself mentally as he voiced his gratitude.

"Thank you. I wouldn't want to delay your plans."

Perhaps I should have thought to warn him to dress warmly, Tau mused as she took in Xanthrall's appearance. In her time here, Tau had discovered that the young prince seldom dressed so finely as he had those first few days. While his lightweight shirt and pants were still made of fine cloth, the cut was not far different than what any moderately well-off young man might wear. There was no embroidery, and he wore none of the trappings of rank, only a simple sword on a sturdy belt. He didn't need any embellishments, in Tau's opinion; he cut quite a figure just as he was.

Magla, Tau addressed her maid gently, pleased at the woman's mild surprise at being mindspoken to. The first time Tau had summoned the young woman this way, the poor thing had nearly gone into a panic. Now she was used to Tau's occasional mental summons; sometimes, it was simply easier.

The prince needs clothes appropriate for flying. Something warm, but not too bulky. And nothing loose. Please have something brought to the roof of Lilae's tower right away.

She felt the woman's understanding and consent, and then closed the connection as Xanthrall made his greetings. She did not miss the look Ramira shot her when Tau confessed her trick with Magla, but she chose to ignore it. Xanthrall's look of relieved gratitude was more than worth any reprimand Ramira might feel she deserved.

"Adept," she said, addressing the older woman in a cool tone, "you are welcome to stay until we are ready to take flight, though I do recommend you remove yourself from the rooftop before we lift off. The winds can be a bit rough, so close."

Ramira obviously knew she'd been defeated; she made no further attempt to protest, but instead made her polite farewells and retreated to the stairs.

Tau watched her go for a moment, then turned to Xanthrall with a smile tugging at the corners of her mouth.

"She reminds me in too many ways of my father sometimes." She shook her head fondly for the thought of him, remembering the way Ramiq tended to react to such shows of willfulness from her.

Xanthrall chuckled slightly as the memory flashed through her mind and faded. "Magic does seem to breed certain types."

She shot him a suspicious look at that, then laughed ruefully herself at his pointed stare.

"I suppose it does, at that!" She held out a hand to him and half turned to face Lilae. "Come; while we wait for your clothes, we can go over a few of the basic things you'll need to know."

His eyes lit up as he took her hand and joined her for the few steps to Lilae's side, and Tau's stomach flopped excitedly in reaction to his proximity.

Xanthrall's time with Tau was typically nothing if not interesting; even if all they did was discuss culture and policy, somehow Tau always managed to make the interaction memorable – often through her presence alone. His brief lesson in draconic flight proved to be an even more fascinating conversation than he had come to anticipate from the young Sennorran mage.

"My everyday saddle is only made to carry one," she began, "but we were able to rig up a rudimentary harness that I will use. That way, you have a more secure seat."

He moved up beside her to examine the contraption strapped to Lilae's body about two-thirds of the way down her neck. It actually looked rather similar to a simple jumper's saddle: there was no horn, and the pommel was so low as to be almost non-existent. The seat was a bit deeper than the saddles he was used to seeing, and there were narrower saddle flaps and knee rolls, but the rig was familiar enough that he could recognize it for what it was.

The extra straps she had referred to were just that: wide leather straps arranged so that a small loop hung down to either side of the great copper dragon – to act as makeshift stirrups, he surmised. When Tau pointed out several sturdy D-rings and tie straps – not normally found on a jumping saddle, but obviously helpful here – he breathed a sigh of relief that he would not have to balance so precariously as he had half expected. No doubt falling from a dragon would be far worse than taking a tumble from atop a horse.

I would not let you fall, Princeling.

Xan started guiltily, wondering if the dragon had broadcast her thoughts to Tau as well. He watched in amazement as the dragon turned to look at him and slowly lowered one scaly eyelid in what he swore was a wink. He felt himself grin in response as he folded his hands behind his back to keep from rubbing them together in boyish anticipation.

"Now," Tau said, pulling him back to the here-and-now, "riding a dragon is both similar to and vastly different from riding horseback. The motion is different – it's more of a lift-and-drop rolling movement, kind of like taking a jump – but the principles are the same. Move with her, not against her, and lean into the turns to keep your balance."

It sounded simple enough, but Xan had no doubt that the execution would not come so easily as she made it sound. He was about to say as much when the sound of footsteps on the stairs drew both of their attention. As he watched, Lyle came into sight and made his obeisance to the two of them.

"Highness, I was told you required warmer clothing?"

He sounded dubious; the day was quite warm by Devalian standards, and Xanthrall was not known for taking a chill.

"Yes, Lyle, thank you. The Lady Dafrin tells me that flying requires somewhat warmer clothing."

The older man's eyes widened as he cast a half-fearful glance at the immense dragon behind them.

"Flying, Highness?"

Xanthrall smiled sympathetically at the man's discomfort as he stepped forward to relieve Lyle of his burdens.

"Yes, Lyle, flying."

He took a moment to look over the clothing and was pleased to see that everything was similar to what Tau already wore. There was even a pair of fur-lined leather gloves.

Tau watched in silent bemusement as Xanthrall took his clothes and dismissed his servant. The poor man looked positively appalled at the thought of his prince flying. Had anyone but Lilae been the one taking them up Tau could have understood his concern, but she knew there was no danger so long as they were astride her guardian.

She watched as Xanthrall pulled a light tan leather jacket on over his shirt, and then had to hide a small smile when he looked around sheepishly, pants in hand.

"I'm afraid I'll need somewhere to change into these."

Tau managed not to laugh and gestured to the merlons behind Lilae.

"Between the stone and the dragon, I should think your modesty well protected."

He flushed at her comment but did not respond as he moved around Lilae and out of sight. After a few minutes he emerged, now garbed far more appropriately for flight in a leather getup not far different from her own. Tau nodded her approval, thinking to herself that the fitted leathers suited him quite well.

"Much better! Now, come over here and we'll get you strapped in."

Lilae shifted herself so that she was no longer laying, but rather crouched, her weight supported on her well-muscled legs. Tau double-checked the flying equipment and straps to ensure that everything was secure, then moved back to allow Xan room to approach the dragon.

"Step there, on her foreleg, and use the straps to brace so you can pull yourself up."

He managed to mount with less trouble than Tau had anticipated, though he did look a bit awkward trying to scramble atop the huge dragon. Once he sat astride, Tau set about helping him lower the stirrups – his legs were a few inches longer than hers – and strap himself securely into the saddle.

When she was confident he was well-situated, she stepped atop Lilae's leg herself and struggled astride. She had positioned herself in front of the prince, and the necessity for her to mount without kicking him in the head complicated the process. She reached down to slip the leather loops over her boots and tested her weight against them experimentally. They would do.

"Now, the launch is going to be the roughest part; she's going to have to work pretty hard to get enough height to level off. You'll want to rise up a bit in the stirrups and lean forward; grab onto the saddle or brace yourself against her neck to help yourself balance."

She demonstrated as she spoke, then craned her head to look over her shoulder and check his form.

"Good. Well, Xan, if you're ready?"

His affirmative was scarcely out of his mouth before the dragon had unfurled wings which spread a good twenty meters to either side of her body (a span that astounded him every time he saw it) and thrust them into the air with a powerful leap.

Despite Tau's instruction and previous warning, the force of the dragon's jump took him by surprise. The air rushed out of him in a painful wheeze when the saddle rose to meet him with unexpected suddenness. The pain was such that his knees

buckled, and had it not been for the straps which held him in place he would certainly have lost his seat when Lilae dropped slightly before the first powerful wingbeat lifted them higher.

He did his best to balance as he had been shown, but his legs still felt like water. As a result, he jounced around painfully until – finally! – Lilae leveled out and settled into a long glide, punctuated occasionally by another stroke of her massive wings.

It took some time before he was able to think past the pain; he was fairly certain that he'd be sporting long, purple bruises for a few days where the straps had strained against his legs. Once he was finally able to see straight, he looked around himself in wonder.

The land spread out below them like a living map. From their height the people on the road looked like ants, the houses stones. Sunlight sparkled across the water of the lake as they flew over, and he spied a few small boats bobbing across its surface.

"Wow," he breathed, the word instantly ripped from him by the wind. Now that Lilae had settled down into a steady flight, he found the rhythm of her movements as smooth as Tau had promised. It was easy to move with her once he had adjusted to the unfamiliar motion.

He leaned forward slightly and placed a hand on Tau's shoulder to catch her attention.

"It's beautiful," he yelled, hoping she could hear him.

Isn't it? He startled when he heard her speak into his mind, and then grinned behind her back. Mindspeech *would* be much more practical in flight.

He berated himself for not thinking of such an elegantly simple solution for a second time today.

I've never seen the city like this. He shook his head in wonder.

Would you like to go higher?

His eyes widened. *You can go higher than this?*

In answer Lilae began to climb, her wingbeats taking them ever-further from the ground. He watched the scene below them dwindle with a breathless sense of awe. In moments they were amongst the clouds; the moisture beaded on his skin and dampened his hair, causing him to shiver slightly in the cool wind of their passage.

Presently they were above the layer of clouds, and Lilae leveled off again to glide above them, the powerful strokes of her wings stirring the water vapor with the force of her movement.

Xanthrall found himself at a loss for words as he looked about himself. It was as though the three of them had entered an entirely different world. He could hear no sound over the rushing of the wind in his ears, and though he spied the occasional bird, otherwise they were alone.

Tau raised her hands from her grip on the strap that secured her to Lilae's neck and spread her arms wide in a pale imitation of the dragon's expansive wings. She laughed aloud, the sound ripped from her by the speed of their flight.

I've missed this! Tau felt more than heard the dragon's rumble of agreement; it vibrated from somewhere deep in her guardian's chest.

It is good to fly together again.

Tau glanced back over her shoulder to meet Xan's eye, but the prince was looking below them, watching the clouds swirl as they passed.

What do you think?

He gave a guilty start and looked up to meet her gaze with a sheepish grin.

It's incredible! I've always wondered what it would be like to touch a cloud. His eyes danced merrily as he loosed one hand from the saddle and spread it beside him in a broad gesture. *Now I know!*

Tau smiled in answer and nodded.

I was amazed the first time we flew this high. I was a child; I had yet to learn that clouds were made of water. I had always imagined them to be soft and fluffy, like down. She shook her head with a rueful smile for the fancies of her youth. *I was so disappointed to learn otherwise!*

Xan's grin stretched in answer to the laughter in her mindvoice, and Tau's eyes lit with mischief as an idea occurred to her.

Are you up for something a bit more exciting?

His eyes widened. *More exciting than flying?!*

When she nodded, he grinned again and gave an enthusiastic affirmative.

Xan wasn't quite sure what Tau had in mind – her eyes had danced with mischief when she'd turned back around – but he was not left to wonder for long.

Brace yourself.

He shifted his position slightly in the saddle and tightened his grip on the pommel – just in time. Lilae dipped a wingtip and spun almost in place, throwing him against the straps with the sudden change in direction.

Lean into the movement, the way you would with a horse.

He nodded, though Tau wasn't looking at him to see, and centered his weight in the saddle again. This time he at least had a little warning. He considered himself a good horseman, and he was finding that riding the larger beast had some similarities he hadn't considered.

Lilae's head craned slightly as she looked left, and then her muscles bunched and he felt her position shift. He forced himself to be less rigid and moved with her into the turn. The experience was much more pleasant this time, and he found an exhilarated laugh bubbling out of him.

Much better! Tau praised, and he grinned at the warmth of approval in her mental tone.

They tried a few more turns, and just when Xan had the feel for how to anticipate the dragon's movements, she did something he did not know how to brace for. She cupped her wings and went into a barrel roll, spinning them upside-down, then right-side-up, then upside-down again.

He wasn't sure if it was his heart or his stomach in his throat as he caught a glimpse of the clouds above him – below him – above him – but he found that whichever it was made it impossible for him to swallow down his sudden panic.

I would not let you fall, Princeling. You are as safe on my back as in your own bed.

Still, she righted herself and few levelly for a time until his pulse slowed and his breathing resumed.

That was wicked!

I only wanted to see how he would respond! Lilae's mindvoice was contrite.

Well, now you know!

Lilae's wordless affirmative held a tinge of sheepishness that made Tau smile and slap the great copper neck affectionately. A few moments more passed, and then, **There is a sizeable herd of buffalo below.**

Tau nodded and glanced back at the prince as Lilae began a lazy downward spiral.

Lilae will drop us off so she can hunt before we fly back. The landing should not be as rough as the take-off was for you, but be prepared to absorb any impact with your legs, as you would to take a jump on horseback.

She felt him nod and adjust his position, and before long Lilae was backwinging to a gentle landing in easy walking distance of a grove of trees. Tau could hear Xan loosening the straps that held him in place, and she freed herself from her own ties before swinging a leg over and sliding down to a sturdy copper foreleg so that she could help him.

In short order, he balanced beside her on the dragon's upraised limb. Tau quickly showed him how to remove the saddle; there were a few more pieces to this one than those he was used to.

Once they had both made it safely to the ground and retreated to a safe distance Lilae gathered herself and with a great thrust of her powerfully muscled hind legs leapt skyward, her wings pumping strongly to help her gain altitude. Tau watched until Lilae had leveled off high above them and was headed in the appropriate direction before she turned to face Xanthrall with a grin.

It was a long while before Xan could bring himself to tear his gaze away from the retreating form of the immense dragon. When at last she had dwindled to little more than a speck in the sky, he lowered his gaze to find Tau grinning at him with a knowing gleam in her lively green eyes.

"Well? What did you think?"

He laughed aloud in answer and threw his arms around her, lifting her off of her feet and twirling with her before he set her down again. She squealed with surprised delight, and he smiled more broadly at the flush in her cheeks.

"What do I think?" On impulse, he leaned forward and kissed her quickly. "I think that is the most wondrous thing I have ever done!"

Tau's cheeks were bright when he pulled back to answer her, and she looked at him in surprise for one breathless moment. Then, what he had just done seemed to register with him and he hastily moved to release her, stammering an apology.

Without allowing herself the time to consider the consequences, Tau reached out to hold his arms in place around her and closed the distance he had opened between them with a step. This time when her lips met his he tensed in surprise. After a moment, though, he relaxed and tightened his arms around her waist.

When at last the kiss ended they stood for a bit, each considering the other. Dancing green eyes met heat-filled gray ones, and Tau felt warmth flush through her under his scrutiny.

"Well." He had to clear his throat before he could continue, "I stand corrected."

A thrill shot through her at his words and she laughed in exhilaration, feeling as though she were flying higher now than she ever had a-dragonback.

Chapter 36

A year passed far too quickly. The weeks, and then the months, went by in a blur of lessons, diplomatic meetings, and courtly events. Her stolen moments with the prince had been few and far between, but the memories of them held the rosy glow of a young girl's first romance.

She stood now in the main courtyard, her guardian to her right, facing south towards Sennor as she watched the bustle of travel preparations being completed in the gray of dawn's first light. Though she longed for home – there had been many nights she'd lain awake, unable to push aside the deep ache of loneliness and the desire to see her parents and friends – she was sorry to be leaving. And not just because of Xanthrall, though the handsome and charming young prince was certainly at the top of the list of people she would miss.

She stifled a sigh as she watched the teams being hitched to their wagons and the seemingly-endless line of trunks holding the party's personal belongings being loaded. She wished she could simply skip the tedium of cross-country travel. *She* could, but she owed some loyalty to her traveling companions. While in many ways her presence would endanger them, with Lilae by her side the pair of them afforded a great deal more in the way of protection than anything else.

"It's all a bit overwhelming, isn't it?"

Tau did not jump at the voice beside her; even without turning to watch, she had been able to follow Ramira's approach. The woman's magical presence was both unique and powerful; Tau couldn't have missed her if she'd tried.

"It is organized chaos." She smiled and turned to face her mentor, inclining her head in a show of respect. After a year under Ramira's demanding tutelage, Tau had been raised – under Devalian standards, at least – to the rank of Master.

"It is that." Ramira smiled at her, then looked up to meet Lilae's slitted green eye. "Good flying, Lilae. Take good care of our Tau. She is precious cargo."

The dragon inclined her head slightly in acknowledgement.

To none more so than I, Adept Ramira. I always take good care of her.

Tau was about to retort when she spied Xanthrall approaching them from across the courtyard. She snapped her teeth shut over her comment and turned to greet him, smiling brightly. This would be nothing more than a formal farewell; they had already said their more personal goodbyes last night.

"Your Highness." Tau inclined her head and offered him a formal bow, carefully gauged to the proper degree based on her elevated rank.

"Master Dafrin. We are sorry to see you go. Please know you are welcome at our court any time you wish to visit."

"Thank you, Highness. On behalf of Queen Sennorra, please know that the same open invitation is extended to you and yours. Sennor would be honored to host you any time you wish to visit."

She reached out and clasped his hand, almost choked with emotion. She would miss him terribly!

"I would be honored." He smiled and gave her hand a gentle squeeze before he released her and turned to face those assembled. As Tau turned too, she saw that the last chest had been loaded, the final team hitched.

When Xan opened his mouth to address those gathered, Ramira wove a quick spell on the air which made his words ring from the stone walls around them.

"On behalf of the Crown of Devali, thank you all for the time you have spent with us. You have greatly honored our nation with your show of trust. Know that each of you leaves here not as a diplomat, but as a friend. May you have a safe and speedy return, and may the next time we meet be as two nations united!"

The last words resonated in the air for a moment before the cheers rose to drown them out. After a brief embrace with Ramira and a customary peck on both of Xan's cheeks, Tau turned and mounted her dragon.

Once everyone had cleared away, she gave the great beast the go-ahead. With a powerful thrust of her hind legs Lilae leapt skyward, her fragile-seeming wings pumping to gain altitude. Before long, they were aloft – and headed home at last.

Chapter 37

Tau had always known the goal of peace was a controversial one, but on the trip between the capitals she had witnessed first-hand just how volatile the matter had become. She still had numerous occasions to be grateful for the party's additional guards; they were assaulted not only throughout the Devalian countryside, but within their own borders as well. She had no few opportunities to exercise her healing abilities.

Now, at last, she and Lilae spiraled down to land in the castle's courtyard, where their arrival was awaited by the queen herself. It was not Her Majesty's presence, but rather Sennora's companions that surprised her; she had not expected to see her parents until she returned to the fort.

They hurried forward to welcome her, and Tau accepted their embrace gladly.

"What are you two doing here?"

They exchanged a look before her father answered.

"We couldn't wait another day to see you! So I brought us here."

Tau frowned slightly, considering her parents suspiciously. Her empathic senses screamed to her that something was off. At a quelling look from her mother, Tau snapped her jaw shut on the question that had been forming and instead released them and turned to greet the queen. She bowed respectfully.

"Your Majesty."

"Tau! Rise, child. You must be tired from your travels."

Tau straightened and smiled warmly at the queen. She'd met Sennorra a few times already when she'd accompanied her father on some of his visits to the capital. She was a warm and friendly woman, so long as you didn't cross her. She tended to listen to Ramiq's council as well as that of her other advisors, but had been known to go her own way when she disagreed strongly enough. Tau rather liked her.

"Let us keep the formalities brief so that you might go refresh yourself."

Tau's smile faltered as she took a breath before speaking.

"I would request a more private audience with you instead, Majesty, if you would permit. There are things I think it best you know right away.

Tau had expected surprise or shock to meet her report. Instead, she looked at three faces set in grim resignation. The queen answered her puzzled look first.

"This dissent is not news to us; it has been going on since the negotiations first opened. It has only grown worse as we come nearer to peace between us. Our people *need* this war to end, but too many cannot see past their fears and prejudices. Still more see less profit in peace than war, even here amongst our nobles."

Tau turned disbelieving eyes to her parents as Sennorra shook her head sadly.

"If this has been going on for so long, how is it I am only now learning of it?"

Tsuga reached out a hand to stop Ramiq from answering; he snapped his mouth shut and shot his wife an anguished look. She patted his arm and shifted her attention back to their daughter with a sigh.

"We kept as much of it from you as we could. We wanted you to have a chance at a real childhood before you were thrust into the turmoil of this war. As it is, we had hoped peace would begin before you learned of this."

Her mother paused and exchanged a meaningful look with Ramiq before taking a deep breath to continue.

"Our position on the border is not incidental, Tau. Under normal circumstances, the Queen's Mage would never be permitted to live so far from his monarch, but these are rather unique times. We are not stationed where we are merely because we are a school that fosters peace; that is only a very small part of our purpose."

Tau looked from her mother to her father in confusion. The bottom had just dropped out of her world in a big way; she had been lied to and deceived by her own parents, the very people she was supposed to be able to trust beyond all others. She wasn't quite sure what to make of this.

"We are a base – one of several – for the queen's eyes and ears on the border and even into Devali. We help her keep a finger on the pulse of the war. But now…."

Tsuga trailed off, looking beseechingly at her daughter. Tau drew back before she could stop herself, and Tsuga flinched as though she'd been struck. Unable to bring herself to look at her parents just now, Tau shifted her gaze to the queen.

"But now?" she prompted.

"But now things have grown too heated, too volatile with these warmongers," Sennorra picked up the thread of conversation. "I've had to request that your parents take a more active role. They've been assigned joint command of a large force – hopefully one sufficient to quell the uprising. Devali's king has agreed to commit a similar number of troops to join ours in a combined effort to help establish the peace."

Tau shook her head, overwhelmed at this news. She looked from the queen to her parents.

"And what am I to do?"

Her father spoke up for the first time, the look in his green eyes – so like her own – anguished.

"Your training is still incomplete, and unfortunately I need to be at the front. You will have to join us, at least for a time."

Tau sighed and leaned her head back against her chair. Sixteen years old, and embroiled in war and politics.

I suppose, she mused, *I should be grateful they enabled me to stay free of it this long.*

With only the three of them needing to return to the front, and two of those three being mages skilled in teleportation, transportation was a simple enough matter. Tau sat alone astride Lilae and took in the sight of the large camp below, watching people the size of ants scurrying about on their business.

Her father never had truly reached a point of comfort with the presence of a dragon in his life; he was interested in Lilae academically, but otherwise avoided the immense beast whenever possible. Tsuga, still uncomfortable with instantaneous travel even after all this time, had opined that she was better off transferring as close to the ground as possible.

Tau sighed as Lilae spiraled down, aiming for the outskirts of the camp furthest from the horse lines to avoid spooking the mounts. She'd read about war. Some writers glorified it, making it sound a wonderful adventure. But her parents had ensured that Tau was relieved of any such illusions long ago. The first-hand accounts of battle from her mother had been enough to open her eyes, but the stories Ramiq told of the aftermath in the healers' tents had truly driven their point home. As a result, Tau had never lusted for battle the way some youths did; she harbored no dreams of glory won for herself at the expense of others' lives. Yet now here she was, embroiled in the war whether she wished it or no.

She closed her eyes briefly and shook her head as Lilae backwinged and touched down on the ground, offering her rider only the slightest of jolts. She was to be the next Queen's Mage someday – hopefully one still far into the future. She would have to deal with this side of things eventually, she knew.

No time like the present, I suppose.

Resigned, she unbuckled herself and slid to the ground to remove Lilae's saddle. She told herself it was the long-engrained training from her mother to care for her mount even before herself, and not an attempt to postpone the inevitable. She wasn't sure even she believed it, though.

At last, there was nothing left for her to use as an excuse. She drew herself up to full height and squared her shoulders, bracing for the shock of being thrust quite abruptly into the middle of the war.

Chapter 38

*T*au leaned back from the table and raised one hand to pinch the bridge of her nose in an effort to relieve her tension headache.

And this is only for the magical troops, she reflected. *There are more than a hundred regular troops for each mage!*

The maps and charts she had been poring over for the past several hours had all started to look the same to her, and her tired eyes no longer wanted to focus on the crabbed lettering denoting rank and ability, dispatch orders and provisions. She didn't know how her mother could possibly keep up with all of this for her command; the fifty-odd mages − not counting the healers, who were in a class all their own − were a handful; she couldn't imagine keeping track of the kinds of numbers Tsuga had to juggle.

How does she manage without going insane?

She has help. Captains and officials who manage the minutiae so that she can shift her focus to the bigger picture. People who do for her exactly what you are doing for your father.

Tau sighed and scowled at the papers strewn before her. She was too young and inexperienced in the practical application of all her years of study to officially be Ramiq's second in command, but he had given her many of the responsibilities associated with the position − and still managed to save her from the majority of the accountability when something inevitably went wrong or slipped through the cracks.

Because she was the future Queen's Mage, her father would not permit her to enter into battle. Instead she headed the healers' tents in his absence, an arrangement that suited both her preferences and her talents admirably. Management of *those* tents came easily to her. She knew to the drop how much of each potion was on hand, to the thread how many bandages they had. She knew which mage was the best with handling emotional trauma, which the best mindhealer, and who was most useful as a power conduit or in a supporting role.

But none of that knowledge helped her here. She had studied tactics and troop disposition for years, but the actual application of those skills had proved far more complex than she could have ever imagined.

The fire mages couldn't be housed too close to one another; their hot tempers tended to spark fights when too many of them were in one place. A water mage made a nice balance of personality, but water mages tended to band together, and dividing them was no easy task. Earth mages were the next-best choice, as they were steady and grounded, but she needed them more to keep the air and weather mages focused when their minds started to wander.

And those were only the basics! They also had mindspeakers, shape-shifters, battle mages, light mages and illusionists, and more subcategories of talents than she cared to contemplate.

All of this just for living arrangements! Battle assignments were a whole other beast. Tau groaned

and pushed to her feet. She needed some fresh air, a new perspective, and something purely physical to take her mind off of things.

She had been neglecting her weapons' training lately in favor of all her newfound responsibilities. A good hard workout was exactly what she needed. Luckily, she was wearing some of the modified robes she had come to favor: less billowy, cut for riding, and fitted more closely to the body to allow more freedom of movement. They would suit her purposes now admirably.

Anticipating a hard workout, Tau broke into a jog to begin waking muscles too long idle. It was time for a change of scenery – at least for a little while.

Five. Ramiq ran his hands through his wavy sandy-brown hair – scrupulously maintained to avoid the creeping strands of gray that insisted on encroaching more and more frequently – and heaved a heavy sigh. Five healers were not enough for a force this size. Not in a war. Not when only two had achieved Master rank.

He himself was an Adept at healing – one of only about a dozen living that he knew of – but he was needed more on the field of battle. Tau was a Master – she made a third available in the tents – and with her strength as well as Lilae's power to draw on for support she could do the work of three, but even she could only be in one place at a time.

The Devalian troops were due to arrive in about a week. He could only pray to Auriga that they brought with them a sizeable complement of healers, but he feared their situation was far too like his own.

There simply were no more healers to be had; the few who remained were stretched too thin as it was.

The physicians were a help – they could set bones and stitch less mortal wounds, but they could not heal a cracked skull or knit lacerated tissue back together so that it still functioned. They couldn't stop a punctured liver from leaking toxins into the body or re-inflate a collapsed lung. Already they had lost too many fighters because of this shortage.

Auriga, help us. I fear you are the only one who can.

Chapter 39

It was hard to maintain a clinical detachment from her work while covered in the blood of the person she fought to save. Even now, two days after the latest skirmish, there were men and women bleeding out in the cots. With only six mage-healers in the tents – one of which was a mind healer, and so unable to contribute magically to the physical healings – many soldiers had to wait for such care. Those who could survive a day or two without immediate healing had been cleaned up and bandaged.

All of them were exhausted from working in round-the-clock shifts to save every life they could. Her father had even come by to help for a few hours yesterday, though with his other responsibilities he was unable to linger.

Tau finished removing the bandages from around this man's rib cage and fought to keep her face still. He had a jagged gash from his left pectoral muscle – just below the nipple – to just right of his belly-button. It was deepest on his abdomen, and as she delved him with her healer's senses she realized the cut had missed opening his stomach and slicing through his colon and small intestine only by the barest of margins.

He had been sewn up with small, neat stitches, but they had pulled against the skin of his muscled abdomen, making the tissue red and inflamed. It oozed blood – thankfully free of the pus that would indicate an infection – and was warm to the touch of her gently probing fingers. Yes, his body was fighting for survival, using the fever to burn out any infection that might try to set in, but he needed help if he was to succeed. She managed a reassuring smile.

"What is your name, soldier?"

He grunted when her fingers found a particularly tender spot, and she felt his muscles tense in a spasm of pain beneath her hands.

"Jonathan," he answered when the convulsion had passed.

"Jonathan, the axe very narrowly missed some vital organs. You don't have an infection yet, but this fever and the inflammation has me a little concerned. Your medics have managed to slow the bleeding, but your tissue is pulling at the stitches, so they haven't been able to stop it."

He nodded, taking this information in stride, and Tau looked up from examining the wound to meet his bright blue eyes.

She had found that the soldiers appreciated frank honesty in her assessments; these men and women stared death in the face each day and had no appreciation for a sugar-coated diagnosis. She had also discovered that they, like anyone else, liked to know exactly what she was going to do to them. The knowledge, which she relayed in simple, non-magical terms as much as she could, seemed to help prepare them.

"I'm going to take away your fever and close that wound to stop the bleeding. It doesn't look like you need a full healing; you'll recover just fine with rest and a little care. Are you ready?"

She waited for his nod before she gathered her magic about herself and bent it to her will.

"This won't hurt, but it may itch or tingle a bit."

As she finished speaking, Tau set to work. It took surprisingly little time for her to flush the fever from his blood and mend his flesh. She watched with professional detachment as his tissues knit back together beneath her fingers. Once she would have been fascinated by the process, but now this was just another healing in a seemingly-endless procession, and she was too tired to look at it as anything but a task to be completed so she could move on to the next.

When she was satisfied, she withdrew and sat back in her chair, taking a moment to close her eyes and steady herself. When she opened them, Jonathan was watching her with an expression of wonder.

"It's incredible what you can do. Just a slip of a girl, and you can knit bones and mend flesh." He shook his head. "Thank you, lass."

Tau smiled and nodded tiredly. It was nice to hear a thank-you once in a while. Often enough her patients were in a drugged sleep or passed out from pain and blood loss.

"It's the least I can do. You are all out there on the front line, risking life and limb. And I just patch you up so you can get back to it."

He laughed and reached out to grasp her hand. With the deep lines pain had etched on his face eased, he looked a good deal younger. He was certainly handsome, with his square jaw and close-cropped blond hair.

"Don't sell yourself short, lass. You work miracles in here." He smiled, and Tau couldn't help but respond in kind. "Like our very own guardian angel."

Tau gave his hand a little squeeze.

"That's very kind of you. Unfortunately, an angel's work is never through." She stood and released his hand before gathering up his soiled bandages.

"Try and get some rest, soldier. If you're not famished now, you soon will be. I'll send someone with a tray for you."

He nodded and said a final "Thank you," and as she turned Tau could feel his eyes follow her progress across the tent. When she looked over her shoulder, he caught her glance and smiled warmly. She shook her head and hid a smile of her own.

She was used to gratitude, and had even grown accustomed to the shameless flirting and occasional vulgarity of the soldiers; many of them used it as a coping mechanism when faced with pain or the reality of a life-altering wound. But this felt different; it felt genuine.

I don't have time for this, she scolded herself as she deposited the bandages with the rest of the dirties to be taken and cleaned. *I have work to do.*

Tsuga had been keeping an eye on her daughter from afar. She didn't want to smother her, but she couldn't help but worry over the dark circles under Tau's eyes and the increasing gauntness of her child's cheeks.

She knew the young woman was being over-worked – they all were – but she also suspected there

was something more to the pinched and strained expression she had adopted.

Tau was a powerful empath; healing was a bit further down on her list of talents. Working day in and day out to save lives – not all of which *could* be saved – and surrounded by pain and worry had to be taking a toll on her. Even with the strongest shields to keep out the thoughts and emotions of those around her, Tau's natural sensitivity made her especially prone to wanting to ease their suffering.

Tsuga did what she could to lessen the young girl's burden; she made sure to enforce Tau's own schedule, so that the young mage did not work any more than anyone else, as she was wont to do. She made it a point to take meals with her daughter whenever she was not engaged in battle, so that she knew Tau ate. And she made herself available as an ear to listen and a shoulder to cry on whenever Tau might have need.

Still, she worried. It was a mother's prerogative. There was only so much that could be done about it in their present situation; Ramiq had to be here, in the thick of things, and Tau had to be with him to continue her training.

Now, as Tsuga caught a glimpse of her wraith of a daughter emerging from the medical tents, she felt herself reach a decision. She hurried her step to interrupt the young woman's path.

"Tau!"

At the sound of her name Tau staggered to a stop and looked around herself dazedly. Tsuga's heart constricted at the fatigue-addled look in her eyes. She watched as the youth drew herself up and visibly reached for the dregs of her energy to muster a soothing smile.

"Yes, Mother?"

Tsuga sighed and shook her head.

"Relax, child. I am not here to ask anything of you. I only wanted to make sure you were on your way to eat and rest."

Tau deflated slightly and managed a small but sincere smile of gratitude.

"Yes, that was my plan. I was on the way to my tent."

Tsuga nodded and gestured for Tau to resume her trek.

"I'll join you – for the walk, at least. The way you look, I'm afraid you might fall asleep and walk into a hole somewhere."

That comment earned her a tired chuckle.

"I feel like I might do just that!"

Tsuga reached out a steadying hand to support Tau's elbow when her daughter stumbled tiredly as though to prove her point.

"Thank you."

Tsuga nodded absently and tucked Tau's arm through hers, so that a casual observer would see only a mother and daughter walking arm-in-arm. Tau shot her a look of gratitude.

"Don't mention it. How are things going in the medical tents?"

Tau shook her head.

"Most of the urgent cases have been seen to. I won't have another shift until tomorrow evening; by then, we should be back to normal – barring another incident like the one a few days ago.

Tsuga nodded.

"That's good news. You all have been hit harder than anyone lately; there are just not enough of you to share the burden."

Tau sighed. "I know. But we are managing."

"Well, tomorrow *we* will manage. If the need for magical healing has eased, then those of us who must rely on more mundane means of treating the ill and wounded can handle changing bandages and emptying bedpans."

"But –"

"No buts, young lady. You – all of you – are nearly dead on your feet. You are as of now under orders to stand down – for one day, at least – and attend to your own health."

As they had spoken they'd drawn nearer to Tau's tent, set off to one side of the camp near the medical facilities and as far from the stock lines as possible, a location necessitated by the proximity of the rather large carnivore whose head now peeked out from behind the canvas structure.

"How long has it been since you've taken Lilae flying?"

"Well…." Tau hesitated, and Tsuga shook her head firmly.

"Too long, then. Why don't you two go hunting tomorrow? I know you could use the change of scenery, and Lilae looks positively tarnished from the strain you two share."

"But, I –"

"Nonsense. Your patients will be in good hands. Take a day to rest, Tau. You won't do anyone any good if you keel over from exhaustion."

She's right, you know.

Tau let out a sigh as her reluctance evaporated. She really *did* need a break, and she missed soaring through the clouds atop her guardian. Perhaps she *had* earned a day – just *one* day – off.

"Very well," she agreed, to her mother's evident satisfaction. "One day."

She frowned as she looked again to Lilae, whose usually brilliant copper coat had dulled and darkened slightly from the strain of supporting Tau's efforts these last few days. The dragon needed the break just as much as she herself did.

"But first," she continued, gesturing to her tent, "a meal and a good night's rest!"

If you can wait that long, Love?

Of course. I am more drained than hungry – though in the morning, I will be famished.

In the morning you can gorge yourself to your heart's content, my dear.

Then I will wait. Go. Eat. Wash the blood from your skin and soak the soreness from your muscles. Sleep, and in the morning....

In the morning, we fly!

Tau inhaled deeply, eyes closed in bliss as she relished the scent of grass and open air. For the first time in months she caught not even a whiff of blood or a hint of the stench that accompanied thousands of bodies in close proximity.

She moved her arms up to cushion her head from the ground and smiled to herself as she enjoyed the sounds of nature. Those, too, had been missed amongst the cacophony of camp life.

The wind shifted, and she caught the smell of smoke and burning flesh. Moments later she heard

Lilae's teeth crunching through the bones of her prey. She sighed contentedly and cracked one eye to watch the high, white clouds crawl across the sky. She couldn't have asked for a more beautiful day.

The air stirred again, and Tau could hear the snap of Lilae's membranous wings as they worked to lift her skyward once again. This would be the dragon's fifth kill today. Usually three of the large deer she'd taken down already would have slaked the immense beast's hunger.

It has been too long since she has been able to hunt, Tau mused sadly. She had been kept so busy in the healers' tents lately that she hadn't had much chance to see to her dragon properly.

It's time for that to change, she decided. In truth, it was time for much to change. Time for this war to end. Time to stop the incessant fighting over territory or custom or belief or whatever other excuse might be raised to justify this petty conflict.

It is time for peace to become a reality, rather than a goal.

Tau had never been a terribly devout person; she knew Auriga existed, but while she said a prayer of thanks to Her every day for the gift of her guardian, she saw no reason to condemn those who worshiped differently. Ketral's followers had their own place in this world, she believed. Nature had a way of seeking and achieving balance and harmony through diversity. Humankind, on the other hand, tended to fight such instincts, striving constantly to expand their own power and influence rather than accepting the ways of others.

She sighed and rolled up onto her side to look northwest towards the site of their camp, too far away now for her to see. She was next in line to be Sennor's Queen's Mage; as soon as she was raised to Adept, she would share in even more of her father's duties until he was – hopefully – able to let her take the reins completely so that he could live out the remainder of his life in peaceful retirement. Not many Queen's Mages had that luxury.

And then there was Devali. For centuries, each nation had had its own Royal Mage; in each generation, a new apprentice was born to take over in his or her own time. But now, Devali's King's Mage, her own cousin Ramira, found herself aging rapidly with no apprentice of her own.

Tau frowned thoughtfully. This was not the first time such worries had occurred to her. More and more she found herself of the opinion that her status as the only Queen's (or King's) Mage apprentice meant something. Something important.

It is time *for this war to end. And, perhaps,* she continued the thought, *it is up to me to ensure that it does.*

Chapter 40

*T*au bit back her disappointment and inclined her head graciously to the Master healer who had arrived with the Devalians. The only one.

One Master, two Journeymen, and a handful of Apprentices to offset seven thousand new men – and we're already short-handed.

Any help was better than none, she supposed, but she couldn't help feeling this was more of a step backwards than anything. She had held out hope for an Adept, someone to whom she could surrender the burden of responsibility. Now the task she faced weighed more heavily than ever before.

"Well met, Master Eioghan. You and yours are a truly welcome sight. If you will please follow me, I will show you to the tents so that you can all settle in."

"If you please," the tall, thin man forestalled her, "I believe I speak for all of us when I say I would like to see what we are up against first. We … we had heard things here are rather grim."

Tau's lips thinned with worry as she glanced over her shoulder in the direction of the medical tents. She supposed grim was as good a word as any.

"We do everything we can, but we are all exhausted. We are grossly undermanned." She sighed and shook her head. "Very well; you may as well know what you're up against sooner, rather than later. Follow me."

"I need a splint!"

Tau swiped at the sweat and damp hair clinging to her forehead with the back of her arm, leaving a smear of blood in its place. She'd lost track of how long ago the injured had started coming in, but she'd been sharing Lilae's strength almost from the beginning. As a result, she was one of the only healers who had not already either collapsed from exhaustion or resorted to non-magical means of first aid.

The patient below her hands now had taken a heavy club to the thigh; his bone showed through the skin, a glistening, pearly white amidst all the blood. With help, she could set the bone to heal on its own, but he had lost too much blood to survive without at least a little healing.

When the splint arrived she called on a few of the Apprentices, many of whom had been wide-eyed with terror early on in the day. By now the horrors had been so many and lasted for so long that the formerly fresh-faced men and women no longer cringed away from her screaming, writhing patient.

"Hold him still. He's likely to pass out from the pain. Gayle, I need you to take his foot. On my word, pull as hard as you can so I have room to slide the bone in place. Everyone set? Pull!"

How can this be happening?
Despite the generals best efforts, this battle had come down to less of a carefully choreographed dance and more of a melee. The cavalry was useless

in such a situation; with no room to maneuver and no way of gaining the space or momentum to ride down the enemy, the mounted soldiers trapped below were being slaughtered.

The foot was scarcely faring any better. Somehow the rebels had managed to surround their forces, and now their superior numbers were meaningless.

Ramiq, this is out of hand. If you have something up your sleeve, now is the time to use it!

Tsuga sensed her husband's wordless agreement — no doubt he was too focused on his own task to spare her more attention than that — but she couldn't bear to sit by and watch her men and women die any longer.

She had a small force with her here on the rise, some hundred mixed mounted and foot soldiers, as well as a few relay messengers and a banner man. Her other high-ranking officers were scattered at other similar vantage points about the perimeter to ensure that no one targeted attack could devastate the leadership of their forces.

In that split second, Tsuga reached a decision. If she led a charge, the force of their cavalry might be enough to punch through the attackers' line. Her infantry would be close behind to hold the gap. If they could open a route out of this trap and gain themselves some space to breathe, their superior numbers would shortly begin to tell.

"Lyle!"

"General?"

"Raise that banner high. Guard, with me. We ride!"

Spurs dug into flanks at her words, but her Bane, her guardian, lunged forward at Tsuga's thought.

Together they led the charge that was their last desperate hope to turn the tide of this battle.

Ramiq winced as another of his mages gave way to exhaustion.

"Move him out of harm's way," he ordered absently, mentally taking stock of what remained of their magical forces. Their losses were negligible in comparison to the staggering number of lives being extinguished among the common soldiers below, as most of his casualties fell to fatigue rather than the blow of a weapon. Still, their numbers were few enough already that each man who fell took a staggering toll.

Tsuga's plea for help came at a time when he was scarcely in a position to give it. He could see as well as anyone that the tide of the battle had turned against them, but the few mages the enemy had on hand were fighting wisely, causing his own fellows to resort largely to defensive measures in order to save what lives they could.

They're too grouped, he groused to himself, scowling down at the chaos below. The tight knot of fighting provided an easy target for attack; few of the rebel soldiers were very far inside that throng. Their mages could hurl simple, low-energy attacks into the midst of the loyalist troops and wreak havoc almost at will. Well, they could have, had it not been for the efforts of Ramiq and his compatriots.

Together they strove to block, divert, and dispel these attacks. But despite their best efforts, it took more energy to counter these simple but devastating assaults than to form them, and his fellows were falling to fatigue one by one.

In the process of diverting one such attack, Ramiq couldn't answer his wife's request right away. A few moments later he let out a cry of fear as he saw her banner rise and fall in the signal to charge. He could do nothing but watch as she led her small guard in an advance down the slope towards the battle.

"Tsu, no!"

Tau stiffened as the soldier's scream of agony merged with another cry that battered at her mind at the same moment.

"Daddy?"

The word was scarcely a whisper, but she could feel his fear as though it were her own. Something had him so terrified he could scarcely move. Something to do with her mother.

Worried, Tau shook off her paralysis and moved aside so the Apprentices could step in to splint the man's leg. She'd done for him what she could; with luck, he'd live.

A quick glance around the tent showed a momentary lull in the chaos. That could only mean the flow of wounded had been stemmed. What concerned her was *why*. Fretful, she stepped out of the way and leaned against an empty shelf – one that only hours ago had been filled with medicinals and clean bandages.

Lilae?

The two had always shared a bond that went beyond words, and without her having to ask the great copper dragon uncoiled herself from where she lay close at hand, lending her partner strength, and took to the skies.

Once at a safe altitude she circled back to make a pass high above the battlefield, sharing her eyes with Tau so both could see what was happening below.

Tau frowned. It was as she'd feared. Their forces had been surrounded; the influx of wounded had slowed because there was no way for them to flee the field of battle.

What's that?!

Lilae's head swiveled, and she focused on the movement that had captured Tau's attention. Her chest constricted at the sight, and she knew then what had so terrified her father. That was her mother's banner charging down the slope, right towards the enemy's line.

She broke the connection with her guardian and shook her head as she readjusted to her human body and sight. For that brief moment, she hadn't simply seen through Lilae's eyes; she had *been* the dragon. It seemed strange, at first, to feel her arms at her sides instead of wings cupping the air. She took a deep breath to steady herself.

Her mother was an experienced warrior, and one of the best strategists there was. Though Tau feared for her, riding headlong into danger as she was, she had to trust that Tsuga knew what she was doing. She couldn't let fear paralyze her as it had her father. She had a job to do.

Chapter 41

As they charged towards the battle time seemed to slow, as it often did for Tsuga in such situations. Her senses sharpened until she was acutely aware of the snort of Devilsbane's breath, the bunching of the horse's muscles beneath her. The clamor of the battle faded to a dull roar, and her focus narrowed to the foes she now thundered towards.

Ramiq's cry of fear was felt and dismissed as she adjusted her grip on her sword and positioned her shield to protect her off side. That was all she had time for before their charge impacted the enemy's line.

She felt a brief surge of elation as she realized that they had taken their foes by surprise; the din of the battle had covered the sounds of their approach. Few men turned in time to meet the charge, and Tsuga's guard crashed into and shortly through them. By the time she had managed to swing Bane about in the milling throng, the foot soldiers had arrived to hold the gap.

It was too crowded here for her to hope for another charge; she scarcely had room to move, let alone build up any momentum. Grimly, she set about herself with her sword, hacking and slashing at anyone that came too near. Bane laid about them with tooth and hoof as Tsuga fought, the two becoming a team that dealt death everywhere they looked.

Once the encircling line had been broken, more of the trapped soldiers were able to join the few of her personal guard and gain the room to fight. The breach began to widen, and before long it was obvious that the tide of the battle had begun to turn.

Tsuga looked about herself for her banner; it was time for her to retreat before she suffered more than the few glancing blows she'd already taken. She and Bane both bled from a dozen minor wounds, and neither had any desire to take anything more serious today.

It was with a brief flash of alarm that she realized she had become separated from her men as she had fought her way through the milling throng.

Damn.

Grimly determined, Tsuga cast about for the best route of escape, almost absently cutting down a man that had come too close to crushing her kneecap with his mace. As he fell screaming, something about what she had been seeing all this time registered. She had been surrounded, cut off from any hope of assistance from her comrades.

Stupid. Of course her banner had been recognized. The enemy knew she'd been the one to break their line and rally her troops. She had been strategically maneuvered into isolation; all she saw around her now were faces of the enemy.

With a cry of despair, she embraced her magic and did that which she had sworn never to do again: she sent fire among her foes and used it to kill. Tears streamed down her face as the acrid stench of burning hair and leather mixed with the smell of roasting flesh and made her stomach turn.

"I'm sorry!" she screamed at them as she turned her ire on another. "I'm sorry!" She screamed it until her throat was raw and all she could manage was a hoarse croak. She nearly choked on the smoke she created, hating herself for what she did but unable to fight her own instincts of self-preservation.

Blinded by tears and smoke, she never saw the soldier behind her. Bane's shriek of agony was almost human as her belly was opened. Tsuga managed to tumble free before her guardian fell, but in the chaos she lost both sword and shield.

"BANE!"

She wasn't sure if her shriek of agony was verbal or mental, but the pain and despair ripping through her could only mean one thing: her guardian was dead. Devastated, Tsuga reached for more power, pulling more deeply at the currents that surged around her than she ever had before.

As she gave herself over to the primal urging of the fire, she sent out one final thought to Ramiq, who she now had to leave.

I'm sorry.

Chapter 42

$\mathcal{T}$au knew the moment her mother died. One minute her familiar presence was there in the back of her mind, waiting to offer comfort, and the next it was gone. She stopped where she stood, pausing in the midst of stitching an ugly gash across a woman's midsection as the realization staggered her. She was only granted that too-brief moment of recognition before a more pressing matter intruded on her stunned thoughts.

Daddy, NO!

She had always had a close mental and magical bond with both parents; they were never more than a thought away, and unless she actively shielded against them – which she seldom did – their presences had always sat in the back of her mind, much like a pale imitation of the guardian bond she shared with Lilae. Now that bond bucked and writhed in pain. Without hesitation Tau locked onto her father's mind, straining to hold him away from the twin dangers of suicidal grief and insanity.

Lilae! Help me!

A surge of strength pulsed into her at the request, and Tau bolstered herself with the dragon's support. Her hold steadied, and Tau reached out to touch her father's devastated mind.

Daddy?

She's gone, she's gone! Let me go! Let me follow her! I'll kill them; kill them all, just like they killed her!

Tau reeled from the alternating waves of murderous rage and crippling grief, but she held firmly to her sense of self. Lilae's anchoring presence helped.

You know she wouldn't want that. She died fighting for peace. *If you avenge her now, where does the killing stop?*

She felt despair wash over him then, all of the fight fleeing him at her words.

Then just let me go. Let me go to her.

You can't. Not yet.

She had expected ranting and raving in protest to her declaration, but instead all she felt was an intense frustrated longing.

Why?

This war is not over. The army needs you. Daddy... I need you. To finish my training. To guide me through this. I'm not ready to fill your shoes. If you go now, the world may never know peace. She wanted that; you know she did. Don't we owe her that much? Don't you owe it to her to at least try?

She felt the last of the resistance flow out of him then, leaving behind a shell full of little more than despair. Tau's heart ached for him, as well as for her own loss. As she came back to herself, she realized that she had no time for such feelings. There was still a steady influx of wounds to close and soldiers to heal.

"Finish these stitches for me," she instructed as she passed her needle across the surgical table to the Apprentice who had been helping her. She wiped

her bloodied hands on the front of her equally stained apron as she turned to find a fellow Master.

"Something has happened. I must go to my father; I will return as soon as I can. No doubt he could do with a stint here, at this point."

When she received his acknowledgement, Tau braced herself against the exhaustion that pulled at her, thankful once again for the wonderful Goddess-sent gift of her Lilae, and teleported to her father's side.

From this vantage she could see the battle still going on below, though it looked to be all but decided in their favor, now that the rebel line had been broken.

She did it.

Tau looked down to her father where he knelt before her, a crumpled heap devoid of any will to live. She sobbed, feeling the tears close off her throat, and fell to her knees beside him, pulling him into her embrace.

Chapter 43

In the months since her mother's death, life had grown increasingly more hectic for Tau. While she had been able to relinquish the duties of running and coordinating the healers' tents, they were still short-handed, and so she continued to work long hours knitting bones and sewing flesh. In addition to these already-strenuous duties she had also taken on increasingly more of her father's responsibilities – partly as part of her training, but largely because he simply no longer had the will to see to them himself.

He was not doing well. Tsuga's death had been hard on him, as Tau had known it would be. It was as though all the vitality had fled him, leaving behind a husk of a man who only went through the motions of living without really being present in his own life.

Pain Tau had been prepared for. She knew how to comfort sadness, how to coax joy from long-forgotten moments. But this blankness, this utter lack of emotion was beyond even her strong empathic gifts.

It was not uncommon, lately, for her to swing between self-loathing for the selfishness of keeping him here and anger at him for not trying harder. Both helped to distract her from the truth of her feelings: fear. Fear that she wasn't ready. That she would fail.

Fear that she would disappoint everyone who counted on her.

It was only times like this, when she lay alone in her tent in the stillness of night and tried to persuade herself to sleep, that the fear crept in to strangle her and squeeze her heart.

Lilae?

She reached out to the dragon mentally, seeking the stoic comfort of her oldest friend.

I am here.

Tau sighed as the pressure in her chest lessened and rolled onto her stomach on the cot, seeking a more comfortable position.

What if I can't do this?

Her guardian was the only one to whom Tau felt safe voicing her worries now that the support system of her parents had been lost. Lilae always seemed to know just what to say.

You are only human. You will do your best, and that will be enough.

But what if it isn't?

It will have to be. Even you cannot do better than your best.

Tau felt a strained smile tug at the corners of her lips at those words. The dragon saw things simply. Often, that simple outlook was exactly what Tau needed to help put things in perspective.

No, I suppose I can't.

Still worried but feeling somewhat comforted, Tau lifted her head to adjust her pillow and then burrowed further under her thin blanket. Before long exhaustion got the better of her and dragged her down into the realm of sleep.

Tau stood in the small audience chamber, alone save for the pair of guards on both doors, and brushed her hands nervously down the front of her multihued mage's robes. They were some of her best, but still she felt under-dressed for such an occasion as this.

Her father had always taken care of delivering the reports in person; this would be her first time taking on this particular duty.

You look fine.

Tau sighed and fought down the urge to adjust the fall of her overcoat yet again. Lilae awaited her outside, once again atop "her" tower in the Devalian castle. She had brought the guardian with her, despite being able to teleport herself alone with far less effort. She needed the dragon's steadying presence today.

There was no fanfare announcing the approach of any notables; the sound of voices was the first warning she had of their presence. She turned to greet them with a nervous smile and bowed, the tight braid twisted about the crown of her head pulling slightly with the shift in position.

"Rise, my dear."

The deep, rich voice unsettled her, and Tau straightened quickly and clasped her hands behind herself to keep from running them down the front of her forest green trousers.

The man who stood before her was tall and well-built, neither lanky nor too heavily muscled. His salt-and-pepper beard was trimmed close to his jaw line, and striking blue eyes looked out at her from above a well-proportioned nose. It was only belatedly that she registered the crown perched atop his graying hair.

"Your Majesty."

Arrayed behind him, she spied several faces she recognized – and a few she didn't. She surmised the strangers to be his military leaders by the stripes of rank they wore. She had met most of the country's nobles and court mages during her year in residence here. Ramira stood just behind the king to his right, and to his left –

Xan.

Her breath caught, and her heart hammered more loudly in her chest. She hadn't allowed herself to hope that he might attend today's meeting.

He offered her an encouraging smile, and she hastily inclined her head to both him and her cousin in turn.

"Prince Xanthrall. King's Mage. It is good to see you both again."

The king waved off the formalities and gestured for the guards to close the door through which they had entered.

"Let us get straight to the business at hand, Lady Dafrin. I have received reports that your father is not doing well after the general's death. I presume that is the explanation for your presence here today?"

Tau inclined her head in acknowledgement, firmly stamping down the anger that threatened at his callous words. Such emotions would do her no good, here.

"Yes, Majesty. He is … not himself. I have been standing in for him more and more lately in preparation to step into the role of Queen's Mage.

"Apologies, Sire, but if you truly wish to get down to the business of the day, it seems to me that discussions of my father's condition are less than pertinent."

Several of the nobles made sounds of protest at her audacity, but she caught the quick grin on Xanthrall's face and the gleam in Ramira's eye. The king considered her briefly, his expression unreadable, and then nodded to her briskly.

"Right you are. Come, then; tell us of how things stand at the front."

Chapter 44

Tau stood next to Lilae, resting her forehead against the smooth warmth of the dragon's side. She took a deep breath, inhaling the comforting scents of sunbaked stone and spice that were so distinctly draconic. Her shoulders slumped with relief; she had survived her first debriefing in front of Devali's most powerful men. Somehow, the same meetings with the Sennorran war councils had never been quite so intimidating.

We have company.

Tau started and drew herself back up to a proud posture as she stepped away from her guardian and turned to face the intruder.

Xan cleared his throat and offered a stiff bow – first to her, and then a lower obeisance to Lilae.

"Lady Dafrin. Lady Lilae."

Tau returned the courtesy stiffly.

"Highness."

They looked at each other for another tense moment, and then Xan broke into a grin and strode quickly to close the distance between them and embrace her.

"You were splendid in there."

Tau sighed and relaxed against him, a sense of relief washing over her as she registered the sincere fondness in his voice.

"Do you really think so? I was so nervous!"

Xan laughed; she could feel the sound vibrate up through his chest from where her head rested against it.

"I thought the advisors might have choked on their own tongues when you put Father in his place –" Tau winced, and Xan's arms tightened around her waist "– but you were right to do so. He was testing your mettle."

Tau sniffed and pulled back slightly to give him a suspicious look.

"Because I'm a woman?"

"Because you're new." He waited until she had settled against him once more before adding, "And because you're a woman."

She pushed him away in mock-irritation and sniffed disdainfully.

"And how did the king find my mettle, then?"

Xan grinned at her, his gray eyes dark with emotion as he watched her movements.

"He was impressed – as I knew he would be." He moved closer once more to gather her against him, his hands resting on her hips. "As I have been, from the very first moment I saw you."

Tau flushed with pleasure at his words, and when he moved to kiss her she did not resist. She was breathless by the time they separated, and she lay her head against his shoulder, not yet ready to break their embrace. After several long moments, Xan broke the silence.

"So you have spent the morning speaking of how the army fares, how the supplies hold out, and what the outlook of this war may be." He paused. "But how are you? You have lost your mother. Reports say that you have all but lost your father. None of this can be easy on you. How are you holding up, Tau?"

She took a shaky breath, suddenly emotional at his words. She had to blink away tears before she could clear her throat enough to answer him with anything but a sob.

"It's hard – really hard. I've been so busy taking care of him and carrying out his duties that I haven't even had time to mourn my own mother."

She choked on the last words, and now the tears did fall, hot against her skin. Xanthrall didn't say anything, but his arm tightened around her and one hand moved up to stroke her back.

"She's gone, Xan. She's been there my whole life, always waiting to offer advice or support. And now she's not."

She swallowed loudly, the task made more difficult by the hard lump of emotion in her throat. Now that this outpouring had finally begun, it seemed disinclined to stop until it had run its course.

"And now I don't even have Da for support. Maybe I should have just let him go with her, like he wanted. He's not himself anymore. The most life he ever shows is when he's teaching me, and even then I know it's because he wants me ready so I'll let him follow her."

The words, once started, tumbled out of her, many of them lost in the sounds of her tears.

"I'm so afraid, Xan. Afraid I can't do this by myself. I'm not ready. Look at me! I'm just a girl; how am I supposed to advise a queen and help rule a country?"

Xan lifted one hand to produce a handkerchief with which he dabbed her tears. After a moment he lifted her chin until her eyes rose to search his face.

"I *am* looking at you, Tau, but I don't see 'just a girl.' I see a beautiful, talented, capable woman. You have been through a lot these last months, but you are still here, still fighting. And I *know* you. You'll never stop fighting, stop trying. That's who you *are*. Who your parents raised you to be. They may not be able to say it now, but I know they're proud of you."

Tau managed a watery smile, but a moment later she broke down again, the sobs returning with a vengeance. He held her a long while, eventually moving with her to pull her down beside him to lean back against the warmth and comfort of Lilae's soft belly.

At length her sobs subsided and her tears dried. She suspected she had simply cried them all out. When she pulled back from him and lifted the cloth he'd given her to wipe her face and swipe at her stuffed nose she noticed her eyes felt swollen, her cheeks raw. She managed a weak laugh.

"I must look a mess."

Xan smiled and held out an arm to her, pulling her back to nestle against him.

"You look as though a weight has been lifted."

She took a deep breath – through her mouth; she doubted she could get any air at all through her nose just now – and nodded slowly. She did indeed feel lighter than she had in a very long time.

There was a long pause, during which Tau watched the last sliver of sun sink below the horizon. She should have returned to the front hours ago, but somehow she couldn't bring herself to feel guilty for the stolen moments here atop the roof.

"She was a hero, you know."

Her voice was soft. When Xan shifted she knew even without craning her neck to look up at him he must be considering her profile where she sat cradled against him.

"All we were told was that she died in battle. Do you know what happened?"

Tau closed her eyes against the twinge of pain the memory brought, but she nodded.

"I didn't see the whole thing; I was in the tents. But I saw enough."

As she spoke the pressure in her chest began to loosen, and she found a sense of relief in sharing with him the pride and awe she held for her mother's final acts of heroism.

"The rebels had us surrounded. She led her personal guard in a charge to break their line." Tau shook her head, remembering the image she'd seen of her mother's banner clashing with the enemy forces. It was the last glimpse of her she would ever have.

"She succeeded. Because of her, the rebels were driven back and countless lives were saved. But not before...." She trailed off, unable to finish the thought.

Xan leaned forward to give her a kiss atop her head, and Tau sighed.

"She was a spectacular woman. Just like her daughter."

Tau managed a sad smile and leaned back against the joint support of the prince and her guardian to

watch as the evening's first stars began to shine. She really should be getting back to the front....

Just a few more minutes, she determined. After all, she'd already been gone this long. *Just a while more before I have to go back to it all....*

The camp below them was quiet, only the occasional guard moving about amongst the tents. Here and there torches dotted the darkness with their pinpricks of light. Tau sighed, enjoying a last few moments of peace before she asked Lilae to descend.

Chapter 45

There had been a time when mage lessons with her father had been the highlight of Tau's whole day. They had always shared a love for magic, and exploring it together had been a joy. She longed for those times now with a sense of nostalgia.

These days her lessons were a painful chore. There was no joy in her father's eyes when he explained the intricacies of a new technique, no pride swelling his chest when she successfully mastered a new skill. She still progressed, but she missed the way things had been before.

"Now, weather manipulation of any sizeable scale would normally take several mages working together. Even powerful weather mages have a limited scope when working above. Most are not powerful enough to affect an area larger than a small village. However, as a Queen's Mage you have the ability to accomplish this on your own. Weather magic is taught as a skill in and of itself, but in reality it is merely a combination of several abilities used in the correct proportions.

"Water and air in the right combination will create clouds. Add in enough static charge, and you make lightning. Increase water by the right amount for rain; tweak the temperature with ice magic and tease the wind for sleet, hail, or snow. The right balance of cool air and warm water creates fog, and so forth."

Tau nodded, sighing heavily at the monotone that once would have been lively and animated when discussing this topic. She knew all of this in theory already, but today would be her first time to attempt an actual change in the weather.

"Weather magic is very finicky, and a small change here could cause massive disruptions elsewhere. For that reason, it is best to only push what is already building, or to set a small change in motion that will affect your end result and let nature take its course."

He tilted his head back to squint up at the sky, and Tau's gaze lifted as well to consider the patchy cloud cover. The formations had the towering, ominous look of building thunderheads.

"Normally, those clouds would take at least until tonight to build to anything significant, but they *are* supposed to let loose on us by morning. Let's see if you can't help them along."

Tau nodded and took a deep breath as she reached for the power that always hovered at her fingertips, ready to be taken up again. When she fell into mage sight, the power behind the slowly-building storm became evident.

She began by building upon the existing clouds, feeding them with water until they darkened ominously. Next she teased the tension in the air, charging it until her hair prickled and her skin tingled with the static. The first crack of lightning and its accompanying thunderous boom almost took her by surprise. She pulled on the wind, cooling the air and whipping the trees with its passing.

The next crack of lightning came of its own accord, and a few moments later she felt the first drop of cool rain kiss her cheek. Before long the scattering of droplets became an outright downpour.

Tau released her magic and threw back her head, mouth open and eyes closed, to enjoy the fruits of her labor.

"Well! I was sure that storm wasn't meant to blow in until tonight!"

Tau's eyes popped open at the new voice and she whirled quickly to find Ramira carefully picking her way across the rapidly-muddying clearing.

"Cousin Ramira!"

The older mage smiled and reached up one hand to swipe dripping hair aside.

"Hello, child! I see you've been witching the weather."

Tau flushed slightly. "Only learning."

"Well, I'd say you've done an admirable job with this rainstorm!"

Tau laughed, and startled when her father spoke from immediately behind her; she hadn't heard him approach.

"Tau, why don't you invite the King's Mage in out of the rain? Our lesson is over for the day, at any rate."

Tau inclined her head in acknowledgement, suddenly a great deal sobered.

"Yes, Daddy. Lady, if you will follow me?"

There had been a time – not all that long ago, in truth – when Tau might have simply removed the water from their hair and clothes magically, but not anymore. She handed Ramira a towel and a clean set of her own robes and showed her where to change while she did the same. Energy – both the magical and the physical – was a precious commodity to her these days, and she had come to appreciate all too keenly that a magical indulgence now could mean one less life saved later.

When Ramira returned, damp hair wrapped in the towel much like Tau's own mane, the two embraced briefly.

"Not that I am not happy to see you, Cousin, but why are you here?"

Ramira smiled as the two separated, and Tau gestured for her to sit while she moved a kettle to the fire to boil some water for tea before moving to join her.

"Your father sent for me."

Tau felt her eyebrows raise in surprise. "Oh?"

The King's Mage nodded. "He tells me you will soon be ready to test for Adept – by Sennorran standards, that is, which I now realize are quite different than what I am used to."

Tau felt her stomach clench uncomfortably at this pronouncement. She wasn't quite sure how to feel about this news. On the one hand, she was proud and excited to be so close to the culmination of all her efforts at last. On the other….

"Then he will go."

She sighed. That had been their deal, after all. He had stayed to complete her training, but once she was raised to Adept and had officially taken up the mantle of Queen's Mage there would be nothing left to hold him here. She would be on her own.

Not so long as I am here.

Tau smiled weakly at Lilae's staunch declaration. The dragon could always tell when Tau most needed her simple words of encouragement.

"Yes, dear," Ramira responded quietly. "Then he will go."

Tau shook her head, confused and slightly resentful that she should have to share what might be her father's last few days with anyone, and frowned.

"So, if you'll pardon my bluntness…. Why are you here, Ramira? This is a Sennorran affair, after all."

She could see a muscle in her cousin's cheek twitch as the older woman clenched and unclenched her jaw, but when she spoke Ramira's voice was surprisingly gentle.

"Your father and I have discussed this at length, Tau. You are linked to both of us – to both lands – both magically and by blood. We believe that Ketral has not sent me a new apprentice for a reason. That reason is you."

Distracted from her resentment, Tau's gaze sharpened and she sat a little straighter in her chair. She had long suspected something like this, but to hear her own private theory voiced by her older, wiser cousin made it suddenly much more real.

"Me?"

Ramira nodded. "Yes, child. Our nations are on the cusp of peace for the first time in generations. It cannot be a coincidence that you were born into the position you were, the family you were. It is our belief, Tau, that you were born to be the first Royal Mage in two hundred years."

Tau took in and then released a deep breath, almost dizzy with the weight of responsibility. A few things suddenly came clear to her as she took in her mentor's words.

"That is why he wished me to train with you in the first place – and why you're here now, isn't it? He wants me raised to Adept by both countries' standards, so that when you…. I mean…." She stumbled to an awkward stop, flushing uncomfortably. Ramira continued for her, unperturbed.

"So that when I die, there will be one less obstacle to your taking on the role you were born to play."

Tau jumped when, at that moment, the kettle let loose with a shrill whistle. She rose, a trifle unsteady, and moved to pull it from the fire.

"Tea?"

Chapter 46

*T*au had lain awake much of that first night after Ramira's arrival, mulling over the information the King's Mage had given her. Royal Mage had become an archaic title, one few had ever thought to see revived – until now, it seemed.

Tau had always known that as the future Queen's Mage her life would not be her own to live. She must go where the queen directed, attend diplomatic and political conferences, and live her life completely exposed to the public eye. A Royal Mage's life would not be far different, she supposed.

She sighed as she strode towards the field they had set aside for their daily mage lessons, the dew from the tall grass dampening the lower inches of her robes. Ramira had warned her that according to Devalian tradition, she could not be told for certain when her test would occur. To ensure no added precautions were taken, the time of the exam must come as a surprise.

Hopefully it will not be today, she mused, feeling the strain behind her eyes that was only one effect of her long and restless night. The attacks had slowed lately, and for the first time in nearly a year they had actually been able to begin a pursuit of their antagonists, rather than awaiting the next attack. With any luck, the rebels would soon be routed.

This possibility, of course, presented them with a whole new set of complications. Until now their main camp had been stationary, a semi-permanent arrangement. Many of the soldiers had even created rough wooden dwellings that were better comfort than the standard issue oiled canvas tents. If the rebels were driven out, the unified forces would have to pursue them to be sure this rebellion was ended once and for all. Which meant moving the wounded.

As her mind mulled over the logistics of executing such a move, Tau's strides drew her within sight of her destination, where both Adepts watched her approach. She came to a halt a few feet away and inclined her head respectfully to both of them.

"Adept Nevarn. Adept Dafrin."

"Master Dafrin," they answered together. There were a few beats of silence, then her father spoke up in the lecturing monotone he so often used in their lessons these days.

"You are familiar with the standards for being raised to the rank of Adept in Sennor. You have already achieved many of them. It is time now for your final test. After much discussion with Ramira about the Devalian customs, we have agreed upon a single trial that will fulfill both of our nations' requirements."

Ramira nodded as Tau groaned inwardly at the prospect of having to undergo such a trial after the restless night she'd had. She hastily brought her focus back to the present when Ramira picked up speaking where Ramiq had left off.

"Sennorran queens depend on their Mages for counsel and to act as an extension of their authority.

Because magic runs so strongly in the Sennorran bloodlines it is rare for a queen to require specialized magical protection; most can maintain a base level of defense on their own.

"The Devalian line, however, is far less prone to magically strong monarchs. Our mages are taught to wage war, and so many are lost at a young age, just as our soldiers are. The primary duty of a King's Mage is to act as a sort of magical bodyguard, a last line of defense for the king. As such, it is vital that a King's Mage be proficient in both defensive and combative magicks."

"Because the test for a Sennoran Adept consists largely of a demonstration of judgement, quick thinking, and endurance through a display of proficiency with more advanced skills," her father picked up, "and the Devalian standard requires much the same in addition to a show of combative prowess, we have determined that the best way to let you prove your abilities is through a mage battle."

Tau inhaled sharply as she felt her stomach turn over nervously. She had never been in a mage battle; the closest she had come had been when she'd helped with the shielding during that long-ago attack on the fort.

"And who will be my opponent?" she managed to ask past the hard knot of nerves that threatened to choke off her words.

The two Adepts exchanged a look before returning their attention to her.

"We will."

Before Tau had time to absorb this revelation, she found herself under attack from two directions at

once. Ramira buffeted her with a howling wind that tore at her clothes as it spun around her and shredded her shields, slicing through her defenses like a thousand shards of glass through her skin.

She cried out in pain as the magical backlash of her destroyed shielding began to buffet her and reached for her magic, trying desperately to erect new ones – only to have them ripped away before they could be completed.

Meanwhile, as Tau strove to regain her footing in the battle against Ramira, she felt the air around her harden until she was locked into place, unable to move. Frantic, she tossed her head, tensing against the restrictions, and darted her gaze back and forth between the two mages.

Air. They were both attacking her with variations of air. Tau closed her eyes and took a deep breath, slowly in, slowly out, focusing on the feeling of her lungs expanding and contracting as she did so. When she opened her eyes she turned her attention to the onslaught from her cousin.

Ramiq had taught her about mobile shields and how to tie them to something other than the ground years ago. Devalians were limited in their thinking, that way; everything had to be anchored. She took another slow breath and quickly wove a shield centered only on herself, rather than one tied into the flows of power around her. As she had known it would, it caught in the magical wind and began to rotate, spinning ever faster as the mini tornado revolved around her, the motion only serving to make its protection more effective.

Now safe from this onslaught, Tau shifted her attention to her father's attack. An elemental mage had to learn to embrace nature, to be able to take its fury and stand untouched by it. Tau took in another deep breath, flexing her magical will as she did so, and then exhaled, puckering her lips and forming the air into an edge with which she severed the bonds that held her.

She shrugged her shoulders as though freeing herself from a physical restraint and gathered her own attack, lashing out furiously and thinning the air around both mages, moving it away from them until the deprivation should have made their vision swim.

With an audible *pop* her pressurized bubble burst, and then Tau found herself blinded by a strike of lightning that exploded only inches in front of her. Her ears rang from the clap of the accompanying thunder as she leapt back with a startled cry she couldn't hear and attempted to blink away the after-image – to no avail. Her eyes watered unmercifully from the flash, and in exasperation she closed them, stretching both her magical and physical senses to their fullest the way her mother had taught her.

The pressure of the air changed, and Tau felt power building around her. Just before it reached its peak she lashed out and diverted it, forming a magical conduit to carry the attack away from her. Seconds later the ground shook as a second bolt of lightning – she recognized its power, even if she could neither see nor hear it – struck somewhere to her right, peppering her with the debris from its impact.

This time she went on the offensive, calling on the power that ran beneath their very feet. The earth began to tremble, and then to shake.

Tau wasn't sure at what point she had been driven to her knees by the constant barrage of attacks, but despite her beaten and battered state, she fought on. Still deaf and blind from the lightning strike, she had learned quickly to adapt to her handicaps, stretching her other senses in ways she'd never dreamed possible.

Unable to see the flow of magic, she found that she could *feel* its ebb and flow as though she stood in a river and felt its currents swirl around her. She found also that many magicks had a distinct smell – the odors of fire and water would have been obvious even to a child, but Tau found the sharp scent of metal and the dryer smell of stone accompanied many earth magicks. When someone – she could no longer differentiate which attack came from whom – sent a flock of crows swooping down to peck at her and slash at arms and face, Tau could smell them coming and feel the movement of the air beneath their wings.

She wove light and air around herself to create an illusion of empty space. A few of the birds hit her, flying blindly, but most passed over or around her in confusion. With a simple use of her animal mindspeech, the flock was dispelled.

Tau no longer hand any sense of how much time had passed. So far she had been frozen, incinerated, half-drowned, and buried to her waist in a ground that became like quicksand beneath her very feet. She was scratched, bruised, and bleeding from a dozen small – and not-so-small – cuts all over her body. She felt her hands shake with fatigue as she lashed out with a bolt of raw mental energy – a desperate move that would temporarily (or permanently, if done with more force) stupefy her opponents.

The attack was rebuffed, and Tau cried out in pain and frustration as the power rebounded on her, thankfully buffered somewhat by what remained of her fractured shields.

She knelt there in the fire-baked muck, chest heaving as she gasped for breath, and waited for the next onslaught. Her entire body trembled with fatigue; she could no longer muster the energy to think beyond her own defense to attack.

She waited – for how long, she didn't know – but nothing happened. At length she felt a cool, gentle hand on her forehead, and then her vision began to clear. As her sight returned Tau looked around herself, distantly noting that the ringing in her ears had faded and been replaced by an almost deafening silence.

When the healer – the Master who had arrived with the Devalians, she realized – moved away, Tau was able at last to see past him and look around what had not long ago been a peaceful clearing.

The ground was scorched in several places from explosions; a single long furrow of smoking and tortured earth marked where her diverted bolt of lightning had struck. Here and there were puddles of dirty water. There were the charred remains of the vines she had grown to bind her opponents' hands; in several places the earth was torn, as though the very rock beneath their feet had exploded – which it had, thanks to someone's wielding of the volatile battle magic. Not a blade of grass stood untouched for as far as she could see, and even a few of the distant trees looked as though they had simply exploded.

Tau shuddered at the sight of so much destruction, briefly closing her eyes against the horror of it. She devoutly hoped she would never have to partake in such a battle again.

When she opened her eyes she spotted two more healers helping Ramiq and Ramira – both as bloody and battered as she herself no doubt still was – to their feet. She struggled upright as well, swaying a bit as her vision swam with the sudden change in altitude, then made her slow way over to her mentors. She respectfully inclined her head to each of them, then took a deep breath and looked up to meet their stares.

Ramira grimaced as she tried putting weight on her left foot and promptly shifted off of it. From the rubble in her father's hair, she would almost have thought he'd climbed out from a collapsed building. Both regarded her coolly for a long moment, during which Tau's stomach clenched painfully – though whether from nerves or hunger, she could not have said.

Finally, Ramira's expression warmed and the King's Mage broke into a wide grin. Ramiq even mustered a ghost of a smile – the first she could remember seeing him wear since her mother's death a year ago.

"You have done well, Tau." Was that a hint of pride in his voice, or only her own imagination, fueled by her longing to hear it there? Ramira nodded approvingly.

"Indeed you have. I declare myself satisfied. What do you think, Ramiq?"

Her father nodded, his eyes glistening with unshed tears. Tau's heart lurched to see him display so much emotion after all the time he'd spent walking about like a ghost of himself. She had all but given up on his ever truly *seeing* her again.

"I agree." Solemnly, each reached out to grasp one of her arms and intoned together, "Tau Dafrin, it is our honor to name you now Adept. Congratulations."

Chapter 47

*T*au examined her reflection in the tall looking glass, her eyes lingering on the large bruise on her cheek that had finally begun to fade to a sickly-looking green-yellow. At least it wasn't nearly black, as it had been two weeks ago.

She sighed, running her hands nervously down the front of her bodice before clutching them in her skirts. She wore a hyper-feminized version of traditional Sennorran mages' robes, with a tucked-in waist and long, flowing skirts covered by a sheer, billowy robe – nothing like the modified versions she'd come to favor. The colors were an intentional combination of the national colors of each country: a filmy black robe with silver trim over a gold bodice and white skirt, the latter embroidered in a flowing pattern with thread-of-gold. Her long hair, glowing with auburn undertones in the sunlight streaming through the window, had been swept into an intricate up-do, and the dagger that held her mage stone hung from the white sash wrapped about her slender waist.

I look tired, she decided, taking in the pinched cheeks and dark circles under her eyes. *But strong,* she amended as she took note of the set of her jaw and the lift of her chin.

She *was* tired, in truth. This war had taken its toll on all of them for far too long. Even had she not lain awake most nights fretting over her future or mourning the upcoming loss of her father she would have been strained and exhausted – and looked it.

She turned from the looking glass with a sigh at the knock on her door and strode across the plush carpet covering the stones beneath her feet to open it.

"Yes?" It was a servant she didn't recognize – though that was hardly surprising, as this was her first visit to this particular border castle. The location for today's ceremony had been carefully chosen to help foster unity between the two countries; they had settled on one of the long-disputed structures that skirted the Dubai Plains. It had changed hands countless times over the course of this war, but for the last decade or so had stood abandoned.

After a thorough cleaning and airing out the place had been refurnished and decorated, and though the elegant old architecture still showed the scars of the many battles it had played host to, it was undeniably grand.

"Adept Dafrin, I was sent to summon you to the ceremony. It is set to commence shortly."

Tau inclined her head gracefully and gestured for the young woman to precede her down the long, straight hallway. She did so only after a second curtsy, her strides so hurried that Tau found herself having to step lively to keep pace.

A spiraling staircase and another long, straight hallway later, her guide stopped in front of a tall oak door with heavy ornamental ironwork. Tau arched an eyebrow in question.

"This doesn't look like the grand audience chamber."

The servant curtsied again; Tau stifled her impatience with the overly formal gesture as the woman shook her head.

"No, Lady. This is one of the council rooms. I was told to escort you here."

Tau nodded and moved forward to open the door, but the other woman beat her to it, hastily pulling the heavy wooden structure aside with yet another unnecessary bending of her knees. Tau fought down a sigh and swept past her with a nod of thanks. Once inside, the door closed behind her.

Before her, Tau saw two faces she had expected to see – her father and cousin – and two she had not. She politely dipped a shallow curtsy to the king of Devali and her own country's queen, all that was required to show them homage from someone of her current station. After today's ceremony, that curtsy would be reduced to a mere bending of her neck, but that was to come later.

"Your Majesties."

Sennorra smiled warmly at her.

"You will shortly be raised to Queen's Mage, young lady. In private I am only Sennorra, if you please."

Tau flushed slightly and inclined her head in acknowledgement of the gesture.

"You honor me, Sennorra."

"Tau," Ramira broke in, "we summoned you here prior to the ceremony for a reason. There is something we would have you know before it begins."

"Oh?" Tau's gaze swept across the four faces before her, but none of them so much as hinted at what was coming. Ramira went on.

"We all know that after today, your father will have stepped down as Queen's Mage. You also know that I have never found an apprentice of my own. Due to these … unusual circumstances in which we now find ourselves, it has become obvious that some concessions need to be made, some changes to our traditional way of doing things."

Tau nodded. She had long known that uniting their two peoples would require a great many changes in the way things were done. Ramira went on.

"Normally, a new Queen or King's Mage is raised only upon the death or retirement of her predecessor, and therefore has many years at the side of her mentor to observe and learn prior to shouldering the full responsibility of the role. With the situation with your father being what it is, we all feel that you should be provided with a bit of guidance as you navigate these new waters.

"There *will* come a day when you are sworn in as the first Royal Mage in over two centuries, but that day is not today. Instead you will take your rightful place as Queen's Mage and be appointed my successor, so that none may dispute my wishes for you. We will work in concert, as your father and I have been, so that I can help guide you when you may stumble. Does that suit you?"

Tau paused for a moment, taking in the faces of the others in the room, and then let out a long sigh of relief and nodded with a smile.

"It suits me quite well. I had been somewhat concerned, I will admit."

Ramira reached out to clasp her upper arms gently, a gesture of comfort, and Tau found that she had to fight back tears at the sudden sense of relief she felt.

The king moved forward then, and Tau shifted her attention to him.

"Take a few minutes to gather yourself. The ceremony is set to commence shortly."

Tau nodded and swiped at her eyes, taking a deep breath to steady her nerves.

I am here.

She smiled, gratefully reaching out to the steadfast, comforting presence of her guardian. With Lilae at her side, she knew she could face down any challenge.

The ceremony passed in a blur. Somehow she must have managed to say and do the right things, for she distinctly heard the queen intone, "People of Sennor, I present to you your Queen's Mage, Adept Tau Dafrin!"

As the crowd cheered her, Tau found her gaze drifting first to her father, who wore a sad little smile, and then to Xanthrall where he stood just behind and beside his own father. His smile was more reassuring, and she managed a shaky one in return.

How she made it through the celebratory feast Tau would never know, but at long last she found herself blessedly alone in her large, empty suite of rooms. She sank into one of the comfortably over-stuffed chairs beside the cold fireplace with a sigh and closed her eyes for a moment, drinking in the welcome silence.

The cacophony of the celebration had grated on her already-raw nerves, and she felt stretched thin from the strain of enduring the evening graciously. She had just begun to contemplate rising to ready herself for bed when a knock sounded at her door, so softly that had she not been in her little oasis of stillness she might never have heard it.

She sighed, wishing she could tell whoever was there to go away and leave her until morning, and rose tiredly. As she crossed to the door she stretched her mental senses, probing gently to get an idea of who her late-night visitor might be. Her step quickened; by the time she pulled the door open to reveal Xan standing in the dancing shadows of the torch-lit hallway she was smiling.

He was striking as always, his dark hair and pale skin accentuated by his gold-trimmed black ensemble. She ushered him inside, and as she closed the door softly behind him she felt his arms wrap around her waist from behind. His breath tickled her neck as he moved to rest his chin on her shoulder, and Tau let out a sigh of contentment and leaned back against him, enjoying his solid presence.

His breath smelled faintly of the wine he'd been drinking, but this close the odors of the feast which lingered on his clothes were overwhelmed by the spicy scent she had come to associate with him. His lips brushed her neck and Tau sighed again.

"I'm glad I found you still awake. I thought you might be tired."

Tau smiled slightly and nodded.

"I am. Exhausted, actually." She felt him begin to pull away from her and turned in his embrace, her skirts rustling softly with the movement as she reached up to drape her arms around his neck.

"But I am glad you're here."

His hands tightened on her waist again and she dipped her head to kiss him, relaxing her body further against his. When they separated Tau pulled away, bending to remove the dainty silver-and-gold slippers she'd worn with her gown.

The colors of the two countries' flags had blended beautifully, as she had known they would. She'd thought it a nice touch, in light of recent events. She wobbled slightly when she bent to remove the second shoe, and Xan reached out to grasp her arm supportively. She gave him an appreciative smile when she straightened.

"Thank you."

He nodded, and when Tau raised her gaze to meet his eyes she saw a heat burning there she had never seen before.

"Xan?" Her voice was hoarse, but he didn't answer her. Instead he moved to stand behind her again, and when his hands rose to her hair she closed her eyes and sighed in pleasure at the release of pressure that came as, one by one, he removed the pins holding the elaborate style in place.

Before long her hair tumbled free in a kinked brunette waterfall, brushing her lower back as he ran his hands through it against her scalp. She moaned in pleasure, closing her eyes as she reveled in the sensation. His hands slid down to her shoulders, and he turned her to face him.

She opened her eyes with a smile and looked down into his gaze for a long moment, taking in his hungry expression and the firmness of his grip on her. She wavered for a moment – but only a moment – before she closed the small distance between them and buried her hands in his hair to give him another kiss, this one longer and deeper. Her own need rose to match his, and her hands shook as she moved them down to unfasten his ridiculously ornate sword belt from around his waist.

She could feel Lilae silently withdraw, offering her the chance to experience this moment alone as she slid her hands under his tunic to touch his bare skin, so hot she thought briefly it must surely burn her.

He caught her lip between his teeth and she gasped in mingled pain and pleasure before he released her and turned her again to begin unlacing the back of her dress, pausing frequently to scatter kisses along her neck and across her bared shoulders. She heard him curse under his breath as he fumbled with the strings, but once he had it started the laces loosened quickly.

She turned again before he could slide the gown down over her shoulders and started on his trousers as he pulled his coat and tunic off over his head. He kicked out of his boots clumsily – this time it was her turn to steady him – and then the two stood for a moment, staring at each other.

Tau experienced a brief moment of doubt, fear and uncertainty warring with desire, but when he stepped forward to cup her face in his hands and kiss her more sweetly she felt the last of her hesitation dissolve.

The sensation of the gown's soft folds of fabric sliding against her skin as it fell to the floor was the last thing she registered clearly for a very long time.

Tau woke slowly, feeling groggily content. She was tired even after the extra hours of sleep, but felt more relaxed than she could remember being for a very long time. She turned her head on its pillow to look to where Xan lay beside her, sprawled and still sleeping deeply. No doubt he had imbibed a good deal of the strong wine last night.

She sighed contentedly, her jaw popping when it turned into a yawn, and rolled up onto her side to admire the musculature of his back as he breathed in and out rhythmically. She knew she should regret what they had done – he was the prince, and some day she would be his advisor – but she could not find it within herself to do so.

She reached out her free hand to stroke her fingertips lightly along the bare skin of his back, smiling to herself when he twitched under her touch and sighed with pleasure. When she lifted her gaze once more to look at his face she found his eyes open and a sleepy smile stretching his swollen lips.

"Good morning."

His voice was raspy with sleep, and Tau resisted the urge to wrinkle her nose at the rank stench of his breath; no doubt hers was just as bad.

"Good morning, indeed."

Her own voice was only slightly less hoarse, and Tau cleared her throat hastily when she realized how she must sound.

Afternoon, actually.

Tau flushed slightly at this correction from Lilae, briefly battling against a sense of guilt. So long on the front lines had made her unaccustomed to the luxuries of rest and quiet, but the rebels had been routed and she was no longer needed to oversee the magical forces there. Much of that army had been dispersed already, released to their normal duties. Only a small contingent had been left to finish rousting out the last of the rebellion's forces.

For the first time in a long while Tau had absolutely no reason to feel guilty over taking a bit of time for herself – though her choice of bedmate offered reason enough to feel contrite.

Her flush cleared as she looked at Xan, and her smile warmed as he stared back at her drowsily.

"Sleep well?" she asked him.

"Mm, once we finally went to sleep."

She chuckled slightly at that, stretching stiff and tired muscles beneath the plush comforter with a satisfied smirk. When she finished she realized he had rolled onto his side to face her, the hungry look back in his gray eyes. When he reached out to pull her to him she pretended to resist, arching an eyebrow at him coyly.

"Again?"

He growled softly in answer and pulled her to him, kissing her passionately. She smiled against him as he pulled back enough to mumble, "Again."

Chapter 48

The countryside was quiet, the only sounds those of the wind rustling through the sun-baked grasses of the plains and the buzzing of insects. Even the wildlife had fallen silent, thanks to the scent of dragon on the breeze.

The Dubai Plains were beautiful this time of year, the waist-high grasses bleached to a crisp amber and the sky above so startlingly blue that it made her heart ache with its beauty. Or perhaps it ached from the weight of the moment. The time she'd so dreaded was upon them at last. She turned to her father with tears in her eyes.

"You're certain this is what you want?"

Ramiq nodded, his expression more at peace than she had seen it … well, she couldn't recall ever seeing him so calm and relaxed before.

He looks as though he has finally laid down his burdens.

He has. She looked down with a smile as Lyra brushed against her legs and bent to scoop the red fox into her arms for a hug. **All but one.**

Me? Tau sighed at Lyra's sympathetic affirmative.

He needs to know you'll be alright.

Tau gave the fox a final stroke before putting her down, the tears at last spilling over as she stepped forward to pull her father into a tight embrace.

"I'm going to miss you, Daddy. All of you. Every single day." She pulled back with a wobbly smile, looking into eyes so like her own that the thought made her smile broaden. "But I'll be okay. You and Momma made sure of that."

They embraced again, and Tau closed her eyes against the pain when her heart constricted even as her father's arms tightened briefly around her.

"You have become a strong, beautiful young woman, Tau. Your mother was so proud of you. As am I."

Tau sobbed loudly as they stepped apart, reaching up absently to swipe at the hot, salty tears spilling from her eyes.

"Tell her hello for me, won't you? And that I miss her?"

Ramiq smiled at her and gestured to the empty plain around them. They weren't far from where her mother had fallen, but this section of the Plains had been untouched by recent bloodshed.

"She knows, my dear. She has been watching over you every day, waiting for time for me to join her. She is here with us now. Don't you feel her?"

Tau would have liked to let herself think that the sense of peace his words brought her had something to do with the presence of her dead mother, but she knew better. Her father's words were only that: words. A delusion he had held on to in order to bring himself comfort. She managed to nod, though, which seemed to satisfy him.

"Are you ready, then?"

Ramiq nodded.

"I have been ready for a very long time. But now, my child, I sense that *you* are ready at last. It is time."

Tau sobbed again as she took another step back and watched Ramiq – her teacher, her Daddy, and her friend – embrace his magic for the final time. She had known that he'd planned to end his life magically somehow, but when instead of pulling power into himself for one final, grand magical feat he instead plunged his consciousness into one of the deepest currents of old magic, she caught her breath in wonder.

She had been warned her entire life about the dangers of these ancient, powerful currents. They were not for human use; these were the sources from which dragons and other ancient races drew their life-force and what they manipulated with the natural ease of instinct to accomplish their own magical deeds.

But her father did not try to control this ancient power; instead, Tau watched in awe as he surrendered himself to it completely. Both he and Lyra began to glow, surrounded by so much raw magical energy that its effect was visible even to the naked eye. Before long they shone so brightly that she had to look away. There was a sound like a great sigh, something that seemed to come from the very earth, and a warm breeze lifted a few of her stray hairs as she opened her eyes and turned to look where her father had been.

She sobbed again, no longer able to manage even a tenuous show of composure, and dropped to her knees. He was gone.

Earth

The ability to manipulate elements found within the earth; i.e. dirt, rocks, etc. Most earth mages are stronger in one of the sub-categories than the others. It is not uncommon for an earth mage to be very strong in one of these categories and have no ability for the others. Earth mages tend to be most grounded in the past; some have been known to claim knowledge of long-distant history that no non-magical person could possibly possess.

Plants – The affinity for growing things, and the ability to accelerate growth and know instinctively which plants have what properties.

Metal – The affinity for metals or things containing metal ore, including location, manipulation, purification, and shaping. Metal mages make spectacular blacksmiths.

Stone/Gems – The affinity for gem stones. Most stone mages will be particularly sensitive to one particular stone, and can locate them by magical sense. They make excellent miners, and because they are able to tell if a stone is flawed with a mere glance, many also profit from becoming merchants.

Air

The ability to manipulate the air. Specific talents include creation of wind, the thickening or thinning of air, as to restrain someone or steal their breath, and a limited ability to levitate. Air mages are occasionally found to be acting as prophets or founders of new religions, using their ability to walk into the very air to manipulate people into following them. Air mages are most centered in the spiritual, and tend to have visions of possibilities rather than anything concrete or real. Many doomsday prophets have small talents in air magic they are unaware of, and are unable to properly interpret their visions.

Water

The ability to manipulate water. Specific talents include extracting water from the surrounding air, plants, or ground and the ability to move water magically. It is known that water mages can also manipulate the movements of people and animals against their will by using the water found in the body and blood, but this is generally frowned upon and seen as a very dark use of magic. Water mages are most focused on the present, and have been known to use the still surface of water to look at what is occurring elsewhere. Rulers often keep them close to use as advisors and spies.

Fire

The ability to create and manipulate fire, even without physical fuel. Often sought as mages for battle, they have a reputation for being destructive and violent, though some few of them manage to live peaceful lives using their talents for more mundane tasks. Fire mages are also notoriously lucky, and occasionally some will have premonitions of the future, though their visions tend to be clearer and more concrete than those of air mages.

Mind

The ability to use one's mind to manipulate the thoughts or feelings of others. Mind mages must walk a thin line between what is ethical and what is a gross misuse of their powers.

Mindspeech – The ability to speak into the minds and hear the thoughts of others. Many mindspeakers have gone insane before they have been found and taught how to use their abilities and shield themselves from the unwanted intrusion of the thoughts of others.

Empathy – An ability which can be either projective or receptive, empathy is the manipulation and sense of others' emotions. Empaths tend to be very in tune with the moods of those around them, and talented empaths are often kept close to a ruler to help them judge the intentions of those around them.

Animal Mindspeech – Less defined than its more common counterpart, animal mindspeech is the ability for a person to communicate mentally with animals. A bit of a misnomer, animal mindspeech rarely includes speech of any kind; rather, it is an ability for a person to interpret the thoughts of an animal, usually in the form of instinctive meanings of scents, sights, and sounds, into something humans can understand, and conversely to shape their own thoughts into a form animals can comprehend. Most often, an animal mindspeaker will have an affinity for a specific type of animal, but there are the rare ones who are able to communicate with any they come across.

Combinations

Combination magicks occur only when one mage has some abilities from one or more of the other categories or two or more mages work in concert. They are not uncommon, but do tend to be oddly specific.

Weather – A combination of water and air, weather mages can create and manipulate storms and read the weather for days or sometimes weeks in advance. Most commonly referred to as a weather witch, this magic tends to be very weak, and few weather mages seek special training outside of their own villages or towns, which often have a mentorship program for when a new weather witch emerges.

Ice – A combination of water and fire, ice mages are fairly rare. Rather than the ability to add

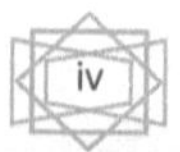

heat to an object until it ignites, ice mages remove the heat until something freezes. Working in concert with a weather witch, ice mages can create devastating winter storms, though on their own they are mostly limited to very localized events.

Battle – A combination of fire and earth, battle magic is highly destructive, and very prized among warlords. Consisting mostly of the ability to rip up great swaths of earth and create massive explosions, battle mages' desirability is limited, but Devali has specifically sought them out and bred them over the centuries, resulting in their becoming far more common than they might have been otherwise.

Other

The other magicks do not fall clearly into any of the above categories, but are rather something entirely separate.

Healing – The ability to heal others' bodies magically. Healers are highly prized, and because they are sought after and encouraged, they have become fairly prolific. Healers of different strengths can cure illness, knit flesh and mend bones, though most tend to use their magic as little as possible and let the body do most of the work. Healers are unable to heal themselves, but have an alarming propensity for putting themselves in danger to save *others*.

Mindhealing – The ability to heal the minds of others. Mindhealers deal with things like mental trauma, emotional strains, and other mental

ailments. They typically are unable to heal physical injuries, and often work in concert with other healers on battlefields or other places where mental ailments are common.

Light/Illusion – The ability to manipulate light to create images or illusions. Light mages are often employed as court entertainers or act as magicians, though some of the most powerful have been recruited by armies in the past to intimidate their enemies.

Lightning – The ability to create and control lightning. No one is really sure what category to put this rare talent into. From small static sparks to destructive lightning strikes, these mages come in a variety of strengths, but most are feared for their strange abilities and so tend to be reclusive and secretive by nature.

Teleportation – The ability to instantaneously transfer one's self and others from one place to another magically. Teleporters are very rare, and though kings and queens have sought to use them to transport armies in the past, the limitations of their powers have proved that to be impossible. Mostly, they tend to be used as messengers for information that is time-sensitive.

Necromancy – One of the darkest talents, necromancy is the ability to communicate with – and occasionally resurrect – the dead. Necromancers are typically avoided except by the desperate, and no one knows very much about them.

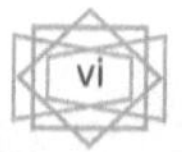

Shapeshifting – A talent possessed only by those
blessed by Ketral, shapeshifting is the ability for a
human to shift his or her form into the likeness of
an animal. While in this form, the human takes on
all traits and abilities – and lack thereof – of the
animal, but retains their human thought patterns
and intelligence, as well as all of their memories.

*C*hristina's (right) love for story telling began at a young age, and has long been an integral part of her life. She currently lives in Cuero, Texas with her fiancé Travis (left) and their two dogs, Tau and P.I.T.A.

It has been observed that Tsuga's tendency to hoard weapons might have its roots in the author's penchant to do the same; her collection of decorative, historical, and functional weaponry is quite varied.

Family has always been one of the most important things in Christina's life, and she enjoys spending time with her numerous relatives. She also enjoys volunteering with the local Barlow Horse Kamp during the summers and horseback riding when she gets the chance.

Christina is eagerly anticipating her wedding to Travis next fall, and has already begun work on her third book.